Skulduggery Pleasant
DARK DAYS

Also by Derek Landy:

DEREK LANDY

HarperCollins *Children's Books*

First published in hardback in Great Britain by HarperCollins *Children's Books* 2010
HarperCollins *Children's Books* is a division of
HarperCollins*Publishers* Ltd
77-85 Fulham Palace Road, Hammersmith, London W6 8JB

Visit us on the web at www.harpercollins.co.uk

Skulduggery Pleasant rests his weary bones on the web at
www.skulduggerypleasant.co.uk

And has a bebo page at
www.bebo.com/Profile.jsp?MemberId=3605555366

1

ISBN 978-0-00-732596-2

Printed and bound in England by
Clays Ltd, St Ives plc

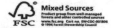

This book is dedicated to Laura.

I'm not going to make any jokes here, because apparently you are the one person on Earth who does not find me even remotely funny.

I am HILARIOUS. Ask anyone. Ask your sister. She thinks I'm HYSTERICAL (you do, don't you Katie…?)

And yet, even though you refuse to recognise my comedy genius, and you refuse to publically admit how impressed you are by everything I do, you're still getting a book dedicated to you – because without you, Skulduggery wouldn't have his Valkyrie.

You're my best friend and my muse, and I owe you a lot.

(A "lot" being, of course, entirely figurative, and in no way implies that you're getting a share of the royalties.)

1

SCARAB

When Dreylan Scarab had been locked away in his little cell, he'd thought about nothing but murder. He liked murder. Murder and long walks had been two of his favourite things when he was younger. He'd walk a long way to kill someone, he'd often said, and he'd kill for a long walk. But after close to 200 years in that cell, he'd kind of lost interest in walks. His passion for murder, however, burned brighter than ever.

They let him out of prison a few days early, and he stepped into the Arizona sunshine an old man. They had kept his power from him, and without his power his body had withered and aged. But his mind stayed sharp. Try as *they might, the years could not dull his mind. Still, he didn't like being old. He counted how long it took him to cross the road and wasn't pleased with the result.*

He stood there for two hours. The dust kicked up and got into his eyes. He looked around for something to kill, then quelled the urge. The entrance to the underground prison was within spitting distance, and killing something while the guards were still watching was probably a bad idea. Besides, Scarab's magic hadn't returned to him yet, so even if there were something in this desert worth killing, he might not have been able to manage it.

A shape came through the shimmer of the heat haze, solidifying into a black, air-conditioned automobile. It pulled up and a man got out slowly. It took Scarab a moment to recognise him.

"Why the hell didn't you break me out?" Scarab growled. His voice depressed him. In the open air, away from the confines of the prison, even his growl sounded old and frail.

The man shrugged. "I was kind of hopin' you'd die in there, to be honest. You sure you didn't? You look pretty dead. Smell dead, too."

"I'm staying alive long enough to do what has to be done."

The other man nodded. "I figured you'd be wantin' revenge. Eachan Meritorious is dead though. Nefarian Serpine killed him. Few others've been killed since you were put away, too."

Scarab narrowed his eyes. "Skulduggery Pleasant?"

"Missin'. Couple of Faceless Ones came through their little portal ten, maybe eleven months ago. They were forced back, but

they dragged the skeleton with 'em."

"I miss all the fun things," Scarab said without humour.

"His friends have been lookin' for him ever since. You want my opinion, he's dead. For good, this time. You might get lucky though. They might find him, bring him back. Then you can kill him."

"What about Guild?"

A bright, white-toothed smile. "He's the new Grand Mage in Ireland. He's a prime target for you."

Scarab felt a tingle, a slight buzz in his bones, and his heart quickened. It was the sensation of magic returning to him after all this time of being kept locked away. He kept the elation out of his dry, croaky voice. "No. It's not just him. It's all of them. I'm going to make them all pay. Their world is going to crumble for what they did to me."

"You got a plan, I take it?"

"I'm going to destroy the Sanctuary."

The man took off his sunglasses and cleaned them. "You goin' to need some help with that?"

Scarab looked at him suspiciously. "I've got nothing to pay you with, and there's no profit in revenge."

"This would be a freebie, old man. And I know some people who might be interested in gettin' involved. We've all got scores to settle in Ireland." Billy-Ray Sanguine put his sunglasses back on, covering up the black holes where his eyes had once been. "I'm thinkin' of one li'l lady in particular."

2

HOME INVASION

She missed him.

She missed his voice, and his humour, and his warm arrogance, and those moments in his company when she realised that this was when she came alive – finally living, by the side of a dead man.

For eleven months he had been gone and for almost a year Valkyrie had been searching for his original skull, to use as a tool to reopen the portal and get him back. She slept when she had to and ate when she needed to. She let the search consume her. Time spent with her parents grew less and less. She'd been to

Germany, and France, and Russia. She had kicked down rotten doors and run through darkened streets. She had followed the clues, just like he'd taught her, and now, finally, she was close.

Skulduggery had once told her that the head he now wore was not his actual head – he had won it in a poker game. He said his real head had been stolen, while he slept, by little goblin things that had run off with it in the night. At the time he hadn't gone into any further detail, but he had filled in the blanks later on.

Twenty years ago, a small church in the middle of the Irish countryside was being plagued by what appeared to be a poltergeist. The angry spirit was causing havoc, terrifying the locals and driving away the police when they came to investigate. Skulduggery was called in by an old friend and he arrived, wrapped in his scarf with his hat pulled low.

The first thing he learned was that the culprit *wasn't* a poltergeist. The second thing he discovered was that it was most likely a type of goblin, and there were probably more than one. The third thing he unearthed was that the church, as small and as spartan as it was, had a solid gold cross set up behind the altar, and if there was one thing goblins loved, it was gold.

"Actually, if there's one thing that goblins love," Skulduggery had said, "it's eating babies, but gold comes in a close second."

The goblins were trying to frighten everyone away long enough so that they could pry the cross loose and make off with it. Skulduggery set up camp and waited. To pass the time, he sank into a meditative state, to be roused whenever anyone got too close to the church.

The first night the goblins came and he leaped out, screaming and throwing fireballs, scaring them witless. The second night they crept up, whispering among themselves to bolster their courage, and he appeared behind them and roared curse words and they ran off once again, crying in fear. But the third night they surprised him, and instead of sneaking up to the church, they sneaked up on *him* and grabbed his head while he was deep in a meditative trance. By the time he had figured out what was going on, they had disappeared, and Skulduggery had nowhere to put his hat.

Now wearing a head that was not his own, Skulduggery's investigations had revealed that the goblins later ran foul of a sorcerer named Larks, who had stolen their paltry possessions and sold them on. The investigation ended there, as other events began to call for Skulduggery's attention. He had always planned to get back to it, but never did, and so the rest was up to Valkyrie.

The skull, she had learned, was bought by a woman as a

surprise, and somewhat unsettling, wedding gift for the man she was to marry. The woman had then used the skull to beat that man to a bloody and pulpy death after she found him stealing from her. The murder inquiry was undertaken by "mortal" police – Valkyrie hated that expression – and so the skull had been logged as evidence. Now known as the Murder Skull, it had found its way on to the black market, and changed hands four times before a sorcerer named Umbra sensed the traces of magic within. Umbra had acquired it and within a year it came into the possession of Thames Chabon, notorious wheeler, unscrupulous dealer, and all-round shady character. As far as anyone knew, Chabon still had the skull. It had taken considerable effort to even get in touch with him, and Valkyrie had been forced to use quite unorthodox means to do so.

The unorthodox means stood by the side of the quiet street, hands in pockets. His name was Caelan. He had been maybe nineteen, twenty years old when he'd died. He was tall, his hair was black, and his cheekbones were narrow slashes against his skin. He glanced at Valkyrie as she approached, then looked away quickly. It was close to nightfall. He was probably getting hungry. Vampires had a tendency to do that.

"Did you arrange it?" she asked.

"Chabon will meet you at ten o'clock," he muttered,

"tomorrow morning. The Bailey, off Grafton Street."

"OK."

"Make sure you're on time – he doesn't wait around."

"And you're sure the head is Skulduggery's?"

"That's what Chabon said. He didn't know why it's so valuable to you though."

Valkyrie nodded, but didn't respond. She didn't tell him about the Isthmus Anchor, an object belonging to one reality but residing in another. She didn't tell him how it kept the portals between these realities active as a result, or that all she needed to open a portal near Skulduggery was his original head and a willing Teleporter. She had the Teleporter. Now she needed the skull.

Caelan looked across at the setting sun. "I'd better go. It's getting late."

"Why are you doing this?" Valkyrie asked suddenly. "I'm not used to people helping me out for no reason."

Caelan kept his eyes off her. "Some time ago you imprisoned a man named Dusk. I don't like this man."

"I'm not too fond of him either."

"You scarred him, I hear."

"He had it coming."

"Yes, he did."

He paused, then walked away. His movements reminded her of the terrible, predatory gracefulness of a jungle cat.

When he was gone, Tanith Low emerged from the alley on the other side of the street, all blonde hair and brown leather, hiding her sword under her long coat.

Tanith took her home, and Valkyrie stood beneath her bedroom window and swept her arms up by her sides, clutching the sharp air and using it to lift her to the sill. She tapped on the glass and a small light turned on. The window opened and her own face – dark-eyed and dark-haired – peered out at her.

"I thought you weren't coming home tonight," her reflection said.

Valkyrie climbed in without answering. Her reflection watched her close the window and take off her coat. It was as cold inside as it was out, and Valkyrie shivered. The reflection did the same, approximating a human response to a condition it had never experienced.

"We had lasagne for dinner," it said. "Dad's been trying to get tickets for the All-Ireland Championship on Sunday, but so far he hasn't been able to."

Valkyrie was tired, so she just gestured at the full-length mirror inside the wardrobe door. The reflection, having no feelings to hurt, stepped into the glass then turned and waited.

Valkyrie touched the mirror and the reflection's memories swam into her mind, settling beside her own. She closed the wardrobe and realised she hadn't been home in eight days. She had a sudden longing to see her parents and not just settle for the memories viewed through the eyes of an emotionless substitute. But her parents were asleep down the hall and Valkyrie knew she would have to wait until morning.

She took a black ring from her finger and put it on the bedside table. Ghastly, Tanith and China didn't like the ring – it was a Necromancer tool after all. But for what Valkyrie had had to face over the past eleven months she had needed something extra, and her natural aptitude for Necromancy had provided her with the sheer strength she had required.

She undressed, dropping her sleeveless top and her trousers on the floor over her boots. No clothes made by Ghastly Bespoke ever creased, and for that she was quietly grateful. Valkyrie pulled on her shorts and the new Dublin football jersey her dad had got her last Christmas then climbed into bed. She reached out and turned off the light before quickly pulling her arm back under the covers.

Tomorrow, she thought. Tomorrow they would find the skull and tomorrow they would use it to open the portal. Wherever Skulduggery was, the portal would open close by.

Valkyrie thought about this and what she would do when she saw him again. She pictured running to him and hugging him, feeling the framework beneath his clothes that gave him mass, and she tried to imagine the first thing he would say. Something dry, she knew. Something understated and funny. Probably a boast.

When she looked at her bedside clock, Valkyrie realised that she'd been lying in bed for over an hour. She sighed, flipped the pillow to the cool side and turned over, banishing such thoughts from her mind, and eventually she experienced the welcome embrace of sleep.

It was a fitful sleep though, uneasy, and she awoke in the night to find someone standing over her. Her heart lurched, yet even through the shock, she was going through a list of possibilities – *Mum Dad Tanith* –and then the man reached down and wrapped his cold hands around her throat.

Valkyrie squirmed, trying to kick out, but the bedcovers were trapping her legs. She fought to break the chokehold, but her assailant was far too strong. His fingers dug into her throat and blood pounded in her temples. She was going to pass out.

The covers came loose and she slammed her foot into his thigh. His leg moved back, but his grip didn't loosen. She got both feet against his belly and tried to shove him off. The dark shape stayed where it was, looming over her. She was going to die. She took one hand away from his wrist and pushed at the air, but the push was too weak to have any effect. She reached for the Necromancer ring, desperately slipping her finger into it, and immediately she felt the darkness within, cold and coiling. She curled her hand and thrust it at him. A fist of shadow slammed into his chest and suddenly the choking fingers were gone and he was stumbling away. Valkyrie leaped off the bed, snapped her palms against the air and the man shot backwards off his feet. He hit the wall and fell, crashing through her desk. She clicked her fingers, conjuring fire into her hand, illuminating the room.

For a moment she didn't recognise him. The clothes were all wrong – layers of torn and filthy garments, mud-caked boots and fingerless gloves. The hair was longer, untamed, and the face was dirty. It was the beard that gave him away though. The pointy little beard that Remus Crux always wore to hide his weak chin.

She heard her father shout her name and she extinguished the fire. Her parents were about to barge in. She whipped a trail of shadow around her bed and dragged it so that it jammed the door shut.

"Stephanie!" her mother screamed from the other side as the

doorhandle turned uselessly.

Valkyrie turned back to Crux just as he grabbed her and hurled her against the wall. She rebounded and jumped into him, using her knee to drive him back. She jumped again, extending both legs, her feet slamming into his chest. He wheeled back, tripping over her discarded clothes and falling. His head crunched off her bedside table.

Her parents were doing their best to break down the door.

In an enclosed space Valkyrie's knowledge of Elemental magic wasn't going to get the job done. The Necromancer ring was cold on her finger as she drew in the darkness. She focused it into a point and then unleashed it. It hit Crux's shoulder and he jerked back. She did it again, hitting his left leg, and it crumpled beneath him.

"Steph!" her father roared. "Open the door! Open the door now!"

Crux came at her before she could strike him again. With one hand he grabbed her wrist, holding the ring away from him, and with the other he grabbed her throat. He pinned her against the wall, pressing against her, cutting off her weapons. His eyes were narrowed and through them she could see his madness.

The window shattered in on top of them. Valkyrie gasped as Crux was wrenched away from her. Shadows swirled and a thousand arrows of darkness flew at him and he dived, barely avoiding the barrage. He snarled, flinging himself out through the broken window.

Solomon Wreath turned to her, checking that she was OK, while shadows wrapped themselves around the cane in his hand.

The door hit the bed and it moved sharply. Wreath followed Crux out of the window and Valkyrie shoved her bed aside. Her parents barged in, her mother wrapping her in a hug while her dad searched the room for an intruder.

"Where is he?" he yelled.

Valkyrie looked at him from over her mother's shoulder. "Where's who?" she asked, not having to act a whole lot in order to sound shaken.

Her father spun to her. "Who was here?"

"No one."

Her mum gripped her shoulders and took a step back so as to look at her properly. "What happened, Steph?"

Valkyrie scanned the room. "A bat," she decided.

Her dad froze. "What?"

"A bat. It flew through the window."

"A... bat? It sounded like you were being *attacked* in here."

"Wait," her mum said. "No, we heard the window break *after* everything else."

Damn.

Valkyrie nodded. "It was already in here. I think it was in the corner. It must have flown in a few days ago and, I don't know, hibernated or something."

"Stephanie," her dad said, "this room is a war zone."

"I panicked. Dad, it was a bat. A massive one. I woke up and it was fluttering around the room, and I fell against my desk. It landed on the floor and I tried to push the bed over it. Then it flew straight through the window."

Valkyrie hoped it wouldn't register with her parents that all the broken glass was on the inside.

Her father sagged as relief spread through him. "I thought something awful was happening."

She frowned. "Something awful *was* happening. It could have got stuck in my *hair*."

After enduring another few minutes of her parents worrying about her, and checking her feet to make sure she hadn't cut herself, her mother helped her set up the bed in the spare room and finally said goodnight.

Valkyrie waited until she was sure they were back in their own bed before she sneaked out of the window. She let herself drop, using the air to slow her descent. Her bare feet touched wet grass and she hugged herself against the freezing cold.

"He's gone," Wreath said from behind her.

She turned. Wreath stood, tall and handsome in a pale kind of way, dressed in black. He was as tall as Skulduggery, and as calm, but they shared other traits too. They were both excellent teachers. Skulduggery had taught her Elemental magic and Wreath was teaching her Necromancy, but they both treated her as an equal. Not every mage she met did that. Another one of Skulduggery's talents that Wreath shared was the knack of arriving in the nick of time, for which Valkyrie was particularly grateful. "What are you doing here?" she asked. She didn't thank him. Wreath didn't believe in thanks.

His eyes gleamed when he looked at her. "I heard Remus Crux had been sighted in the area," he said. "Naturally, I assumed he was coming after *you*. It seems I was right."

"And why didn't you tell me this?" Valkyrie asked, her teeth chattering.

"Bait doesn't needs to know it's bait. Crux might have sensed a trap and that would have sent him scurrying back into the shadows."

"I don't appreciate being *bait*, Solomon. He could have gone after my family."

"He doesn't want to hurt your family. We don't know *why* he's after you, but at least we now know that he *is*."

Wreath wasn't offering her his coat. Skulduggery would have done that by now.

"I don't want this happening again," she said. "My town is off-limits to this stuff. China Sorrows can put up symbols and sigils to make sure he can't get into Haggard. Tomorrow that's what I'm asking her to do."

"Very well."

"Solomon, next time something like this comes up, I'm expecting you to tell me about it *before* I'm attacked."

He smiled. "I'll try to remember that. It's quite safe for you to return to your house. I'll keep watch until morning."

Valkyrie nodded and positioned herself beneath the spare room window.

"Oh, and the skull?" he asked. "Are you close to retrieving it?"

"We're meeting the seller tomorrow."

"And you're sure he has the one you're looking for? You've been disappointed before..."

"This time it's different. It has to be."

He bowed his goodbye then tapped his cane to the ground and invited the shadows in around him. By the time they had scattered, he was gone. It was a Necromancer trick, similar to teleportation but with far less range. It used to impress her.

It didn't any more.

She swept her arms up and a gust of cold wind lifted her up the side of the house. She climbed through the window and closed it behind her then wiped her feet on the carpet to dry them. She scrambled under the bedclothes and lay there, curled up in a shivering ball.

She didn't get much sleep.

3

THE PLAN, SUCH AS IT IS

The next morning Valkyrie went back to her own room. It was freezing. There was glass all over the floor and the desk was in pieces. She called China Sorrows and told her what she needed. For the past six months China had been instructing young sorcerers in the language of magic, and she said she would send her students to construct a warning system around the town.

Valkyrie thanked her and hung up, then opened the wardrobe and touched the mirror. Her reflection stepped out then crawled under the bed to hide while Valkyrie dressed in her school uniform and went downstairs. It had been over a week since she'd joined her parents for breakfast and she was anxious to enjoy their company. She was also determined that today was the day she'd get Skulduggery back.

Her parents talked about the broken window – her father was confident he could replace the glass himself, but her mother wasn't so sure – and then her dad announced his plans.

"I'm taking a half-day," he said. "I'm off to meet a few clients, take them out for a quick nine."

Her mother looked at him. "A quick nine what?"

"I'm not sure," he admitted. "It's a golf term. Men my age say it all the time. I wanted to take them to the football final on Sunday, but golf this afternoon will have to do."

"You don't play golf," his wife pointed out.

"But I've seen it on television and it looks pretty straightforward. Hit the ball with the thing."

"Club."

"What could be easier?"

"Your hand-eye co-ordination isn't the best though, and you hate long walks and carrying things. And you also regularly say that you think golf is stupid."

"Golf *is* stupid," he agreed.

"Then why would you want to take your clients golfing?"

"Primarily, it's the outfit. The V-neck jumpers with the diamond patterns and the trousers with the socks pulled up."

"I don't think people wear those any more."

"Oh."

Valkyrie often thought her parents were ideally suited to one another. She doubted that anyone else would be capable of appreciating just how odd they really were.

She finished her breakfast and went back to her room to change into her black clothes. The reflection took each item of school uniform as it was removed and put it on.

In a town called Roarhaven, almost two years earlier, Skulduggery had shot the reflection and killed it. Its original purpose had been to fill in for Valkyrie while she was with Skulduggery, but as a result of its overuse, it began developing certain quirks of behaviour, a problem compounded when it "died". They had returned the body to the mirror, and the reflection came back to its imitation of life, but after that it became even more erratic. It had broken free of some of its own boundaries – the changing of its clothes being a primary example – and every now and then there were short gaps in its memory.

But Valkyrie didn't have time to worry about any of that now. She needed to get Skulduggery's head. Besides, *someone* had to go to school today and it sure as hell wasn't going to be *her*.

She buttoned up her black trousers and pulled on her boots, letting the trouser turn-ups fall over them. The top was sleeveless but warm, and when she slipped into the coat, it was like she was suddenly wearing thermals. The material reacted to the environment and to her body temperature, keeping her in comfort no matter what. The coat was black, but its sleeves were the dark red of dried blood. A Ghastly Bespoke creation.

The reflection picked up Valkyrie's schoolbag and left, closing the door behind it.

Valkyrie rang Fletcher Renn and he stepped out of empty space beside her. The phone crackled in her hand as the network struggled to compensate, then gave up. His blond hair was painstakingly untamed, and his grin was the usual mix of cocksure and mocking. He wore old jeans, scuffed boots and an army jacket, and the only problem with how he looked was that Fletcher knew he looked good.

"What happened here?" he asked, the grin vanishing as he noticed the mess.

"I was attacked."

His eyes widened and he grabbed her, as if making sure she was still alive. "Are you OK? Are you hurt? Who did it?"

"I'm fine, Fletcher. I'll tell you about it when I tell the others."

"It wasn't the vampire, was it?"

"What?"

Fletcher let Valkyrie go and stepped back. "What's-his-name, from yesterday. Mean and moody vampire boy."

"His name's Caelan. And no, of course not."

He nodded slowly. "OK then. And you're sure you're all right?"

"I'm fine."

"What did he say anyway? The vamp."

"He set up the meeting, like he said he would."

"No chit-chat then?"

"He's not the type."

"Strong and silent, eh?"

"I suppose. Also the sun was going down."

"Ah, OK. He probably didn't want to turn into a horrible monster and tear you apart on your first date."

"I'm sensing that you don't like him very much."

"Well, no, on account of the horrible monster part. Do *you*?"

"Like him? No. I don't even know him."

"Well, all right then." Fletcher seemed satisfied. "Can I ask you a question?"

"You already did."

"Can I ask you another?"

"Can you ask me somewhere my parents won't hear?"

He took her hand and in an eyeblink they were standing on the roof of Bespoke Tailor's. These days, teleportation didn't even make Valkyrie dizzy.

"Ask away," she said.

He hesitated and then said, very casually, "Do you think things will return to normal for you when we get Skulduggery back? You and him, out solving crimes and having adventures and stuff?"

"I expect so. Don't see why they wouldn't."

"That's good," he nodded. "It's nice that it's finally coming to an end, isn't it? After everything we've all done and been through."

"These past few months have been terrible," Valkyrie admitted.

"Yeah, I know. But at the same time, like, I've actually been, you know, enjoying it."

Valkyrie said nothing.

"Not in a bad way!" he added, laughing. "I didn't enjoy the fact that he was lost, or that you've been so worried about him. I just mean that, for me, being part of everything, it's been good. I've liked being part of a team."

"Right."

"So, I mean, I was thinking, I was wondering, do you think he'd let me tag along on your cases?"

Valkyrie took a sudden breath. "I... I really don't know."

"I'd be pretty useful, you have to admit. No more driving everywhere in that ancient car of his."

"He loves the Bentley. And so do I."

"I know, I know, but still, maybe you could mention it to him, when he's back."

"I will," she said. "I'll mention it."

"Unless *you* don't want me around."

Valkyrie raised an eyebrow. "Did I say that?"

"No, but... Actually, yes, you have said that, a lot."

She shrugged. "That's only when you annoy me."

"Have I annoyed you lately?"

"You're annoying me *now*..."

Fletcher grinned and Valkyrie held out her hand. "Downstairs."

He took her hand and bowed. "Yes, m'lady."

Instantly, they were in the backroom of Bespoke Tailor's.

"You can let go of my hand," said Valkyrie.

"I know I can," Fletcher responded. "I just choose not to."

She rotated her wrist, forcing him to release her in a relatively painless manner.

They smelled coffee and heard conversation, and emerged into the shop to find Tanith and Ghastly Bespoke sitting at the small table by the wall. Ghastly was shaking his scarred head in disgust.

"What's wrong?" Valkyrie asked.

"Dreylan Scarab got out of prison yesterday," Tanith told her.

"Who's Dreylan Scarab?" asked Fletcher.

"He's the assassin who killed Esryn Vanguard."

"Who's Esryn Vanguard?" asked Fletcher.

Valkyrie was thankful Fletcher was around. Finally, somebody who knew even less than she did.

"Vanguard was an ex-soldier who became a pacifist," Ghastly said. Valkyrie noticed the edge of a bandage poking out beneath his shirt collar. She didn't mention it. "This was, what, maybe 200 years ago? He talked about a peaceful resolution to the war with Mevolent, one that didn't require one side vanquishing the other."

"Common sense in other words," said Tanith. "This was well before my time, but I remember my parents talking about him."

Ghastly said, "Mevolent grew tired of him constantly chipping away at his troops' morale and conviction, so he sent Scarab to assassinate him."

"And 200 years later," Tanith said, "Scarab completes his sentence and is freed. I'm surprised he lasted that long actually. After a couple of years in a bound cell, sorcerers start ageing again. I think everyone expected old age to finish him off."

"He should be dead," Ghastly said quietly. "He murdered a great man."

"Do you know who *else* should be dead?" Fletcher asked brightly. "Valkyrie. Someone attacked her last night."

Tanith and Ghastly stared and Valkyrie sighed, then told them about Crux.

Ghastly narrowed his eyes. "Wreath just *happened* to be passing while all this was taking place? For all we know he could have orchestrated the whole thing just so he could swoop in and save the day."

"He didn't save the day," Valkyrie said somewhat defensively. "I'd have stopped Crux. Somehow."

"Ghastly's right," said Tanith. "We don't know what Crux has been up to since Aranmore. That glimpse he caught of the Faceless Ones snapped his mind, Val. He could very well have fallen under Wreath's influence."

"Solomon Wreath's on our side," Valkyrie said, already tired of this argument. It was one they'd had a dozen times before.

"And why would he send Crux after me? What would he have to gain?"

Tanith shrugged. "*We're* close to getting Skulduggery back, and *he's* close to losing his prized pupil. He gains your trust, and your confidence, and if he's lucky, you choose Necromancy over Elemental magic."

Valkyrie felt the ring on her finger. She hadn't taken it off all night. "We'll worry about that later," she said.

"A lunatic attacks you in the middle of the night," Tanith said with a raised eyebrow, "a lunatic who, even when he was *sane*, detested you and you want us to forget about it?"

Fletcher peered at Ghastly and then said, with his usual tactfulness, "Hey, what's with the bandage?"

Ghastly adjusted his collar. "It's nothing," he said gruffly.

"Did you cut yourself shaving? Did you cut yourself shaving a *lot?*"

Ghastly sighed. "I asked China if she could help me blend into a crowd. I'm sick of disguises. So she came up with a façade tattoo. That's all."

"What's a façade tattoo?" Tanith asked.

"It's not important."

"Then tell us what it is so we can get *on to* something important."

"It's a false face," he said, trying to hide his embarrassment with impatience. "She tattooed two symbols on my collarbones and when they've healed, in theory, they'll make me look like I'm normal for a short period of time."

"Normal?"

"No scars."

"Wow."

"Like I said, it's not important."

"When can you try it out?"

"Another few hours. It mightn't work, but... it's worth a try. It's better than having to a wear a scarf every time I go out. I think we should get back to the matter at hand. Chabon's plane lands in an hour, right?"

"He'd be here by now if he'd let *me* pick him up," Fletcher said.

"He doesn't trust us," Valkyrie told him. "He buys and sells and the people he deals with aren't always as honest and trustworthy as *we* are."

Fletcher shrugged. "I'd have just nicked the skull off him and teleported back here."

Valkyrie sighed. "Do we have the money?"

Tanith kicked a duffel bag on the floor beside her. "A bit each from our various bank accounts. Good thing money doesn't mean a whole lot to people like us."

"Speak for yourself," grumbled Fletcher.

"You didn't contribute *anything*," Tanith frowned.

"Is contributing *time* not enough?" Fletcher replied archly.

"Not when you're trying to buy something, no."

"Oh."

Tanith looked back to Valkyrie. "And Val, relax, OK? We've thought of everything."

"Skulduggery told me once that only *he* can think of everything, but he doesn't do it very often because it spoils the surprise."

This raised a smile on Tanith's lips. "Then we have thought of everything that we four are capable of thinking of, and we can't think of anything else. There is absolutely no reason to think that this won't be as easy as meeting up, handing over the money, getting the skull and saying thank you. This afternoon we take a trip up to Aranmore Farm and Fletcher opens the portal. Then we go in, find Skulduggery and bring him back. Easy as proverbial pie."

"Unless something goes wrong," Valkyrie said.

"Well, yes. Unless something goes horribly, dreadfully wrong. Which it usually does of course."

4

BRING ME THE HEAD OF SKULDUGGERY PLEASANT

Chabon had picked a café on Duke Street for the exchange to take place. Valkyrie and Tanith sat facing the door. Fletcher was beside the window, reading a comic and drinking a Coke and doing his best to look inconspicuous – not an easy feat with that hair. Only Ghastly was absent. His scars were too difficult to conceal from the public for any length of time.

A little after midday, a man with a suitcase entered. He

spotted them immediately and approached. He wasn't what Valkyrie had been expecting. His clothes were casual and he didn't have a pencil-thin moustache for a start.

"Afternoon, ladies," he said, smiling politely. "Do you have my payment?"

"Show us the skull," said Valkyrie.

Chabon put the suitcase on the table and patted it. "You're not seeing the merchandise until I know you have my payment. That's how it works. That's how these things happen."

Tanith lifted the duffel bag and opened it, allowing Chabon a peek at the money within. She closed it and held it on her lap.

Valkyrie reached for the case, but Chabon grabbed her wrist.

"You're very eager," he said, his voice cold. He turned her wrist, eyes narrowing when he got a closer look at the ring. "You're a Necromancer? I thought you people didn't even leave the *Temple* until you were twenty-five."

She took her hand back. "I dabble," she said. "Your turn."

Chabon flattened his palm on the case and the locks sprang open. He raised the lid, enough for Valkyrie and Tanith to see what it contained.

"That's the Murder Skull?" Tanith asked. "You're sure?"

"Positive."

"If you're lying to us..." Valkyrie began.

Chabon shook his head. "Don't threaten me, girl. I've been threatened by professionals. I had this discussion with your vampire friend, and all the facts we established then are still true today. So, unless you're planning on double-crossing me, and using that fella with the stupid hair by the window, what do you say we conduct our business and part ways? I've got a plane to catch."

Valkyrie glanced at Tanith, who put the duffel bag on the table. Chabon reached in and touched the money.

"It's all there," Tanith said.

After a moment, Chabon nodded. "Yes, it is." He withdrew his hand and stood, taking the bag with him and leaving the case on the table. "Been a pleasure," he said and they watched him walk out.

Fletcher came over and Valkyrie raised the lid slightly. The case was lined and cushioned, the skull sitting comfortably within. A huge smile suddenly broke across Valkyrie's face.

They had it. They had it, and in a few hours they'd pass through the portal and get Skulduggery back. All her hard work would pay off and, by the end of the day, her life would be allowed to resume. She closed the case.

"I just want to make sure," she said and hurried to the door. She stepped out and saw Chabon just as he turned the corner on to Grafton Street.

"Hey!" she roared, a furious look on her face.

Chabon turned. If the skull *was* the Murder Skull, he would have no need to panic. If it wasn't... Chabon panicked and broke into a sprint.

"It's a fake!" she shouted to the others and bolted after Chabon, with Tanith and Fletcher following.

Valkyrie barged into the crowd, fighting to keep Chabon in sight. She leaped over a busker's coin tray and dodged around a man painted silver. Chabon turned right, into a long, bright lane, the duffel bag swinging wildly.

If the lane had been empty, Valkyrie would have wrapped a tendril of shadow around his ankles and pitched him forward on to his face. But there were maybe a dozen people wandering by shop windows, and a woman begging for spare change just ahead of her. Out of the corner of her eye, Valkyrie saw Tanith dart into an alcove and run up the side of the building. Valkyrie chased Chabon to the next street, where he glanced up and saw Tanith moving over rooftops to cut him off. He knocked over an old man and ran into the Powerscourt Centre. Valkyrie took the street adjacent, moving parallel to him. Through the windows she saw him crash through the lunch crowd at the restaurant, slowing him down.

She reached South William Street as Chabon staggered out of the Powerscourt Centre. He saw her, cursed and kept running, through Castle Market and straight into the old Victorian building that housed the George's Street Arcade. She knew she had him. He didn't have a hope of getting away now.

The stalls were set up down the middle of the arcade, funnelling the shoppers down paths on either side. There were clothes stalls and jewellery stalls and a fortune-teller behind a red curtain. Chabon chose the left path, knocking people out of his way. He stumbled over a box of old paperbacks and Valkyrie piled on the speed and jumped, her knees slamming into his back. He sprawled to the ground and she ignored the startled looks from the people around her. He reached for the fallen bag and she stomped on his hand. He shrieked, kicking, and her feet swept from beneath her. She landed just as he got up, the bag in his uninjured hand, but she grabbed one of the straps and wouldn't let go, and Chabon remembered too late that she wasn't alone.

Tanith came flying over Valkyrie and her boot-heel connected with Chabon's sternum. There was a crack and he went down and rolled a few times before curling up. Valkyrie got to her feet as Fletcher joined them, puffing and panting like someone who hadn't needed to run anywhere in quite a while.

"Here you go," Valkyrie said as she pressed the duffel bag into Fletcher's arms. She smiled at the crowd. "This poor boy got his bag snatched by that nasty man."

Fletcher glared at her as the crowd applauded, and Tanith picked up Chabon and escorted him away. Valkyrie and Fletcher followed.

"That was unnecessary," Fletcher seethed.

"If you'd been faster," she said quietly, "maybe you could have been the hero – but you weren't, so you're the innocent victim. Get over it."

Tanith took Chabon far enough away from passing pedestrians so that they could talk without being overheard. She pressed him back against the wall. He was holding his hand against his chest, obviously in a great deal of pain.

"Where's the real Murder Skull?" Valkyrie asked, keeping her voice low.

"I gave it to you," Chabon tried. She prodded his hands and he hissed. "OK! Stop! I had it, I swear I did. When I talked to you on the phone, I had it."

"So what did you do with it?"

Chabon was looking quite pale. His injury was making him sweat. "There's a... Look, there's a rule, in what I do. If you find something that one person is willing to pay for, odds are there's someone else who's willing to pay more."

"You *advertised?*"

"I didn't know anyone would be *that* interested, so yeah, I mentioned it here and there, and someone came to me with a better offer."

"Who?"

"I don't know."

Valkyrie made a fist and crunched it against Chabon's hands. Tanith struggled to keep him standing upright.

"A woman," he gasped. "I met with her an hour ago. She paid me triple. I didn't think you'd ever know. It's the Murder Skull. What's so important about it?"

"What did this woman look like?" asked Tanith.

"Dark hair. Pretty enough. All business."

"A name," Valkyrie said. "A number, address, anything."

"She called me. Kept her number private. We met in the arrivals area in the airport. She had the money so I gave her the skull. I brought a second one for you lot."

"You'd better give us something we can use to find her," Fletcher said, "or I'm teleporting you to the middle of the Sahara and I'm leaving you there."

Chabon looked at him, like he was gauging whether or not the threat was serious. He obviously decided it was.

"She's American – Boston by the accent. And she's got that eye thing – one green eye, one blue."

"Heterochromia," Tanith said. "Davina Marr."

Valkyrie's stomach dropped. Davina Marr had been brought in by the Irish Sanctuary to assume the role of Prime Detective. Valkyrie had had a few run-ins with her already, and had found her to be ambitious, patronising and ruthless.

"If she bought the skull," Valkyrie said grimly, "then Thurid Guild has it by now, and he's going to lock it away to make sure Skulduggery *never* gets back."

"So what do we do?" asked Fletcher.

"We steal it," said Valkyrie.

5

THE REVENGERS' CLUB

It was raining. Again.

Scarab didn't like Ireland. Every great misfortune in his life had happened here. Every major defeat. Even though he had done his time in an American prison, he'd been arrested here in Ireland – and it had been raining then too.

The castle was cold and there were draughts everywhere. Most of the doors had recently been blocked off, sealing away the dungeons and various unsavoury places. They were still accessible through the many secret passages, but it was proving quite difficult to get around. Also the plumbing was terrible. The cell that had been his home for two centuries had kept him alive, kept him nourished, kept his body clean and his muscles from atrophying. For 200 years he had not even needed to visit a bathroom. Where did all the waste go? Was there any waste to begin with? He didn't know and no one had come around to tell him.

And now, suddenly, he had to eat and wash and visit the bathroom at worryingly frequent intervals, and the toilet wouldn't flush. He'd searched for another bathroom and had quickly got lost. He had stumbled around in the dark for half an hour before finding his way back to where he started.

"Where have you been?" Billy-Ray asked, hurrying by. "They're here." He disappeared into the next room.

Scarab shuffled to the door and heard Billy-Ray welcoming their guests. Scarab's bladder was still full, and he wondered if he had time to find a potted plant or something. Not that a place like this would have a potted plant.

"You're wonderin' why I called you here," he heard Billy-Ray say. "You're lookin' at the guy sittin' next to you and you're goin', hey, don't I hate that guy? Didn't that guy try to kill me once? The fact is, yeah, we all probably tried to kill each other a few times over the years, but y'know what? So did plenty of other people.

"And that, gentlemen, is why we're here. That is the bond we share. This is our common affliction and so it provides us with our common goal. I got someone I want to introduce. You may have heard of him. He's the man who killed Esryn Vanguard. Boys, I'd like you to meet the man, the legend, Dreylan Scarab!"

Scarab straightened up and walked in, keeping his steps purposeful and strong.

Four men sat at a table, with Billy-Ray taking the fifth seat. Scarab strode forward but didn't sit. He knew each of the men, though they'd never met. His son's descriptions were more than adequate.

Remus Crux was the ex-Sanctuary Detective, now a raving lunatic who didn't bother washing. He was a recent convert to the Faceless Ones, according to Billy-Ray, and he'd developed a murderous fixation on the girl called Valkyrie Cain after she'd killed a couple of his Dark Gods with the Sceptre of the Ancients. Scarab had always believed the Sceptre to be a fairytale, and he'd never had much time for the Faceless Ones. He'd agreed to Crux's inclusion, however, because while having a madman on board was a risk, sometimes risk was all you had.

The dark-haired man beside Crux was pale and dressed in black. Cain, a girl who was sounding more and more like a real and viable threat, had cut a slash across Dusk's face with Billy-Ray's straight razor, scarring him for life. Vampires were known for their grudges. Dusk was another unpredictable entity, for a vampire was more creature than man. But for sheer physical power he was an asset that could not be discounted.

Sitting across from Dusk was the self-proclaimed Terror of London, Springheeled Jack. His lanky frame curled into the chair, one knee drawn up to his chest. His suit was old and ragged, and his top hat was perched at an unsteady angle on his head. Hardened fingernails drummed a slow rhythm on the tabletop. Scarab didn't know what manner of monster this was, but he knew that Jack had been driven out of England and was being hunted across Europe. Scarab liked people that had nowhere else to turn. Those were people he could rely on.

The fourth member of this little society, this Revengers' Club, was the one about whom they knew the least. Billy-Ray had informed Scarab that this man claimed to be a killer beyond compare, who had suffered at the hands of the skeleton detective and his partner, but that was all they knew about the mysterious and deadly Vaurien Scapegrace.

Scarab stood at the head of the table and summoned all the dreadful authority he could muster.

"You've heard of the things I've done," he said. They looked at him without speaking. "You've heard of the people I've killed. Most of these stories are true. I have killed and laughed and killed again. As have all of you.

"Gentlemen, we are a dying breed. A hundred years from now, people like us will be taken down before we've done anything wrong. We will be put in prison for the thoughts we think and the things we feel. We are the last of the truly great and the truly free. And they want to take that away from us.

"Sanguine was talking to you about a bond we share, a burning desire that lights within us all. We are free men, and to be free we must reject the rules and the laws that do not define us and do not apply to us. We must strike against our enemies, bring them down and grind them beneath our boots."

"I am here because I am curious," Dusk said. He spoke calmly, without *effort or emotion. "Why should I help you?"*

"I busted you out of prison for this," Billy-Ray said. "You owe me, vampire."

"I owed Baron Vengeous," Dusk said. "But to you, I owe nothing. So I ask again — why should I help you? Why should I help any of you? I don't think everyone here can be trusted anyway. Seated at this very table is someone who saved the life of Valkyrie Cain, after all."

Springheeled Jack smiled. His teeth were narrow and sharp and many. "I stopped you from killin' her cos I didn't like you lot lyin' to me, and I didn't like your boss. The chance to mess up your plans, therefore, was too sweet to resist. Tell me, you still sore from that hidin' I gave you?"

Dusk met his eyes. "If we were to meet on equal ground, I'd tear you to bloody, quivering pieces. Here for instance."

"It ain't even night yet," Jack grinned. "You sure you can be let off your leash so early?"

Dusk launched himself across the table and Jack laughed and rose to meet him. They crashed to the ground, knocking Scapegrace out of his chair. They flipped and rolled and went at each other again, snarling deep in their throats.

"Quit it!" Scarab roared and the scuffle broke. He pressed on before they had a chance to resume. "We're fighting ourselves? That's how you want this to go? This is an opportunity to shake the world to its foundations, and you want to kill each other? Let me tell you — and I'm speaking from experience here — there are always more *deserving people out there to kill.*

"This is our opportunity to strike back against our enemies. We have a chance to succeed where everyone else has failed. We've seen those failures. We've seen where people like Mevolent and Serpine have gone wrong, and we have learned from their mistakes."

"I nearly killed Valkyrie Cain last night," Crux announced.

They all stared at him.

"You what?" said Billy-Ray.

"My hands," Crux said, "around her throat. Squeezing. I could see fear in her eyes. Real fear. Almost had her."

Dusk turned to him. "You know where she lives?"

Crux nodded. "Can't get there now though. Saw a lot of mages marking symbols around the town. Got a perimeter there now. Can't get in without alerting the Cleavers. Don't like the Cleavers."

"Why didn't you tell us?" Billy-Ray snarled. "We could've gone in, got her, torn her to pieces—"

"I kill Cain," Crux said, pointing a finger back at himself. "Me. Not you, not the vampire, not the idiot."

Scapegrace frowned. "Who's the idiot?"

"She killed the Dark Gods," Crux continued, "but they will rise again."

Scarab could see the anger growing in Billy-Ray and Dusk. He could use his own knowledge of the language of magic to bypass this magical perimeter, but in doing so he'd lose most of his team before they'd even started on his mission. He needed them to stay thirsty for revenge. He spoke quickly to calm the situation. "Mr Crux, if you want the Faceless Ones to return, you've got to make it happen. And the first thing we do is get rid of the opposition. And we have a plan to do just that."

Dusk took his eyes off Crux. "You *have* a plan," he said.

"Yes, it *is my* plan," Scarab said, "but it belongs to all of us. We're going to steal the Desolation Engine."

Three of the men smiled. One of them looked confused.

"What's a Desolation Engine?" asked Scapegrace.

"It's a bomb," Billy-Ray said. "There's no big explosion or loud bang, just the instant disintegration of every single thing in its radius. It all turns to dust. So we're goin' to steal it an' we're goin' to use it to destroy the Sanctuary."

"The other Sanctuaries around the world have always looked at Ireland with envy," Scarab took over. "They'd like nothing better than to come in here and take over, ransack everything magical from this little pipsqueak of a country and take it all back home with them. We're going to make sure they get their wish, and we're going to kill a few of our most annoying enemies right along with it."

"They've dismissed us in the past," Billy-Ray said. "They don't rate us – not compared to Vengeous or the Diablerie, any of those guys. We're the hired help. But we're goin' to show 'em. We're going to show 'em that they should've been scared of us all along."

"They think they know what's coming?" Scarab asked. "They think they know what to expect? They have no idea."

6

INTO THE SANCTUARY

Skulduggery had once told Valkyrie that the best plans are the simple ones. Her plan was not a simple plan, but it was the only one they had, so they were stuck with it.

"Here's what we do," Valkyrie said as she paced the floor of Ghastly's shop. "We go to the Sanctuary and ask to see Guild. Guild will keep us waiting, as he always does, because he won't want anything to appear different until he knows for sure that we know he has the skull."

Tanith, Ghastly and Fletcher looked at her and nodded.

"However," she continued, "he'll also be assuming that we *do* know, so he'll be waiting for us to make a move. Fletcher won't be with us, which will make Guild suspect that he's already teleported in."

"And where will I be?" Fletcher asked excitedly.

"I don't know, fixing your hair or something. The point is his attention will be in two places – where *we* are and where the *skull* is."

"And how do we find out where the skull is?" Tanith asked.

"The reasonable place to put it would be the Repository," Ghastly said. "Put it with all the other artefacts and magical objects and keep it there. But he's not going to do that."

"It's too obvious," agreed Valkyrie. "That's the first place we'd look. It's also the first place we're *going* to look."

Fletcher frowned. "But it's not going to be there."

"No, but the cloaking sphere *is*."

"The invisibility ball?" said Fletcher.

"Cloaking sphere," insisted Valkyrie.

"Invisibility ball sounds better."

"Invisibility ball sounds stupid." She turned to the others. "Once we get it, we call Fletcher. He arrives, we let them close in on us and then we use the sphere."

"And they think we've teleported out," Tanith finished, smiling.

Valkyrie nodded. "And then, hopefully, Guild sends someone to check on the skull. We follow, grab it and *then* we teleport out. If it doesn't pan out like that, we can at least search for it without being seen."

"China will have to be ready," said Ghastly. "Once they realise what's happened, Davina Marr and the Cleavers will come after all of us."

"Can I just point something out?" Fletcher asked. "That is an *awful* plan. On a scale of one to ten – the Trojan Horse being a ten and General Custer versus all those Indians being a one – your plan is a zero. I don't think it's a plan at all. I think it's just a series of happenings that are, to be honest, unlikely to follow on from each other in the way in which everyone's probably hoping."

"Do you have a better plan?" Valkyrie asked.

"Of course not. I'm a man of action, not thought."

Valkyrie nodded. "You're definitely not a man of thought."

"Why are you in charge anyway? What do *you* know about organising something like this?"

"I have faith," Tanith said.

"As do I," said Ghastly.

Valkyrie smiled at them gratefully. "So you think the plan will work?"

"God, no," said Ghastly.

"Sorry, Val," said Tanith.

Valkyrie stood with Tanith outside the old Waxworks Museum, letting the rain drench her hair. The windows were boarded up and there was a rusted gate pulled across the door. Even before the museum had closed down, it had never been impressive. She remembered school visits, trudging through dark corridors, gazing blankly at wax statues of boring politicians. She often wondered how things would be now if, as a little girl, she had wandered away from the tour group and found the hidden door.

If she had entered the Sanctuary *then*, would she have been taken under Skulduggery's wing that much earlier? Or would the Cleavers merely have chopped her head off the moment they saw her? Probably the latter.

At least, back then, Eachan Meritorious had been Grand Mage of the Council of Elders. These days they didn't even *have* a Council, only the Grand Mage, Thurid Guild, whom Skulduggery had once suspected of treason. Even now that Valkyrie knew he wasn't guilty of *that* charge, she still viewed him as a dangerous individual with his own agenda.

And Guild had the skull.

Needing a replacement for Remus Crux, Guild had poached

Davina Marr and her subordinate, Pennant, from one of the American Sanctuaries, and provided them with whatever they needed to do their job. Guild's first decree had been that the portal never be opened again, lest more Faceless Ones come through. He had known Valkyrie and the others were hunting for the skull, and until today they had managed to stay one step ahead of him. But now, it seemed, Guild had overtaken them at the last hurdle.

The wind took the rain in at an angle and Valkyrie pulled her collar tight. She had called China, who had listened to the plan, such as it was, and assured her that if it did in fact work, then she would be available to help. She also said that there were two Sanctuary agents watching her at all times, and another two at Aranmore Farm. She had barely been able to send out her students to set up that perimeter around Haggard without the agents noticing. Valkyrie didn't care. Only one thing mattered.

A bald man in a nice coat smiled as he passed them. Tanith ignored him, but Valkyrie returned the smile politely. There was something very familiar about him. He walked on and she looked around, wary of anyone trying to sneak up behind them.

"Ladies."

She looked back. Ghastly stood where the bald man had been a second ago. Valkyrie was about to ask him what was going on, but Tanith figured it out before she spoke. "The façade tattoo," she said, astonished. "It works!"

Ghastly smiled. "No more hat and scarf disguises for me, thank you very much. I can only use it for half an hour each day, but China's working on a way to extend that."

"Show me!" Valkyrie demanded, unable to stop her own smile from spreading.

Ghastly pulled apart the collar of his shirt and she saw the small tattoos, freshly burned into either side of his neck. He touched them and unblemished skin flowed upwards, rippling over his scars until it covered his whole head.

"Oh my God," she said.

Ghastly smiled. "What do you think?"

"Oh my God," she said again.

His features were strong, his jaw square and his skin, though slightly waxy, was clear and unscarred.

"China wanted to give me hair, but I thought that would be just a little *too* much, you know?"

"Oh my God."

"You keep saying that. Tanith, what do you think?"

"I like it," Tanith said. "But I dig scars too."

He smiled, and touched the tattoos, and the perfect skin melted back into them, revealing the scars once again.

"Are we ready?" he asked, looking at the Waxworks Museum.

"I don't like going anywhere without my sword," Tanith grumbled. "You do realise that if the Cleavers come for us, they won't care that we're on the same side. They'll cut us into itty-bitty pieces just because they can."

"If that happens," Ghastly said, "you'll at least die comforted by the fact that you had the moral high ground."

"Well, that'll be nice," she muttered.

They went around the back of the Waxworks Museum and entered through the open door. It was dark and the corridor they walked along was narrow. They passed three wax statues. Valkyrie wasn't surprised they'd been left here when the museum closed down. They weren't very good and only one of them had a head.

They finally came to a wax statue that looked like the person it was supposed to be – Phil Lynott from the band Thin Lizzy. It turned its head as they approached.

"Hello," it said.

"Hi, Phil," replied Valkyrie.

Tanith, who had actually known the real Phil Lynott when he was alive, found the figure too unnerving, so she stayed at the back and didn't look at it.

"We request an audience with the Grand Mage," Ghastly said.

"Do you have an appointment?" the figure said, looking down at a page it had stuck to the back of its guitar. "You're not on the list."

"We don't have an appointment, but we request to be seen."

The wax head of Phil Lynott frowned. It didn't like its new role. It was originally supposed to only open and close the door, but now that the Sanctuary didn't have an Administrator, its job description had expanded.

"I'll tell him you're here," it said and closed its eyes.

While they waited, Valkyrie became aware of how fast her heart was beating. If this didn't work, they could all be arrested and it would be her fault. Worse, their one opportunity to get Skulduggery back would pass, and she'd never see him again.

The wax figure opened one of its eyes. "Any of you going to the final?" it asked.

Valkyrie took a moment. "I'm sorry?"

"The All-Ireland," the figure said. "Dublin versus Kerry. Going to be a good one. I asked if I could go. I've never been to Croke Park. The Grand Mage said no. He said it would raise some questions if I'm recognised."

"He's probably right," said Valkyrie slowly.

The figure opened both eyes. "The Grand Mage has been informed," it said. "He has instructed a guide to take you to the

Greeting Room, and he will be with you as soon as his schedule allows."

"Thank you," Valkyrie said, and the wall beside them rumbled and parted, and they went through.

They got to the bottom of the stone stairs and a sour-looking man beckoned to them impatiently. Valkyrie glanced at the grey-clad Cleavers as she passed them, their faces hidden behind visored helmets. She used to find them threatening, but compared to the White Cleaver who stood with the Necromancers, they were positively cuddly.

The impatient sorcerer herded them quickly through the corridors.

"I don't have time to be doing this," he griped. "I've got work to do, for God's sake. Don't they know I have work to do? Showing you people where to go is an Administrator's job. Do I *look* like an Administrator to you?"

"No," Tanith said. "You look like a remarkably grumpy man."

He glared at her and she narrowed her eyes. He looked away.

"In there," he said, pointing to a room. "The Grand Mage will be with you when he's with you. If you want anything, tea or coffee, get it yourself and don't bother me any more."

He stalked off and they looked at each other.

"Guild wants us left alone so that we'll go after the skull," Ghastly said quietly. "He wants us arrested and thrown in the cells. He's just waiting for us to make a wrong move."

"Let's not disappoint him then," Tanith responded. They ignored the Greeting Room and took the first corridor to their right. The people they passed didn't even glance at them.

They passed the Gaol, where the sickest, most evil sorcerers in the country were kept in cages hanging off the ground. An average criminal would be sent to one of the maximum security prisons, but the Gaol was reserved for the worst of the worst.

Beyond the Gaol was the Repository. Making sure no one was watching, Tanith pushed open the double doors and they crept inside. Ghastly held up his hand and read the air, feeling any disturbances.

"We're alone," he announced and all three of them immediately strode among the dimly-lit shelves, looking for a wooden sphere about twice the size of a tennis ball.

Valkyrie hurried to the place where the cloaking sphere had been kept the last time she was here, but the space was empty. She quickly checked the rest of the shelf, her eyes skimming over the arcane objects. The collection of magical artefacts in this room was enough to make collectors like China Sorrows envious.

They searched for five or six minutes and came up with nothing.

"This isn't good," Ghastly muttered when Valkyrie passed him.

She clicked her fingers to summon a flame into her hand and searched the darker recesses of the room. This wasn't good at all.

"Do we have a Plan B?" Tanith called out from behind a stack of scrolls.

"We barely have a Plan A," Valkyrie muttered.

Ghastly had his ear to the door and he stepped away. "They're coming," he said.

Furious, Valkyrie whipped out her phone and called Fletcher. Her plan hadn't worked. The only thing they could do now was get out before they were caught.

"The Repository," she said into the phone and Fletcher appeared behind her. Symbols flashed on the walls and blue lightning darted to where he was standing. He screamed as the lightning danced through him. When the symbols faded, he collapsed with a moan.

It was a trap and, right on cue, the double doors swung open and a dark-haired woman walked in, a squad of Cleavers behind her.

Ghastly and Tanith converged on Valkyrie as she knelt by Fletcher.

"Get us out of here," she ordered, but tremors coursed through Fletcher's body.

"Can't," he mumbled.

Davina Marr looked at them and smiled. "Welcome to the Sanctuary. You are all under arrest."

7

BACK TO ARANMORE

The Interrogation Room was bound. Valkyrie could feel the low ebb of her magic, just out of reach. She didn't like that feeling. It added to her uneasiness.

She sat across from Marr and did her best to ignore Pennant, standing beside the door. Having the door in front of her was their mistake. Anytime Skulduggery had used this interview room, he'd positioned the suspects with their backs to it. It meant they had to crane their necks to see whoever walked in. The way Marr had arranged it, it was almost like this was Valkyrie's office and she was sitting at her own desk.

Valkyrie worked at looking calm and hiding the panic she was feeling. This had been their one chance to get Skulduggery back. If Guild hid the skull or worse, destroyed it, their one chance would disappear. She went cold inside thinking about it.

"Valkyrie," Marr said eventually, raising her different coloured eyes from whatever it was she was reading. Valkyrie doubted the file had anything to do with her. It was probably just some random collection of pages Marr thought might intimidate her. "You're in quite a lot of trouble."

Valkyrie said nothing and rubbed the fingers of her right hand against each other. Her Necromancer ring had been taken. She missed it.

Marr had dark hair, cut short at the neck. She was pretty, in an unremarkable way. "You were caught trying to steal Sanctuary property. Do you know how serious that is? Do you know how long you could be put in prison for?" Marr sighed as if disappointed. "This isn't a game, Valkyrie. You're part of something that is turning out to be very dangerous. Ghastly Bespoke and Tanith Low are looking at twenty years in prison at the very least. Twenty years, Valkyrie. What is it you were trying to steal anyway?"

Valkyrie fixed her eyes on a speck of lint on Marr's collar and didn't answer.

"We have Skulduggery Pleasant's head. I know you're here to steal it, and let me assure you, we do understand. Skulduggery was a friend of yours."

"*Is* a friend," corrected Valkyrie.

"Was I referring to him in the past tense?" Marr asked, looking ashamed. "Oh dear, I'm very sorry. Yes, he *is* a friend of yours and I'm sure you consider him a very *good* friend. We *all* have good friends and we would do a lot for those friends – within reason, naturally. But this crusade of yours, to open up the portal, it's... quite frankly, it is *not* within reason."

"I don't know what you mean," Valkyrie said.

Marr's smile was becoming as irritating as her manner. "Of course you don't," she whispered conspiratorially. "But let's pretend you did. Let's pretend, and this is without incriminating yourself – that means to get yourself into trouble – that you *did* want to open the portal to try and bring your friend back. It would mean that you'd *also* be opening the portal for the Faceless Ones. Do you see that? Do you understand?"

Valkyrie was becoming fixated on Marr's little nose. It was like a target, begging to have a chair smashed into it.

"The only reason they came through the last time was

because they had been signalled," Valkyrie said. "Hypothetically speaking, if we were to open that portal now, they wouldn't be waiting. But Skulduggery *would*."

"The Grand Mage has expressly forbidden that portal to ever be opened again. I'm sorry."

"I don't work for the Grand Mage."

"The Sanctuary polices the entire magical community in Ireland – not just the people who work there. Valkyrie, I hate to be the one to tell you this, but your friend is most likely dead."

"Of course he's dead. He's a skeleton."

"For almost a year he's been trapped on a world with the Faceless Ones. We can only imagine the horror and the agony he must have been put through before they finally decided to end his existence. We can only imagine what they reduced him to – the screaming, the crying, the begging. Sweetheart, in a way you're lucky he's gone. If he ever did return, I'm sure you'd find him a little... pathetic."

"Don't call me sweetheart."

Marr blinked, surprised. "Oh. OK."

"And *never* call him pathetic."

Marr leaned forward, resting her elbows on the table between them. "I can help you. I want to help you. Tell me who planned this and you can walk away. We'll drop all charges against you. Help us punish the people who deserve to be punished – Ghastly, Tanith and China. Oh, yes, we know she's involved. She's mixed up in every seedy little operation in the country. Sanctuaries all over the world want Miss Sorrows behind bars for the things she's done in the past. You'll be doing everyone a great service."

When she didn't get a response, Marr shook her head. "This is a one-time offer, Valkyrie. The moment I walk out that door, you'll be taken back to your cell to await transport to a Gaol. You'll go to prison, sweetheart. Please, I don't want to see that happen to you. Talk to me, let me help you and you can walk away."

Valkyrie met her eyes. "And Fletcher?"

Marr nodded. "Mr Renn is doing fine. We installed that security system to temporarily disrupt certain electrical impulses in his mind. He can't teleport if he doesn't have a clear head, now can he? But I assure you, he's fine now."

"Are you going to offer the same deal to him?"

"Do you want us to? Is there some kind of... connection between the two of you? I'll be honest, Valkyrie, if you help us, I think I can persuade the Grand Mage to release him. I think I can do that."

"And Guild will let him go? He won't want to hang on to

him? Fletcher *is* the last Teleporter alive after all."

"I really, really don't know, sweetheart, what the Grand Mage has in mind. If you're asking would he like Fletcher to work for this Sanctuary, then yes, I'm sure he would. Fletcher has a unique and sought-after ability. Maybe, how about this, maybe you *both* could sign up? Would you like that? Become an official Sanctuary agent? You might make a good team."

"Why doesn't Guild want us to get Skulduggery back?"

Marr shook her head. "You wouldn't understand. The Grand Mage has to weigh up everything about this. He has to evaluate the risk against the reward. It's a big, important decision that he's made and I think he's made the right one. Skulduggery made a sacrifice. He died so that we could live. The Grand Mage is respecting that and we should too."

"Guild said Bliss made the sacrifice. He said Bliss saved us all."

"Mr Bliss gave his life, Valkyrie."

"I know he did. I was there. I saw it happen. You didn't, but I did. I saw Bliss die and I saw what happened next. I saw Skulduggery get dragged through that portal. He reached out to me, but I couldn't save him."

"That's very sad," Marr said gently.

"But Guild ignored all that. He gave all the credit to Bliss because he didn't want to admit that he was wrong about Skulduggery."

"No, Valkyrie, that's not what happened."

"Guild doesn't want us to even *try* to get Skulduggery back because Guild doesn't *want* Skulduggery back. He hates him. He always has."

Marr pinched the bridge of her nose. "China Sorrows has brainwashed you," she said sadly. "I can't take it any more. I'll order her arrest immediately."

"China's done nothing wrong," said Valkyrie angrily.

"You'd do anything she tells you to," Marr sighed, gathering up her papers. "Detective Pennant will take you back to your cell."

Pennant opened the door and Marr walked over to it.

"You'll regret this," Valkyrie said.

Marr turned. "Are you threatening me, child?"

"No. I'm just saying you'll regret this. Anyone who stands against Skulduggery always regrets it. The Detective before you, for example. Remus Crux. Have you heard from him lately?"

Marr's face went taut and she didn't answer.

"He stood against Skulduggery," Valkyrie continued, "and then his mind was torn to pieces. Everyone regrets it, Miss Marr. You will too."

Marr turned to go, then turned again.

"I've changed my mind," she announced. "I'll escort you back to your cell personally. Detective Pennant, you may leave us."

Pennant smiled and walked out without a word. Marr swept her hand to the door as an invitation. "After you, Valkyrie."

Valkyrie got up and walked over, expecting Marr to shackle her wrists before she left the room, but she walked into the corridor unbound and felt her magic return to her. She led the way down towards the holding cells, Marr at her elbow, and tried to figure out what was going on. Had Marr simply forgotten the shackles? Did she not think Valkyrie was a legitimate threat? Or was it a trap? Was Marr waiting for Valkyrie to attempt an escape? The closer they got to the cells, the wilder her mind spun.

"You said those who stand against your skeleton friend regret it," Marr said as they approached the corner to the cells. "But what about those who stand *with* him? What about Bliss, since you brought him up? How is *he* doing these days?"

Valkyrie said nothing and turned the corner. She frowned. There was usually someone on duty at the desk, but today the chair was empty.

Marr spoke right into her ear. "That skeleton got people *killed*

– friends, people he loved, his own *family*. It's a wonder he didn't get *you* killed before he went. It's a damn shame, if you ask me."

Valkyrie turned quickly and Marr pushed her back and laughed.

"Don't worry, sweetie. I know what it is. All those hormones raging, you have all these conflicting emotions..."

Valkyrie raised her hand to push at the air, but Marr was faster. The air rushed around her and Valkyrie hit the wall and dropped to the floor.

Marr strolled towards her. "You had a crush on him before he was pulled into hell, didn't you? A little one? You can tell me. It's sad and pathetic and highly amusing, but I promise I won't laugh."

Valkyrie clicked her fingers and Marr kicked her wrist. The fire went out and she was hauled up. She swung a punch that missed, and Marr sent her face-first into a cell door.

"No one likes an upstart," Marr said. "If you start behaving, maybe I'll even let you in to say goodbye to his head. It makes a very nice ornament for the Grand Mage's office."

Marr was close and Valkyrie reached out and grabbed her. She got one foot behind Marr's, tried to throw her, but Marr bent her knees and moved. Valkyrie tumbled backwards over Marr's hip. All her weight came down on her shoulder and she cried out. Marr took hold of her arm and twisted it as she kneeled on her ribs.

"Assault on a Sanctuary agent," Marr said sadly. "If you were an adult, that would mean years in prison for you. But seeing as how you're a child... I don't know. Maybe all that'll happen is that you'll be branded with a few binding symbols, to permanently disable your magic. That wouldn't be so bad, would it, you insolent little wretch?"

"Get *off* me."

"Or what?" Marr smiled. "You'll start crying? I can already see the tears in your eyes. Look at you. So helpless. So weak. You don't even have your little ring, do you?"

With her free hand, Marr took the black ring from her pocket.

"Now what's a nice girl like you doing studying a nasty discipline like Necromancy? We don't *like* Necromancers around here, haven't you realised that? Nobody likes them. They can't be trusted."

"Let me up."

Marr let the ring fall to the floor and slapped Valkyrie across the face. "You do *not* tell me what to do." She slapped her again. "You do *not* tell your elders what to do. Do you understand me?" Another slap. "Say you understand. *Say you understand.*"

Through gritted teeth, Valkyrie said, "I'm going to kill you."

Marr pressed her knee in harder against Valkyrie's ribs and Valkyrie cried out again.

"You want me to break your arm, you little brat? You want me to break your ribs? Puncture a lung? Because I can do it. I can do anything I want and no one will question me. So go ahead. Lie there and threaten me some more. See where it gets you."

Fighting back the tears, Valkyrie glared but said nothing.

"Good girl," Marr said, her eyes narrow. "Now apologise."

Valkyrie clenched her jaw.

"I said, *apologise*. There's no one here but us. You've got no one to impress. Apologise and I'll let you up and put you in your cell. If you *don't* apologise..."

Marr slapped her again and raised her hand for another strike.

Valkyrie worked to ignore her pride and the anger that humiliation brought. She swallowed. "I'm sorry."

Immediately, Marr softened. "OK. OK, Valkyrie, that's all I needed to hear." The pressure on her ribs was removed. "Now ask me to let you up."

Valkyrie took a moment then, "Can I get up?"

"Say please."

"Please... can I get up?"

"Of course."

Marr stepped back and Valkyrie turned on to her hands and knees, and started to rise. Suddenly the air was pushing down, keeping her hunched over.

"Say thank you," Marr said, controlling the air with her hand. Valkyrie looked up at her. "Say thank you, Detective Marr, for letting me stand up."

And Valkyrie said, "Thank you, Detective Marr, for giving me back my ring."

Marr's eyes flickered to the ground where the ring had fallen, but it wasn't there any more, and before she could do anything about it, Valkyrie sent a fist of shadows slamming into the detective's chest.

Marr stumbled and Valkyrie straightened, reaching out through the air for the desk. It shot forward and slammed into Marr's legs, and she flipped and fell over it.

Valkyrie opened the desk, snatched the keys up and ran to the cells. She unlocked Ghastly's door and he emerged, tackling Marr as she came at Valkyrie.

"Prisoners are escaping!" Marr roared.

Valkyrie unlocked the second door and Tanith came out, just as Cleavers appeared around the corner.

"Get Fletcher," Tanith said in Valkyrie's ear, "then get Skulduggery back," and she launched herself at the Cleavers.

Valkyrie unlocked the last cell and hauled Fletcher out.

"Stop them!" Marr screeched. Already the Cleavers had Ghastly and Tanith on the ground, arms locked behind them.

"Guild's office," Valkyrie said to Fletcher. He nodded and closed his eyes, forcing himself to calm down and picture their destination.

Then they were outside Guild's door. Valkyrie barged through. The office was empty. The shelves groaned with heavy books and artefacts, and the desk was made out of what appeared to be solid gold. Beside the desk was a cabinet. Skulduggery's skull lay inside.

Shadows curled around her fist and she punched through the glass and grabbed the skull. She felt Fletcher's hand on her shoulder and she blinked.

They were now standing in the maze of bookcases in China's library.

Fletcher looked at her. "Are you OK?"

"Don't worry about me," she said. She could feel the side of her face burning from where Marr had repeatedly slapped her. "We have to get to Aranmore Farm."

"We're opening the portal?" Fletcher asked, concerned.

"Just you, me and China? So who goes in with you?"

"No one. I go in alone."

"No." He shook his head. "It's way too dangerous."

"We don't have time to waste!" Valkyrie said, suddenly angry. "We have to do it now before they find us again and lock us away! This is my only chance to get him back!"

"*Our* only chance," he said.

"Yes. Yes, that's what I... Fletcher, listen, China has to stay with you, on the farm. She has to make sure that you're able to reopen the portal for Skulduggery and me to get back. I'm going in alone and that's all there is to it."

Fletcher looked at her, his jaw clenched. "Fine," he snapped and led the way through the maze.

Valkyrie didn't know any of the sorcerers they passed among the stacks, and none of them raised their eyes from their open books. The library was considered to be a neutral place, where privacy was paramount.

China Sorrows was waiting for them, dressed in black trousers and a simple blue shirt. As usual, her unnatural beauty elevated her outfit to something beyond the ordinary. A delicate chain hung around her left wrist. Her hair, black as deepest sin, framed her face while her eyes, as pale a blue as her brother's had been, watched them approach.

Valkyrie fought down the feelings that were stirring within her. Fletcher wasn't quite so successful.

"I love you," he whispered and was ignored.

"The plan didn't work," Valkyrie told her. "In fact, it probably made things worse. Ghastly and Tanith are under arrest, and agents are coming here to take you in."

China sighed. "And we're going to rescue Skulduggery *now*, I take it? With the full might of the Sanctuary bearing down on us?"

"Yes. Sorry about that."

China shrugged. "You make life interesting, Valkyrie. Just give me a moment, I have two annoying spies to deal with."

Valkyrie looked behind her as a man and woman advanced, shackles in hand.

China tapped her forearms and glowing tattoos rose to the surface of her skin. She flung her arms wide and a wall of blue energy slammed into the agents, knocking them back. They were unconscious even before they stopped tumbling across the floor.

An elderly sorcerer peered round a bookcase and scowled.

"My apologies for the disturbance," China said gracefully. "They wouldn't pay their late fees."

The elderly woman shrugged and went back to her reading.

China held out her hands and both Valkyrie and Fletcher took one. "These shoes will probably be ruined," she said, "but I'm sure one of you will inform Skulduggery of the sacrifices I have made getting him back. Take us to the farm, Mr Renn."

The library vanished and the afternoon sun was without heat. A cold wind blew in across the fields of Aranmore and howled softly through the ruined walls of the farmhouse.

"This boy is handy to have around," China said, but for once Fletcher didn't seem to be taking notice of her. His eyes were on Valkyrie as they walked.

"Have you said goodbye to your parents?" he asked.

"Shut up, Fletcher."

"I just thought you might like to, that's all. One last goodbye before you get yourself killed."

"The only way it would be a last goodbye is if you don't have that portal open for me to get back."

He laughed bitterly. "You're walking into a world run by a race of evil gods. And for what? If Skulduggery isn't dead, he's insane. One glance at a Faceless One is enough to drive you nuts. He's been there for almost a year, Val. How many glances do you think he's had?"

"You don't know him. He's alive and he's waiting for me."

"We're taking a big risk here, aren't we? Like, a major risk?

We're opening a door to a universe of unspeakable evils and hoping they don't notice. Is Skulduggery worth it if this goes wrong?"

"If you're not going to help," Valkyrie said, "I can't make you. But if you are, then shut up. None of us would be here if it wasn't for him, and he wouldn't leave any of *us* over there. Not even you."

They reached the farmhouse and froze. A Sanctuary agent ambled by inside, sipping a mug of tea. He frowned, and turned, and seemed surprised to find three people staring in at him through the gaping hole in the wall.

"Um," he said.

Valkyrie snapped her palm. The air rippled and the sorcerer went skidding across the floor. She stepped inside, using her ring to gather the shadows in the house and bring them crashing down on his head. He didn't get up.

China and Fletcher joined her, and they moved to the hole in the opposite wall, the one that opened up to the yard beyond. Across the yard, standing amid the rusted farm machinery, was the second sorcerer. He saw them and his hand dug into his jacket for his phone.

Fletcher vanished and reappeared instantly next to the mage. He put his hand on the man's shoulder and then they were both gone. A moment later Fletcher was back, standing right in front of Valkyrie. She was about to ask where he had put the Sanctuary agent when she heard a terrified yell, and the agent dropped from the sky and hit the ground hard. He moaned, then stopped moving.

Fletcher pulled Valkyrie towards him, and before she could protest he kissed her. She stiffened in his arms, but as his right thumb brushed her cheek, she relaxed into him. Her belly did flips. And then the kiss was over.

"If we're going to go through with this," he said gruffly, "then hurry it up. It's not everyday I send someone into hell."

China made a circle on the ground and Fletcher knelt in it, holding the skull in both hands. She carved protective symbols around him. If something *did* come out of the portal uninvited, she explained, these symbols would at least give Fletcher enough time to close it before he died. He didn't look comforted, but he didn't say anything.

She activated the symbols and red smoke drifted from them, swirling with the black smoke that rose from the circle. The smoke formed a column that grew more violent as it twisted into the sky.

Fletcher knew what to do this time. Eleven months ago, forced to open the portal, he had to learn as he went. He had to use the Isthmus Anchor – back then it was the Grotesquery, today it was the skull – without sufficient preparation and he said it was like tearing open his insides. Today, from the glimpses Valkyrie caught through the smoke, he had everything under control. He looked determined. Angry, but determined.

A yellow light appeared, like a flattened sun, the edges boiling with flame. It grew wider.

China took Valkyrie's arm, leaning in close to be heard over the roar of the column of smoke. *"You have one hour,"* she shouted. *"In exactly one hour that gate will open again. You'd better be ready – with or without him."*

"I'm not leaving him there," Valkyrie shouted back. *"You just make sure Fletcher's still here when it's time for us to come home."*

China looked at her, her blue eyes bright, and she hugged Valkyrie. "Thank you for doing this," China said into Valkyrie's ear.

China stepped away and Valkyrie turned to the portal. It was taller than she was now. She licked her lips and walked forward. The wind whipped her hair and she could feel the gravitational pull, eager to welcome her. Valkyrie hesitated and then ran, straight into the yellow.

8

CALLING DIBS

Springheeled Jack missed London. He missed its rooftops and its towers and its parapets. He missed the way he could dance, high above it all, watching the people pass below him. He missed the way Londoners sounded as he killed them – like they were offended that anyone would even dare.

Jack hadn't been home in over a year. They were hunting him there. He'd tried Paris, he'd tried Berlin, and he'd liked them well enough, but he knew he was homesick when he realised the only people he was killing were English tourists. That had sent him into a spiral of depression that lasted months. Finally, in an effort to confront this problem, he had made a list of everyone he viewed as being responsible for his exile, and he marvelled at the way the depression quickly turned to anger. Every name on that list worked for various Sanctuaries around the world, and suddenly Jack's mission was clear.

Destroy the Sanctuaries.

And now here he was, serendipity be praised, back in Dublin, working with two men he had never expected to share the same space with again, Billy-Ray Sanguine and Dusk. But since Sanguine was no longer palling around with those Faceless Ones nutters, and since his fight with Dusk hadn't been personal to begin with, Jack was willing to forgive and forget. They were all working towards the same goal after all – revenge on those who had wronged them.

"I want Tanith Low," he said to that other bloke, Scapegrace, while they were lounging about in the castle.

Scapegrace looked up, startled that anyone was talking to him. "I'm sorry?"

"Tanith Low," Jack repeated. "Her of the brown leather and the singing sword. I want to be the one to get her."

"Oh," Scapegrace said.

"In a way, you know, she's responsible for me bein' hunted. She arrested me – put me in that cell where Sanguine found me. If I hadn't agreed to help him in return for freedom, I'd never have been hunted in the first place."

"Right," Scapegrace said.

"What about you then?"

"Me?"

"Who do you want revenge on?"

"Oh, uh, Valkyrie Cain."

"She's a popular one to get revenge on. What age is she, fifteen? Fifteen years old and already four people want to kill her."

"Well," Scapegrace said, leaning forward, like he was confiding, "she's responsible for foiling my plans, you see."

"That so?"

"Oh, yes. I'm an artist. I make murder into art. That's kind of what I do – that's my whole thing. And she has repeatedly stopped me from doing that. Also, one time, she beat me up when I was already really badly injured."

"A fifteen-year-old girl beat you up?"

"When I was badly injured, yes. And she was fourteen at the time."

"Well, I suppose in the right environment, Elemental magic is hard to defend against."

"Oh, she didn't use any magic."

"So she just... beat you up then?"

"When I was injured, yes."

"How injured were you?"

"Very."

"You were very injured?"

"Yes, I was. Have you ever been beaten up by a fourteen-year-old girl?"

"Can't say I have."

"It's not very nice."

"I wouldn't say it is."

"So that's why I want revenge."

"Listen, mate, I don't mean to pick a fight or nothin', but you call yourself the Killer Supreme, right? Have you ever actually killed anyone?"

Scapegrace erupted into horribly forced laughter, desperate and panicky, and Jack could have sworn he started to blush.

Jack didn't much care of course. They were here to make up the numbers, to sit here while Scarab and Sanguine called the shots. And then, when it was time, they would strike.

Jack was looking forward to that bit.

9

DEAD NEW WORLD

The sky was red.

The sun, directly above her, was a ball of fire. It was big and hot, and closer than the sun back home.

Once the city would have been impressive. Its inhabitants would have lived in the towering cliff, using the caves as homes, carving doors and windows from the rock, before extending outwards. The stone houses that they built, on top of each other, jutted from the cliff face and reminded Valkyrie of pictures she'd seen of mountain towns in Brazil. She imagined that it had been a city teeming with life, energy and noise, with hundreds of thousands of people packed in together and forced to get along.

It was quiet now though. Quiet and dead.

The portal closed behind her and Valkyrie was in a narrow alley of white, sun-bleached stone that hurt her eyes. She followed the alley down, her footsteps crunching on the cracked ground. She peered into half-crumbled houses as she passed, but every room was empty, stripped bare by the elements and whatever else was around here.

The alley plateaued and opened into a square, and she walked to the middle and turned in a slow circle, scanning her surroundings. She looked up at the cliff face, the sheer size of it finally becoming clear. It wouldn't have been hundreds of thousands of people living here, she realised – it would have been *millions*. A thought struck her. She was standing on an alien world.

Despite herself, Valkyrie grinned.

She shook her head. She had a job to do and a limited amount of time to do it in. She walked through a street that led to her right. The street curved and she was walking on sand that had blown in from the vast expanses of the dry valley around the city. The sand was a deep gold.

She walked for a few minutes, careful to move in a relatively straight line so she could be sure of finding her way back. Ghastly had claimed that her clothes would regulate her temperature no matter what, but something wasn't working. She was perspiring. A trickle of sweat rolled down her face. She took off her coat and left it at a corner as a marker, and felt the sun on her bare shoulders. She opened her top to let the air in, but whatever breeze there may have been was being blocked by the labyrinth of streets. Then she turned another corner and saw the body.

It sat on the ground, propped up against the wall. Its chest was a gaping hole, the insides long since dried up. The head was smooth and featureless. This had been the body of the man called Batu, a body that had been commandeered by the last Faceless One to come through the portal. There was no sign of life in it now though. To the Faceless Ones, human bodies were mere vessels to be used and discarded. Batu's body was nothing more than a leaky old boat or a rusted car. So much for his masterplan to become a god.

The body was holding something in its right hand, a bone, most of it covered by rags. Valkyrie didn't want to imagine that it might be one of Skulduggery's. She was desperate to call out his name, but the idea of breaking this eerie silence repelled her. She didn't know what else to do though. She could spend months checking this city without finding him. No. No, the portal would have opened somewhere in Skulduggery's vicinity. He was nearby. He had to be.

Valkyrie headed back the way she'd come, scooping up her coat and walking fast. She got back to the alley where the portal had delivered her. She followed it as far as she could, until the alley led into a cave. She dropped her coat again and summoned a flame into her hand. Then she stepped out of the sun into pitch-black.

As she walked, she saw shelves carved from the walls and a table that had once been a boulder. There were large areas of the cave where she didn't even need the flame – the windows had been constructed to drink in the sunlight and spread it around. The cave ended at a wall. As Valkyrie turned to go back, she saw a bone in the dirt and beside it stone steps, leading up. She climbed them.

The sun came in through the three windows along the far wall and Valkyrie let the fire in her hand go out. She stood beside the steps and didn't move. In the centre of the room a skeleton lay. Its clothes were shredded and hung off the frame that had been constructed to give the illusion of mass. From what she could see, the trouser-legs were empty and the skeleton's right arm was missing. It lay on its back, its exposed ribcage dirty and covered in dust, and it didn't move.

Something clutched at Valkyrie's heart and wouldn't let go. She made a sound, like a whimper, but when she tried to say his name, she couldn't. Her first step was uncertain because her legs felt weak. She walked slowly, so very slowly, to the middle of the room.

"Hello?" she whispered. The skeleton lay on the ground and didn't move.

"It's me. I've come to take you back. Can you hear me? I found you."

Not even a breeze stirred the ragged clothing.

She knelt by the skeleton. "Please say something. Please. I've missed you so much and I've worked so hard to find you. Please."

She reached out to touch him, and Skulduggery Pleasant whipped his head to her and roared, "*Boo!*"

Valkyrie shrieked and scrambled back, and Skulduggery laughed hysterically, like it was the funniest thing he had ever seen. He was still laughing when she got to her feet, and when she glared at him, he laughed even harder. Eventually, with bouts of laughter still rattling his bones, Skulduggery propped himself up on the only elbow he had left.

"Oh, dear," he said. "Now I'm deriving amusement from scaring my hallucinations. This can't be good for me, psychologically speaking."

"I'm not a hallucination."

He looked up at her. "Yes, you are, my dear, but I wouldn't

worry about it. Being a hallucination is a state of mind, I always say."

"Skulduggery, I'm real."

"That's the spirit."

"No, I mean I'm really real, and I've come to take you home."

"You're an odd one. Usually my hallucinations do a lot more singing and dancing."

"It's me. It's Valkyrie."

"You'd be surprised how many figments of my imagination say that. You don't happen to have an imaginary chessboard with you, do you? I've had a hankering to play for a while now, and since you're an aspect of my personality, you'd probably be a worthy opponent."

"How do I prove to you that I'm real?"

This made him pause. "Intriguing. It's not as if you can tell me something only we would know because if I know it, my hallucination would know it. But, in the theoretical extension of that approach, if you were to tell me something only *you* would know, then that would prove to me that I'm not conjuring you up in my mind."

"So... what will I tell you? My deepest, darkest secret? My earliest memory? My ultimate fear?"

"How about what you had for breakfast this morning?"

"Honey Loops."

"Well, there you go."

"So now you believe I'm real?"

"Not in the slightest. I may have just made that up."

"I found your skull – the one the goblins took. Fletcher used it as an Isthmus Anchor to open the portal and I came through to take you back."

"My skull?"

"It makes sense, doesn't it? It's possible, right?"

"It's... very possible actually."

"Did you think of it? Did you imagine your skull could be used as an Anchor?"

"I didn't, but then I *have* been preoccupied by the torture and the lack of good conversation."

"So if this is something that you hadn't thought of yet, how could I come up with it if I were just a figment of your imagination?"

"Well," Skulduggery said slowly, "you could be a figment of my *subconscious*."

"I'm not your subconscious. I'm Valkyrie. I'm real. And I'm here to rescue you."

"If you can get me my limbs back, I'll believe you."

"Fine," Valkyrie said, looking around the cave.

He spoke to her as she searched. "To be honest, I've given up hope of ever being rescued, so this entire scenario is kind of redundant. No offence meant. At first, I thought some of the survivors might come for me, but I've reconciled myself to the fact that they're all dead by now."

"Survivors?" Valkyrie echoed. She picked up a leg, fully intact, and brushed off the dust before handing it to him.

"There were survivors when I arrived," he told her, fixing the femur to his hip in that convenient, yet obviously painful, way of his. "This was the last world the Faceless Ones reached and they took their time with it. I got to know a couple of people before they were killed and I was captured. It took me a while to learn their language, but from what they told me, this was once a world full of magic. Then, 300 years ago, the Faceless Ones appeared."

"But the Faceless Ones were expelled from our reality *thousands* of years ago." Valkyrie went down the stone steps to the bone she'd glimpsed earlier. This was his other leg, and she scooped up a handful of what appeared to be toes.

"Ah, but this isn't where the Faceless Ones were exiled to," Skulduggery said as she came back up. "The Ancients expelled them from our world and forced them into a barren dimension. But the Faceless Ones escaped and tore through the walls of reality to a universe teeming with life. Over time, they decimated that universe, killing everyone, destroying suns, laying waste to whole galaxies. And when they were finished, they moved on."

She gave him the pieces of his leg. "To another reality?"

"One after another, snuffing each one out as they searched for their way back home. 300 years ago they arrived here, and could go no further. They've been looking for a way off ever since."

"Oh my God..."

"And all this time we thought the Ancients had exiled them to where they could do no harm. Countless trillions of beings, Valkyrie, killed because of us."

She didn't respond.

"If you're real," he said, "I know what you're feeling. Guilt, yes? A tremendous sense of awful responsibility for something you had no part of. That was my reaction when I first heard the story. I didn't know what to do. Maybe send each reality a card, with a little apology? Then, when the Faceless Ones found us and killed the others and took me, I finally realised that nothing good could come from pointless remorse and I got over it. The constant torture proved to be a good distraction."

"Are you... OK?"

"Not even remotely." He paused, halfway through putting his leg back together. "They haven't killed me, and they haven't taken my magic away, because every day they hunt me. They take turns, I think, in inhabiting Batu's body. They track me down, I fight back, they win easily and they tear me apart. Yesterday, for instance, they pulled off my legs and wandered off with one of my arms. They leave me overnight to put myself back together, so that they can hunt me down again with their pets the next day. It is, as you can imagine, oodles of fun."

"Well, all that's over now. We have half an hour before the portal opens again and we're going through. Come on."

He looked up at her. "I'm missing an arm."

"So?"

"You wouldn't say that if it were *your* arm. I'm not going anywhere without my arm. Fetch me my limb and I'll go through the imaginary portal with you."

"Well, you can help me look for it," Valkyrie said and reached for him. Her hand hit an invisible wall. "What is *this*?"

"Something I've been working on," he replied smugly. "I've had a lot of time with nothing to concentrate on but magic. The Faceless Ones have no problems getting through this little wall of air, but for figments of my imagination like yourself, it's quite tough. I've also taught myself a couple of other new tricks."

"So you're going to sit here while I do all the work?"

"Indeed I am. If I were you, I'd find the body that used to be Batu's. If the arm is anywhere, it's there."

"Yes, I saw it. It's outside, down a couple of streets. We could *walk* there and still be back in plenty of time for the portal."

"And if you *run*, you'll get it to me sooner."

Valkyrie sighed and left him while he finished putting his leg back together, and a muttered rendition of 'Dry Bones' followed her down the steps. She hurried out to the red sky and retraced her path, guided by her footsteps in the sand. She wished she had a pair of sunglasses to offset the glare. Her arms were rapidly turning red under the sun, and she wondered how she'd explain sunburn in September to her parents.

The body sat where she had left it, head down and lifeless. She ran her tongue over her lower lip while she debated the best way to go about this, and then she kicked it in the head. When it didn't try and grab her, she bent down, pulled Skulduggery's arm from its clutches and then her ears popped. She staggered, feeling the goosebumps ripple. The inside of her mouth was tight, dry skin and her beating heart was the drum it was stretched across. She stumbled over the body and fell, and now she was crawling. Her head was filled with deafening whispers.

The Faceless Ones were coming.

10

BLOOD AND BULLETS

China knew when someone was staring at her. It was a sense she'd honed over the last few hundred years, as precise as it was useless. People were *always* staring at her, after all.

She glanced around and Fletcher looked away, embarrassed.

"How long do you think she'll be?" he asked.

China didn't answer. She didn't do small talk. He shrugged and nodded then stuffed his hands in his pockets. He all but started to whistle.

If she bothered with idle conversation, she would have told

the poor boy that this thing with Valkyrie was never going to go anywhere, not when Skulduggery got back. Valkyrie's life revolved around Skulduggery now – she was caught in his orbit, and someone like Fletcher didn't stand a chance.

Skulduggery and Valkyrie were meant for each other. China could see that now. They were meant to find each other, to form this bond and to affect each other's lives. The best the boy could hope for, the best *anyone* could hope for, would be to stand in the wings and look on.

A crescent tattoo faded up on China's wrist and began to burn, signalling to her that someone had breached the perimeter alarms she'd installed.

"Stay here," she ordered and strode off across the yard.

They came around the corner of the farmhouse – a Sanctuary agent she recognised as Pennant and four Cleavers. At a nod, the Cleavers ran at her and China tapped the symbols on her forearms and flung her arms wide. A wave of blue energy struck one of the Cleavers with full force and knocked him back. The other three were ready though, and they twisted into the wave, the magic rolling over their uniforms.

This was no mere arrest, she realised as she dodged the scythes. From the way they were attacking, the Cleavers had permission to use lethal force and they weren't being shy about it. She knocked her fists together and the red tattoos on her knuckles became visible. She ducked a swipe and punched. On impact, the Cleaver's head snapped around and he crumpled and didn't get up. She caught the next one in the gut and he doubled over.

The last Cleaver cracked his scythe's staff against her knee. China gasped in pain and barely managed to avoid the blade that followed it. His uniform was too well protected for this to be any kind of a fair fight.

She collided with him, grabbed his arm and yanked up his sleeve. Her right hand clenched, her fingertips pressing tightly into her palm, activating the symbol she had carved there so long ago. She closed her fingers around his bare wrist. He stiffened and she could have sworn she heard him scream beneath his helmet, and as he collapsed she turned to Pennant and he shot her.

The bullet caught China in the chest and she found herself walking backwards quickly, trying to regain her balance. She brought her hands to the wound, the dark blood gushing out between her fingers. Her legs buckled and she fell awkwardly. Her head hit the ground and she lay there, looking up at the clouds.

"Oh," was all she said.

11

THE FACELESS ONES

Batu's old body stood up slowly. Its back was hunched and its thin arms were curled. From her hiding place, Valkyrie watched it shuffle deeper into the darkness, wondering why the Faceless One was bothering with such a damaged vessel.

The pressure in her ears was back to normal, and while her heart was beating fast, it was no longer threatening to break free of her chest. When she was sure she wasn't going to throw up, she followed at a safe distance. There wasn't a whole lot she could do against a Faceless One, except maybe distract it by dying loudly. If it started to torture Skulduggery again, she'd just have to watch. She didn't much like that idea.

She was still clutching Skulduggery's right arm. It was in one piece, fingers and all, and it clacked slightly as she moved.

The Faceless One dragged itself up the steps and Valkyrie crouched in case it happened to glance back. It didn't of course. Faceless Ones were not the type to "glance". For a start, they didn't even have eyes. Valkyrie waited until it was gone from sight and crept forward. She had a niggling suspicion why Batu's body was still being used – maybe torture was more satisfying when conducted in human form. She climbed the stairs slowly, peeking up to see Skulduggery backing away from the Faceless One as it neared.

"I knew she wasn't real," Skulduggery was saying. "It's all part of some new trick, isn't it?"

He grunted and rose into the air, and suddenly his body locked out straight. Valkyrie watched in horror as an unseen force began separating his bones from each other, centimetre by centimetre. The sounds of his pain started low, then twisted, and he threw his head back and screamed in abject agony as his jaw was slowly pulled from his skull.

Valkyrie bolted into the circle, her Necromancer ring grabbing the shadows and curling them around the Faceless

One's left ankle. She kept running and yanked the shadows with all her strength, but the shadows went taut and her legs flew from under her and she crashed to the ground. The Faceless One hadn't budged. Its blank head turned, and it let Skulduggery drop to a groaning heap. Valkyrie threw his remaining arm to him as she got up.

The Faceless One observed her without moving. She'd experienced this reaction before, eleven months ago. It was China's theory that the Faceless Ones could detect the blood in her veins, the blood of the Last of the Ancients. Valkyrie didn't know if that was the genuine reason, but she took every advantage she could find. She snapped her palms and the air rippled and slammed into the ruined body before her. The rags it wore fluttered in the violent gust, but the body stayed still.

The ring was cold on her finger and it drank in the death this city had seen. She focused the shadows and hurled them at her enemy. A spear of darkness flew into the torso cavity and tore out through the back. The Faceless One staggered and looked down at itself.

Skulduggery sat there, flexing the fingers on both of his hands, and Valkyrie grabbed him and hauled him up. He was surprisingly heavy. They got to the steps, jumped down, and ran on towards the mouth of the cave.

"Faster!" she demanded.

"Why?" he asked. "I'm still not entirely sure you're real."

"I just picked you up back there!"

"That could have been a draught."

They left the cave and Valkyrie grabbed her coat off the ground and looked back. The Faceless One hadn't even reached the steps yet.

She looked at Skulduggery. "I'm not a draught!"

"You look like a draught..."

"That doesn't even make any sense."

"My verbal sparring has been a tad one-sided of late. I should keep moving. You're welcome to come along."

"But this is where the portal opens."

"If the Isthmus Anchor is linked to me, the portal will open near to wherever I am. Come along now, we don't have much time."

"How did it hunt you?" Valkyrie asked as they ran through the narrow alleyway. "It can barely move faster than a walk."

"It has pets," Skulduggery said. "And its pets have pets." He pointed to the red sky. "And here they come now."

She saw them, black against the red, beating their massive wings. Their bodies were the size of buses and their jagged tails were twice as long again. She saw what appeared to be straps, criss-crossing their underbellies, and she realised these beasts had a dozen riders or more saddled on top.

"You'll know they've spotted us when they screech," Skulduggery told her.

The creatures screeched.

Skulduggery and Valkyrie jumped a low wall and ducked through a doorway, moving through the ruined house and out of the window on the other side. The winged beasts swooped low over the streets and the riders dropped from them.

Two riders landed close by. They were skinny things, with primitive tattoos covering their yellow skin, dressed in leathers and furs and wielding thin, wicked blades. Their teeth were sharp and their eyes were dark, and their hair was spiked like porcupine needles.

Skulduggery went to meet them, blocking the first swipe of a dagger and snapping the arm at the elbow. He pulled the screaming rider into the path of his companion, using the momentary confusion to kick out the other rider's knee. He left them and took Valkyrie's hand again, steering them between two houses.

A rider dropped from the roof, but Skulduggery pushed at the air and he flew backwards. Valkyrie spun as another rider dropped behind her. The sword he swung was huge, too big for such a narrow space. She flung her coat into his face then pushed his sword hand down, grabbed his shoulder and kicked his ankle. He fell, smashing his head against the wall.

She snatched back her coat and they ran on, darting into another house as a trio of riders appeared ahead of them. They took the stairs up, ran to the window and jumped through it like they were hurdlers, landing on the roof of the neighbouring house. They jumped from rooftop to rooftop, sprinting to the sheer edge of the city, as all around them, riders clambered up to continue the hunt.

"Do you have a plan?" she called.

"Only rarely," he answered then scooped her into his arms and jumped. There was nothing beneath them but a two-mile drop to the valley floor, and Valkyrie screamed.

"Why are you screaming?" Skulduggery asked in her ear as they tumbled through the air, and she turned her head to him and continued the scream right into his eye socket. He sighed. "Do try to hang on."

Their angle changed abruptly and now they were moving sideways, out of range of the knives that were being hurled at them from the city.

They were flying.

12

DOWN THE BARREL

s China's lifeblood drained away, Pennant walked over to where she lay and aimed his gun at her again. Then Fletcher Renn stepped out of nothing and swung a baseball bat down on Pennant's arm. Pennant screamed and dropped his weapon and Fletcher caught him twice more before he disappeared. A moment later he was back and swung a weightlifter's dumb-bell into Pennant's jaw. Pennant pirouetted like a ballerina and fell to his knees. Fletcher let the dumb-bell fall and vanished, then reappeared with a taser gun. He jabbed it into Pennant's back, electricity crackled and

Pennant jerked and fell forward. The air closed in around Fletcher and he was gone, taking Pennant with him.

China touched the markings at the hinges of her jaw, and the heat started almost immediately, travelling the length of her body and then back again. It focused around the wound and she gritted her teeth. She felt the bullet move and twist, and tears came to her eyes. It worked itself back through the tunnel it had carved, and she cried out as it rose to the surface, now a misshapen lump of lead.

Fletcher reappeared beside her, but she waved him away with a hand slick with blood. The heat intensified and burned away the bacteria that had followed the bullet in. Slowly, far too slowly for her liking, the meat inside her began repairing itself.

13

NO THANKS

alkyrie clung on to Skulduggery and she wasn't screaming any more. She was laughing. He was in a standing position and he moved them quickly through the air with an unnerving casualness. This was what he must have meant by the new tricks he'd taught himself. She looked down. All that empty space beneath them, added to the reality of what they were doing, took her breath away. Then she looked up, at the red sky, and saw the winged beasts swooping down.

Skulduggery altered course, avoiding the claws of the nearest beast. They spun in place then shifted left and a second beast missed them, screeching its displeasure. It was dangerous up here, even more so than in the city, and they flew back over the streets. They dodged another flying creature and passed over the riders, until Skulduggery found a suitable place to touch down. They landed and hurried through a door, into the quiet gloom.

"You can fly," she whispered.

"I got bored walking everywhere," he said.

"Can you teach *me* to fly?"

"You'll need to master everything else about Elemental magic first, but yes. If we live through this, and if you continue your training, and if you're real, then yes, I'll teach you to fly. I'll teach *every* Elemental to fly. It's fun."

"What else can you do?"

He looked at her and cocked his head. "Lots."

A shape loomed in the doorway and Valkyrie's smile vanished. They backed away as the Faceless One came through. Skulduggery clicked the fingers of both hands then thrust them out straight. Twin streams of flame hit the Faceless One, enveloping it completely. Valkyrie stared in amazement. The flame streams were continuous, like two flame-throwers. She'd never seen Elemental magic used like that before – she hadn't even known it *could* be. But it wasn't enough to stop the Faceless

One or even slow it down.

Skulduggery cut off the fire and retreated. "It never works," he muttered. "Nothing I do ever works."

Something bright caught Valkyrie's eye and she looked past the shambling form that had once been Batu, through the door it had come through, and saw the yellow portal.

"The gateway!" she said. "It's open!"

"You better get going then," Skulduggery said dully. His hands had dropped by his sides and he'd stopped walking backwards.

"Come on!" she yelled.

"The mind plays such cruel tricks," he murmured.

Valkyrie ducked past the Faceless One. It turned its head to her then refocused on Skulduggery. She had a clear run to the portal. "Skulduggery!"

"You're not real."

"Please!"

The Faceless One held up its hand and Skulduggery moaned a little. His legs buckled and he dropped to his knees, his bones shaking.

"I have done terrible things," he managed to say.

The riders were running through the streets towards them. The ones out in front had almost reached the portal. She couldn't let them go through. Fletcher would shut it all down if they started coming through.

Valkyrie put on her coat and ran into the sun. She pushed at the air, throwing two riders off their feet. A third slashed at her with his dagger, but she blocked with her sleeve and fed him a faceful of fire. She kicked him back and whipped the shadows at another, catching him across the chest and sending him to the ground. A rider fell on her from behind and got her in a headlock. She kneed the muscle of his thigh and brought her fists crashing against his kidney and groin, then flipped him over her leg and stood on his throat.

She turned and a fist smashed into her cheek. She staggered, overbalanced and fell. The rider came in to kick her, but she jammed her left foot against his shin and swung her right foot over and back so that her heel connected with the back of his knee. She twisted and he yelped as he fell forward, his leg caught in a lock. She rolled over him and heard his leg crack. He screamed.

She threw a fireball that ignited the furs of a rider who was about to touch the portal. He shrieked and danced away, but now there were riders everywhere, coming in from all sides, and Valkyrie turned and turned again, fists raised.

"Skulduggery!" she shouted. "Help!"

And then China Sorrows appeared through the portal.

Tattoos glowed as she flung a wave of blue energy into the riders before they had a chance to even react. She hurled daggers of red light and dodged a rider who came at her with a sword. She slammed her forehead into his face and then went to work on his friends.

Valkyrie launched herself at the rider who tried to sneak up on China from behind. She snatched the knife from his hand and pushed at the air to shoot it straight into the leg of another.

"Skulduggery?" China demanded, breaking a rider's wrist and jabbing her fingers into his eyes.

A rider yanked Valkyrie's hair and she stepped back and rammed her elbow into his nose. "In there," she panted. "With a Faceless One."

"Skulduggery Pleasant!" China roared. "Get out here at once!"

Valkyrie covered her head as two riders leaped at her, but when they didn't land she looked up. They hung in the air, quizzical expressions on their faces, and then hurtled back as Skulduggery stumbled from the doorway, his arm outstretched.

"Two of you," he said, sounding surprised. "But my hallucinations *never* travel in pairs..."

Valkyrie grabbed his hand and pulled him from the door as

the Faceless One reached out to drag him back. China kept the riders away then she took hold of Skulduggery's other hand and all three of them jumped into the portal.

Yellow flashed bright and was gone, and something tangled with Valkyrie's legs and she fell. Instead of falling on to hard ground and sand though, she fell on to grass, still wet from hours-old rain.

She blinked her sight back, realising she had tripped over Skulduggery's feet and that they had both fallen. China had stayed upright of course, and she was commanding Fletcher to close the gateway. Valkyrie watched the portal shrink down almost instantly, then vanish.

They stood up and Fletcher stepped out of the circle. They all watched Skulduggery as he looked around at Aranmore Farm.

"Good God," he said softly. "I'm home."

"How are you?" China asked. For the first time Valkyrie noticed the blood on China's clothes and how pale she was.

Skulduggery's head tilted and he paused a while before answering. "I'm fine," he said. "You've been shot."

"I'm OK now."

Fletcher walked up and handed over the Murder Skull. "I think this is yours."

Skulduggery took the skull in one hand and looked at it. "Handsome devil," he murmured. And then, "Why are there unconscious people lying around the place?"

"Guild sent some of his agents to stop us," China said. "There are probably more on the way."

"Then let's not be here when they arrive." He looked at Valkyrie and took a moment. "You saved me," he said.

"I did," she said.

She was expecting a hug. She didn't get one.

"Good job," said Skulduggery and started walking.

14

THE FACT OF THE MATTER

At the back of Sanguine's mind there lay a question that would squirm, now and then, into his thoughts. How many of these men would he have to kill to get what he wanted?

He was confident he wouldn't have to kill Scarab. Scarab was focused on the bigger picture – vengeance on a grand scale. Springheeled Jack wasn't likely to get in his way either. Jack simply wanted to pay back everyone who'd ever wronged him. Sanguine could appreciate that.

But the others... They all wanted the same thing. Their prime *motivation was revenge on the same person.*

Valkyrie Cain.

Sanguine himself had his own reason for wanting to kill the girl, a pain that had plagued him ever since the day the Faceless Ones had come through the portal. He fully intended to back Scarab's plan as far as he could and so far, he'd done his part. He'd stolen what he'd had to steal, and he'd broken Dusk out of prison by burrowing in and fighting his way out. Dusk was now building up one army and he was building up another. He was co-ordinating and facilitating the plan. And it was, admittedly, a good plan. If everything came together, it was a plan that would destroy their enemies, satisfy their bloodlust and change everything.

It wasn't without its flaws of course – among them Vaurien Scapegrace who, as far as Sanguine could tell, was not the Killer Supreme he'd said he was. This, however, was Sanguine's fault – he'd recruited him after all – and so it was his responsibility to take care of it.

But the plan was, essentially, a good plan and a solid one. However, the moment he saw his chance, he was taking it. He didn't care if it ruined the plan, or got everyone else arrested or killed.

One way or another, Sanguine had decided, Valkyrie Cain was going to die – and he was determined to be the one to kill her.

15

BACK ON
CEMETERY ROAD

Skulduggery's house was cold and the air was stale. Valkyrie checked the messages on her phone while Skulduggery took the head that Fletcher had given him and went to the large room where he kept all his best clothes. Fletcher tried to turn on the TV, but the power had been cut off. Suddenly they heard a sharp howl of pain, and Valkyrie spun in alarm.

"Skulduggery?" she called as she ran from the room. "Are you OK? Skulduggery?"

She hurried through the house, flinging open doors as she passed them. She reached the last room and just as she was about to barge in – "That hurt," Skulduggery said from inside.

Valkyrie frowned at the closed door. "What happened?"

"I was changing my head. It feels good to have the old one back on. And now I have a spare, which is nice."

Valkyrie stepped back as the door opened and Skulduggery emerged. His suit and tie were navy blue and his shirt was crisp and white. He tilted his chin. "What do you think of the head?"

"Uh, it's... it's really nice. Looks a lot like the other one."

"What are you talking about? It's completely different. The cheekbones are higher."

"Are they?"

"Aren't they?"

"I suppose they... might be. Is it comfortable?"

"Very." He walked past her into the room where he kept his hats. "Where's Ghastly? Have you told him I'm back?"

"Uh, no..."

"He mightn't believe you. He might think I'm still hallucinating. You'd better tell him I'm not. I think he'd want to know that he's not a figment of my imagination. I know *I'd* want to." Skulduggery put on a hat that matched his suit, cocked it low over his eye sockets and admired himself in the mirror.

"I have missed this," he murmured.

"Ghastly was arrested," Valkyrie said, trying to get him to focus. "Him and Tanith. They're being held at the Sanctuary."

"What for?"

"For helping me get *you* back. Guild made it clear that we were *not* to open that portal again. He said we couldn't risk something escaping through."

"Hmm. That was very wise of him."

She glowered. "That's not helping me in the slightest."

"Now, Valkyrie, opening that portal *was* very dangerous. Sometimes you've got to admit it when you're wrong."

"You *never* admit it when you're wrong."

"But I'm rarely wrong, you see. You, on the other hand, are wrong a bizarrely large amount of the time. Statistically, it's quite amazing."

He opened a wooden box and slowly reached his gloved hand in. His revolver gleamed when he withdrew it. "Smith & Wesson," he said lovingly. "You had it cleaned?"

"Last week," she said and found herself smiling. "Thought you might want it."

He opened the cylinder, took six bullets from the box and slid them into the chambers then clicked it shut and thumbed on the safety. He tucked the gun into the holster under his jacket.

"There," he said. "I feel complete again."

Fletcher walked in. "Hey," he said.

"Fletcher," Skulduggery nodded. "Did I thank you for opening the portal and getting me home?"

"You didn't," Fletcher said. "But you're welcome."

"You could have been responsible for the end of the human race," Skulduggery continued happily, "but I for one am not going to hold it against you. You may leave us now."

"I may what?"

Skulduggery hesitated for just a moment. "Your hair. It's distracting. I'm sorry, I thought someone ought to tell you."

"You want me to go because of my hair?"

"There's just so much of it, to tell you the truth."

"Are you being serious?"

"Can't you tell?"

"Not really."

"Well, for future reference, this is my serious face."

Fletcher looked at Valkyrie and she shrugged. "We'll call you when some of us are feeling a little more... sensible," she said.

"OK," he said. "Then I'll... I'll go then."

He vanished and Skulduggery turned to her. "Now," he said. "Where is she?"

They went outside and Valkyrie opened the garage. She

grabbed the tarp and pulled it off the car, a 1954 Bentley R-Type Continental, one of only 208 ever made, retrofitted with modern luxuries and the apple of Skulduggery's eye. If he'd *had* an eye. Skulduggery ran his hand over the bodywork.

"Do you even *need* a car these days?" asked Valkyrie. "Aren't you going to just fly everywhere from now on?"

"Flying takes a lot out of you," he said, "and it's not the most inconspicuous mode of transport."

"But the Bentley *is*?"

She heard a sound that may have been a laugh and they got in. The Bentley tore out of the garage and raced to the top of the road, taking the turn at a speed that would have terrified Valkyrie were it not Skulduggery behind the wheel.

"Intriguing," Skulduggery murmured and the Bentley abruptly slowed.

"What's wrong?" she asked.

"We're being followed," he said. "And not very well."

He took a lazy left on to an empty side street then gunned the engine. Valkyrie was pressed back into her seat. He turned into the next left and stopped in the middle of the road. He made sure his scarf was securely wrapped around his face and got out, gun in his hand.

A blue Volvo roared around the corner and brakes squealed

as it swerved to avoid the Bentley. It hit the wall and the engine cut out. Skulduggery crossed to it and smashed the window with the butt of his revolver, then dragged the red-headed driver out and dumped him on the road.

"I don't appreciate being followed," Skulduggery said, an edge to his voice.

"Don't shoot me!" the driver yelled.

"I've had enough of being followed," Skulduggery continued, like he hadn't heard him. "I'm not in the mood for it any more."

Valkyrie recognised the cowering young man on the ground. His name was Staven Weeper. She'd seen him in the Sanctuary a few times. His eyes were fixed on the gun at Skulduggery's side.

"I usually kill people who follow me," Skulduggery murmured, almost to himself.

Valkyrie frowned. "Skulduggery?"

"That's what happens," he continued softly. "They hunt me, they die. Simple. I like to keep it simple. Keep it clean."

He raised the gun and Valkyrie darted forward. She grabbed his wrist. "*What are you doing?*"

He looked at her and cocked his head. "Valkyrie. What are *you* doing here?"

He didn't move for a moment then shook his head and put

the gun back in its holster. He walked over to the Bentley and stood beside it, looking up at the sky. Weeper was staring at him in terrified bewilderment and Valkyrie stepped up to block his view.

"What do you want?" she demanded.

He raised his eyes to her. "I'm here to arrest you."

"What for?"

"You assaulted Detective Marr and you have obviously opened the portal, against the Grand Mage's explicit orders."

"I'm sorry, but I'm finding it hard to believe that they sent *you* to arrest us."

"Well, originally, I was just supposed to watch Skulduggery Pleasant's house," Weeper admitted. "The other Detectives are busy."

"With what?"

"They wouldn't tell me. I heard one of the Sensitives had a vision that they were getting worried about... The Detectives don't really tell me this stuff. I'm not exactly high on the, you know, the totem pole."

Skulduggery wandered over, hands in his pockets, seemingly back to his old self. "You're not here to arrest *me*, are you?"

Weeper shrank away. "I... I don't know."

"Because technically, I have broken no laws recently. I didn't rescue *myself*, now did I?"

"I suppose not..."

"So it's Valkyrie you're after, is that right?"

"Uh, yes."

"Excellent."

"Although..." said Weeper hesitantly.

"Although?"

"Technically, you've just assaulted me and I'm a Sanctuary agent."

"Well, yes," Skulduggery said, "but you're not a very good one, are you? I mean, they told you to watch my house. That's not exactly a high-profile case you're running. How long have you been watching my house?"

"Uh, three... three months."

"Three months. And what is the result of your investigation? Has my house been involved in any illegal activities? Has it robbed a bank? Has it mugged anyone?"

"No..."

"Has it moved, even a little?"

"I don't... think so..."

"Made a prank phone call?"

"No."

"I see. And just now, did I run you off the road? Or did you crash, all by yourself?"

"I suppose I, uh, crashed."

"And I pulled you from the wreckage, did I not? That car could have exploded for all you know. I saved your life and now you want to arrest me for it?"

"Well, not any more..."

"I'm glad to hear it. Do you want to stand up?"

"Yes, please."

"Stand."

Weeper stood.

"My friends have been taken into custody," Skulduggery said. "Ghastly Bespoke and Tanith Low. What do you know about it?"

"Just what I heard on the updates. They broke into the Sanctuary and one of them assaulted Detective Marr."

"Marr," Skulduggery murmured. "Davina Marr? American?"

"That's her," Valkyrie said.

"Oh, she hates me," said Skulduggery. "For no reason, I might add. At least no reason that I care about. Snivelling boy, will you tell the Grand Mage that I have returned, and from what you have seen, I have been slightly unhinged by my dreadful experiences in an alternate dimension? Could you also tell him that I would appreciate it if he released my friends at his earliest convenience?"

"Yes. OK. Sure."

"And then threaten to shoot him."

"Uh... I don't know if that's wise..."

"Nonsense," Skulduggery said, patting him on the shoulder. "The Grand Mage *hates* getting shot. It's quite funny. You'll be fine. Run along now."

"Can I... can I get back in my car?"

Skulduggery pondered the question and shook his head. "No."

Weeper sagged.

16

THE TEMPLE

"You're quiet," Skulduggery said when they were back on the road.

"I am," Valkyrie agreed.

"Are you in awe of me?"

"Something like that."

Skulduggery nodded. "You're in awe of me."

"How are you feeling?"

"Splendid," he replied.

"You sure frightened him," Valkyrie said.

"Who, the boy? Did I?"

"For a moment it looked like you were going to kill him."

"It did?"

"It did."

"Fancy that," he said.

"You said you were unhinged."

"Hmm? Oh, yes, I did. Quite clever, yes? You see, if they think I have been driven mad, they will struggle to predict my actions. I become very, very dangerous to them, and hopefully, that will make Guild do what we want."

"And you're not, right?" Valkyrie said cautiously. "You're not unhinged?"

"Oh, God, no," he laughed. "No, I'm perfectly sane. Now then, do you want to tell me about that ring you're wearing?"

"Oh," she said. "That."

"Solomon Wreath is teaching you Necromancy, isn't he?"

"I needed the extra strength to get you back," she explained. "I'm only a trainee Elemental – I need all the help I can get, you know?"

"And now that I'm back?"

"Sorry?"

"You said you needed that ring to get me back. So now that I'm here, is that it? Are you going to throw it away?"

Valkyrie felt the cold metal around her finger and how

comforting it had become lately. "If you want me to," she said slowly.

"What do *you* want to do?"

"I don't know." Skulduggery didn't say anything so she had to continue. "I suppose throwing away another set of powers, I mean, it doesn't really make sense. It's a weapon I need to get the job done."

"And being an Elemental isn't enough to do that?"

"When I'm powerful enough, sure, and especially with all those new things you can do, but I'm still learning. And I've got another few years before my magic settles, right?"

"That's true," Skulduggery nodded. "You'll probably be twenty, maybe twenty-one, before you have to choose one style over all the rest."

"And after that, I can't switch?"

He hesitated. "It's not impossible. But it *is* rare."

"But I can keep using the ring until I'm about to settle, can't I, and then give it back?"

"As easy as that?"

"Why wouldn't it be?"

"Strength is addictive."

"I can handle it."

"Solomon Wreath is not to be trusted."

"He saved my life last night."

Skulduggery snapped his head to her. "What happened?"

"Uh, Crux got into my house and tried to kill me. I could have handled it. I don't mean Wreath *saved my life*, but he, you know, he helped. China's people set up a perimeter around Haggard though, so nobody magical can get in without being noticed. Except me of course."

"Right," Skulduggery said, yanking the wheel sharply. "I need to have a word with Wreath."

Valkyrie had been to the Necromancer Temple only once before, to see her ring being forged in the shadow furnace. She had imagined, when told of the Temple, a vast building with spires and long narrow windows, of huge doors and possibly some dark and terrible towers. Her expectations were dashed when Solomon Wreath had led her through an old graveyard, to a crypt with rusted iron gates, overgrown with weeds and ivy. Beneath that crypt, however, the Temple lay – a cold and forbidding labyrinth, drenched in darkness.

It was at this rusted gate she found herself again, standing at Skulduggery's side. Her heart beat fast. Not from nerves, or excitement, but simply because she was in a graveyard. She could feel the tendrils of death being drawn into the ring on her finger and soaking through into her body. The thought of it made her queasy, but the sensation was... electric.

The crypt door opened heavily and Solomon Wreath smiled at them, and said, "Suddenly there came a tapping, as of someone gently rapping, rapping at my chamber door."

"How unique," Skulduggery said without enthusiasm, "a Necromancer quoting Poe."

Wreath's smile grew wider. "By the pricking of my thumbs, something wicked this way comes."

"Shakespeare is the happy hunting ground of all minds that have lost their balance," Skulduggery responded. "Are we going to boast about how well-read we are all day or are we going to talk?"

"About?"

"Valkyrie."

"I see. In that case, please come in." The gate creaked open for him and they passed through. "How are you by the way? I hope that alternate dimension wasn't too uncomfortable for you."

"It wasn't all bad," Skulduggery responded. "It gave me time to catch up on some screaming."

They followed Wreath down the stone steps, into the darkness.

"I believe I have you to thank for suggesting my own skull as an Isthmus Anchor," Skulduggery continued. "If it wasn't for you, I'd still be over there."

"Think nothing of it."

"Very well."

Wreath laughed.

Now they were in the dark labyrinth, passing the chambers that were carved into the walls. In some of these rooms people in black robes raised their heads, lamplight catching flashes of skin against shadow. In others the dark-robed figures were too busy with whatever they were doing to bother looking up. Up ahead, people moved quickly.

"There seems to be a disturbance," Skulduggery noted.

"Nothing to concern you," Wreath said. "One of our trinkets has gone missing. We're trying to find it. But enough of the everyday humdrum of Temple life. You are here to talk, are you not?"

"Valkyrie tells me she's been taking lessons with you," Skulduggery said, his voice loud in the cold silence.

"Indeed she has," Wreath responded. "Would this be a problem for you?"

"Necromancy is a dangerous discipline. Not everyone is suited to it."

"Well, now," Wreath said, smiling, "could it be that I have more faith in Valkyrie's abilities than you do?"

"This isn't about ability," Skulduggery said curtly. "This is about aptitude."

"What do you mean?" Valkyrie asked.

"In order for you to make an informed decision, can I assume Solomon here has told you about the Necromancer beliefs?"

Suddenly Wreath did not look happy. "Our beliefs are private. They are not discussed with..."

"With?" Skulduggery prompted.

"Non-believers," Wreath said.

"You can make an exception for me, can't you?" Skulduggery pressed. Somehow, he was now in the lead and Valkyrie realised they were heading for the source of the quiet commotion. "And as for Valkyrie, don't her lessons with you entitle her to hear this?"

"Valkyrie," Wreath said, "you could be considered one of our indoctrinates, one of our trainees, and as such you could expect to be taught these things gradually, over the coming years."

"But you'll skip the formalities," Skulduggery said. "Yes?"

Wreath sighed and spoke to her. "Death is a part of life.

You've undoubtedly heard that before. It's meant as a platitude, to comfort the bereaved and the scared. But the truth is, life flows into death and death flows back into life.

"The darkness we use in our magic is a living energy. You've felt it, haven't you? It almost has a life of its own. It *is* life and death. They're the same thing – a constant, recycling stream that permeates all universes."

"Tell her about the Death Bringer," Skulduggery said, looking around.

"The Death Bringer is not relevant to—"

"Well, you can't hide it from her *now*, can you? So you may as well."

Wreath took a breath to keep his temper in check. "We're waiting for a Necromancer strong enough to break down the walls between life and death. Some people call this person the Death Bringer. We have conducted tests; we've researched; we've taken a very clinical approach to all of this. This isn't a prophecy. Prophecies mean nothing, they're merely interpretations of possibilities. This is an inevitability. We will find someone powerful enough to break down the wall, and the energy of the dead will live alongside us, and we will evolve to meet it."

"They call this the Passage," Skulduggery said. "What

Solomon here is neglecting to tell you of course are the names of a few people whom the Necromancers have proclaimed to be the Death Bringer in the past."

"She doesn't need to know this," Wreath said, anger in his eyes.

"I think she does."

"Tell me," Valkyrie said to them both.

Wreath hesitated. "The last person we thought was powerful enough to possibly become the Death Bringer came to us during the war. Within two years of starting his Necromancy training, Lord Vile was the equal to any of our masters."

"Vile?" Valkyrie said. "*Lord Vile* was your *saviour*?"

"We thought he *could* be," Wreath replied quickly. "His ascension through the ranks was unheard of. It was impossible. He was a prodigy. The darkness was... it wasn't just *in* him. It *was* him."

They turned a corner and followed a passageway to its end, Skulduggery leading the way without appearing to.

"And then he left," Skulduggery said. "And joined Mevolent's army. I bet that still rankles."

"So you've been without a Death Bringer ever since?" Valkyrie asked.

"Yes," Wreath said. He looked at Skulduggery. "Is that why

you are here then? So you could make this clumsy attempt to embarrass me?"

"At first," Skulduggery said. "But now I'm curious as to what trinket you've misplaced. Oh, look where we are. What a nice coincidence."

They had arrived at a small chamber with wooden shelves at odd angles. The two Necromancers within fell silent immediately. Skulduggery went to step inside, but Wreath took hold of his arm.

"We didn't ask for your help," he said firmly. "This is a Necromancer affair."

"It was here though?" Skulduggery asked. "Your trinket? Why don't you tell us what has gone missing and I'll tell you who took it."

Wreath smiled thinly. "You've worked it out already?"

"I *am* a detective."

Wreath took a moment then nodded to the two Necromancers and they left. He stepped back as Valkyrie joined Skulduggery in examining the room. "The missing object is a sphere, about the size of your fist, set inside a cradle of obsidian."

"A Soul Catcher," Skulduggery said.

"One of the last in existence," Wreath nodded.

Valkyrie frowned. "Does that do what it sounds like it does? Why would you need to catch *souls?*"

"The Soul Catcher was used to trap and contain an individual energy," Wreath told her, "to stop it from rejoining the stream. It was a barbaric punishment that we have long since outlawed.

"The last time an inventory was carried out was a month ago. If it *was* indeed stolen, it could have been stolen a month ago or it could have been stolen *yesterday.* The simple fact is, however, I can't see how any thief could have got this far into the Temple without being seen."

"Oh, it was definitely stolen," Skulduggery said. "But the thief didn't use the door."

Valkyrie looked at him. "So who stole it?" Skulduggery pointed up. She clicked her fingers and raised her hand, the flames flickering across the patch of cracked and crumbled ceiling, large enough to fit a man through.

"Sanguine," Valkyrie said.

Wreath frowned. "Billy-Ray Sanguine? What would he want with a Soul Catcher?"

"This is just a guess," Skulduggery said, "but maybe he wants to use it to catch a soul."

17

DEAD MAN TALKING

Vaurien Scapegrace was dead and Billy-Ray Sanguine had killed him.

Scapegrace was pretty sure that's what happened anyway. He couldn't remember all of it.

He remembered Sanguine taking him to one side, and telling him that he'd made a few calls and asked a few people, and nobody could vouch for Scapegrace as a remorseless killer of unparalleled skill, like he'd claimed. Scapegrace had tried to explain then that, fair enough, he hadn't actually killed anyone yet, but it was only a matter of time, and if Sanguine and Scarab could just give him a chance, he'd prove himself worthy to be included in their plans.

At least, that's what he'd planned *to say. He dimly remembered getting as far as "Fair enough" and then... nothing.*

Sanguine had killed him.

He opened his eyes, in a dark and dank dungeon, and looked up to see his Master's face.

"Finally," Scarab said and it was the greatest word Scapegrace had ever heard uttered. Finally. Here is my loyal companion, never to leave my side. *Scapegrace smiled as he lay there.*

"Stop grinning," Scarab ordered. "You look deformed."

"Sorry, Master," Scapegrace said, sitting up. Why was he calling Scarab Master? He didn't know, but it seemed so right, *so he just continued. "Master, what's happened to me?"*

"You're dead," Master Scarab said. "You lied to us, Scapegrace. You're not a killer. Knew it from the moment I saw you."

"Was it because I fell off the chair?"

"It doesn't matter what it was. But because you lied to us, wasted our time, made us rethink some of our plans, we decided to put your death to good use. We killed you and brought you back. Do you know what you are?"

"Very lucky?"

"You're a zombie."

Scapegrace laughed. "No, Master. Not me."

Scarab took a knife from his pocket and stabbed it through Scapegrace's arm. Scapegrace stared.

"You feel no pain," Scarab continued.

"Oh."

"Your corpse is being sustained by magic."

"I'm a... I'm a zombie."

"Yes."

"Am... am I like that White Cleaver person?"

"I've been in prison for 200 years. I have no idea what you're talking about. You are, to be blunt, a fairly basic zombie. You're not one of those fully reanimated, self-healing zombies. You're a lower class. Best I could do with the stuff I know."

"Oh, I do appreciate it, Master."

"Shut up. Do you know anything about zombies?"

"Not really..."

"You have no magic. The magic you did have is being used to keep your body moving and your brain thinking — I wouldn't imagine much magic is required for that particular feat."

"I wouldn't say so, sir."

"The advantage of being such a basic zombie, however, is that you can pass on your condition with simply a bite. See, I want you to go out there and recruit."

"Recruit?"

"One bite'll do it. These people you recruit do not need to be sorcerers — in fact, it would be best if they weren't. The thing is, you're the only one who can bite, you get me? None of the others, and I mean none, can even taste human flesh."

"Why can't they?"

"Because I'm telling you they can't. You are the only one who'll be immune to its effects. They'll be sustained by trace amounts of magic, though they'll decompose faster than you will. The thing is they'll want *human flesh*. They'll need *human flesh*. You've got to make sure they don't get any."

"You can count on me, Master!"

Scarab sighed then looked at him. "You're going to be killing folk, Mr Scapegrace. You're finally going to be the killer you always dreamed of being. Do not mess this up."

18

DARQUESSE

They drove away from the graveyard.

"Have you heard anything about Sanguine?" Skulduggery asked. "Has he been spotted at all since I've been away?"

"He vanished," Valkyrie said. "We didn't know if he was dead or alive. I got him pretty good with Tanith's sword, right across the belly. I suppose a bit of me actually thought I'd killed him."

"Well, you didn't."

"I don't know whether to be disappointed or glad."

"Pick glad. You've got plenty of time to regret the things you haven't done yet."

"I'm... not sure what that means."

"Take it home with you and think about it."

"I will, thanks. So, anyway, we have no way of knowing *when* Sanguine stole the Soul Catcher."

"That *is* annoying," Skulduggery murmured. "Still, it's not our concern."

She frowned. "What?"

"It's not our case. Why should we worry about what someone like Sanguine does? I'm bored with all of them. I need something new. I need a new mystery, with new people."

"And so where are we going?"

"That snivelling boy said the Sanctuary Detectives are worried about a vision one of their Sensitives had. That sounds intriguing, doesn't it?"

"Does it?"

"It does. It sounds new and exciting. I wonder if they've seen the end of the world. I love end-of-the-world visions. They're always so graphic."

"I don't like visions at all."

"Really?"

"I don't like things being inevitable."

"Ah, but visions of the future are *not* inevitable. The very fact that someone sees a *vision* of what will happen automatically *changes* what will happen. Granted, sometimes these changes are too infinitesimal to notice, but they are still changes. I find the whole thing quite fascinating to be honest. After all, you're working against the natural course of events. You are working against your own destiny every time."

"That's one way of looking at it."

"That's my way of looking at it," Skulduggery said happily. "Give me a few minutes and that way will change."

Even at this time in the morning the tattoo parlour was open. The low buzz of the tattooist's needle greeted them the moment they stepped through the door. They climbed the narrow steps, passing all the photos of tattooed body parts.

The parlour's only customer was a fat man lying face down on a tilted table. The skinny tattooist with the shaved head and the Dublin football jersey looked up from his work and a grin broke across his face.

"Skul-man!" he exclaimed as he rushed forward to shake his hand. "How is this possible? Last I heard you were trapped on a dead world overrun by evil trans-dimensional superfiends!"

Skulduggery nodded. "Just got back."

"That's awesome, man. That's really great. So did you get me anything?"

"Like... a souvenir?" Skulduggery asked doubtfully.

"Doesn't have to be anything big. A rock, maybe, or a twig. Just *something* from an alternate universe, you know? It'd be something to show the kid when he's older, tell him it was an early birthday present from his Uncle Skulduggery."

"I'm sorry, Finbar, I don't have anything."

"That's OK, that's OK. I suppose I could just give him any old rock, couldn't I? He'd never know that it wasn't from an alternate universe. He'd be so happy. I can just see him, bringing the rock into school, showing his little friends, carrying it around with him everywhere. I used to have a pet rock when I was a kid, but it ran away. At least, my mother *said* it ran away, but I think my dad just picked it up one afternoon and threw it out the window. I went looking for it, but..." Finbar's voice cracked. "They all looked the same, you know? They all looked the same..." He narrowed his eyes. "Hey, Skul-man – you wearing a new head?"

"Yes, actually," Skulduggery said, sounding very pleased. "What do you think?"

"Oh, man, I like it. Don't get me wrong, I liked the other one, but this is just... better looking, y'know? The cheekbones are higher."

Skulduggery looked at Valkyrie, his better-looking head tilted at quite a smug angle. She sighed then gestured to the fat man on the table. "Is it OK to be talking about, um, business stuff with...?"

"Oh, don't worry about *him*," Finbar said. "He came in as soon as we opened, asked for a growling panther on his shoulder blade. He fainted the moment I started."

"A growling panther?"

"Yep."

"Then why are you giving him a tattoo of a kitten?"

Finbar shrugged. "I'm just in a kitten kind of mood, y'know? So if you're not here to give me a present, why are you here?"

"Have you had any particularly weird or unsettling visions lately?" Skulduggery asked. "We've been hearing about—"

"Darquesse," Finbar said immediately.

Valkyrie frowned. "Darkness?"

"Darquesse, with a *q* and a *u* pronounced like a *k*. It's causing a stir in the Sensitive community, let me tell you. And if *that* many psychics are having the same dream, you know it's got to be trouble. I've been having these really freaked-out visions. They come to me day and night, and they're so... disturbing. It's like watching a horror movie without eyelids. Can't even blink."

"Who or what *is* Darquesse?" Skulduggery asked.

"Darquesse is the sorcerer who destroys the world," Finbar said. "And I mean she *levels* it. I've seen cities flattened, like a nuke had gone off. Everything's burning. I see little snippets as it happens. This woman in black... Mevolent was *nothing* compared to this kind of evil."

"Do you know when this will happen?" Valkyrie asked.

"I don't, but I think Cassandra Pharos may have some idea. The visions are coming to her pretty vividly for some reason. I can take you there if you'd like. Sharon and my kid are at her cult meeting, so I'm not doing anything for the next few hours."

"Sharon's in a cult?"

"Yeah, it's one of those funny ones that try to get the women members to sacrifice their husbands at every full moon or something. I don't know if that's an appropriate atmosphere to bring a kid into, but everyone needs a hobby, am I right?"

Valkyrie didn't quite know what to say to that, so she nodded to the unconscious fat man. "And it's OK to leave him here?"

"He'll be fine," Finbar said, grabbing his jacket. "Will we take your car or mine?"

Skulduggery tilted his head. "Do you have a car?"

"Nope."

"Then we'll take mine."

"Probably wise. I think I've forgoten how to drive."

They left the city and for most of the journey Finbar lamented the fact that his psychic powers could not ascertain who would win the All-Ireland Championship. What good were psychic powers, he asked, if they couldn't tell you who was going to win the Gaelic football?

They drove on until they came to a cottage, surrounded by nothing but fields and meadows and hills, rolling back as far as they could see. A light headache pressed against Valkyrie's temples, but she did her best to ignore it.

"Cassandra's one of the best Sensitives around," Finbar said as they got out of the Bentley. "Skul-man knows her, am I right?"

"You are," Skulduggery confirmed.

"Cassandra's a nice old bird," Finbar continued, leading them to the cottage, "and she has all these fancy little doodads that help her with her psychic mojo stuff. Wait till you see the dream whisperers, Val. They're like something out of *Blair Witch*."

Valkyrie didn't know what a Blair Witch was, but before she could ask the cottage door opened and a woman appeared. She looked to be in her fifties, and her long hair was grey and hung loosely around her shoulders. She wore a faded dress and a light cardigan.

"Cassandra," Skulduggery said, a smile in his voice. "You're looking well."

"You're a liar," Cassandra Pharos said, "but I don't care. It's good to see you again."

"Cassie," Finbar said, "this is Valkyrie Cain."

"I've seen you in my dreams, Valkyrie," Cassandra said. "But in my dreams you're older than you are now. That's a good thing."

"Oh," Valkyrie said. "Right."

Cassandra ushered them into the cottage and closed the door behind them. It was an almost perfectly ordinary cottage. It had rugs, it had a sofa, a TV, a bookshelf, a guitar in the corner and doors leading off into the other rooms. But what set it apart from any other cottage Valkyrie had been in were the dozens of little wooden figures hanging from the rafters.

Each one was about the size of her outstretched hand and was made up of bundles of twigs, bound with strips of black ribbon. Two arms, two legs, a torso and a head. Cassandra saw her looking.

"My abilities don't work the same as Finbar's," she said.

"Mine require a lot more effort for significantly lesser results. For me, glimpses of the future can come during meditation, they can flash into my head without warning or they can come in dreams. I have all sorts of tools of the trade to help me, from every culture and country." She took a twig figure off a shelf. "This is a dream whisperer. Dreams that you forget, that drift from your mind when you wake, they collect. They keep them as long as they have to, and when it's time, they tell you about them. You have to be really quiet to hear their whispers though, which is why I live all the way out here."

Valkyrie did her best to look interested and not creeped out. Cassandra was making it sound like the little figure was alive.

Cassandra smiled and held it out. "Take it," she said. "You look like you have interesting dreams."

Valkyrie hesitated then took it. "Thank you. It's... lovely."

It didn't have any features, no mouth or eyes, but she could still feel it watching her. She smiled tentatively and put it carefully in her coat pocket.

Cassandra led them to a narrow door and they followed her down into the cellar. In stark and unpleasant contrast to the cosiness of the cottage, the cellar was an ugly room of cement brick walls and harsh lighting that made Valkyrie's headache jab at her. The floor was a large metal grille and beneath the grille, coals. Rusted old pipes ran from a red wheel, up the wall and across the ceiling. Sprinklers protruded from the pipes and hung down half a metre below the protected lights. In the middle of the floor was a single straight-backed chair. A yellow umbrella lay beside it.

"This is the Steam Chamber," Cassandra said as she sat in the chair. "This is where I can project what I've seen into images. Sometimes it's hazy; sometimes it's clear. Sometimes there is sound, sometimes not. At the very least, you can get an idea of what's in my head. Before we begin, however, you have to understand something. This future you're about to see is not set. You can still change it. All of you can."

Even though Cassandra was speaking to all three of them, Valkyrie had the distinct impression that the comment was directed solely at her. Suddenly she wasn't altogether certain she wanted to see what Cassandra had to show her.

"Why haven't you gone to the Sanctuary with this?" she asked. "You and Finbar must be better than any psychics they have on the staff. They could probably use the help."

"I don't talk to *The Man*," Finbar scowled. "*The Man* keeps me down."

"In what way?" asked Valkyrie, genuinely puzzled.

Finbar hesitated. "General ways," he said at last.

"Just... general ways, keeping me down, oppressing me."

"We're not too fond of the Sanctuary," Cassandra told her gently. "Any establishment as big and as powerful as that is rife with corruption. I suppose we're still activists at heart, even after all these years."

"Damn *The Man*," Finbar said proudly.

"Now then," Cassandra said, "to business. Skulduggery, if you wouldn't mind...?"

Skulduggery looked at Valkyrie. "This may get a little warm."

He clicked his fingers, summoning flame into both of his hands, and then he tossed the fireballs at the ground. They fell through the grille and he gestured, and the flames spread out and started to burn with the coals.

Cassandra closed her eyes and stayed like that for a minute or two. Valkyrie wanted to ask if she could open the door at the top of the stairs to let some air in because Skulduggery hadn't been lying. It was getting uncomfortably warm down here.

Without opening her eyes, Cassandra reached down, picked up the umbrella and opened it. She rested it against her shoulder, open above her head, and she nodded.

"I'm ready."

Finbar turned the little red wheel on the wall and Valkyrie

heard the water gurgling through the pipes. She stepped back as a few drops started to fall from the sprinklers, and Skulduggery moved her back three more steps just as the full spray came on. Valkyrie stood with her back to the wall, the spray just hitting her boots. The water passed through the grille, hissing as it hit the burning coals, and steam began to billow.

Cassandra sat in the middle of the room, her yellow umbrella doing its best to keep her dry, and then she was lost from sight. The steam was thick like mist, like fog, getting denser with each passing moment. Valkyrie's head was pounding by now.

She heard Finbar turn the wheel again, though she couldn't see him, and the sprinklers turned off. The steam, however, stayed.

Someone moved in front of her and Valkyrie reached out then pulled her hand back sharply. There was another figure behind it and there was movement to her right. They weren't alone in here.

Someone stepped up beside her and she whirled, lashing out, and Skulduggery caught her fist in his gloved hand.

"You're not in any danger," he said.

"There are people in here with us," she whispered.

"Watch," he responded and led her away from the wall, towards the middle of the room.

She turned her head as a figure ran through the steam towards her. She dodged back, but the water had made the metal grille slippery and her boot slid. She stumbled and Ghastly Bespoke ran at her, his body scattering in the steam right before he hit her.

Valkyrie spun, aware of Skulduggery standing beside her, completely calm.

"Think of it as a hologram," he said, "projected on to the steam. None of this is real."

There were buildings now, on either side of them, and a road at their feet. The road was cracked and the buildings were ruined. It was a dead city, dead or dying, and she heard muted shouts in the distance. A figure approached, striding through the street of steam, a gun in his hand. Skulduggery. His black suit was torn.

The real Skulduggery nodded. "At least I'm still looking well..."

The image of Skulduggery disappeared. And then a sound. Someone screaming in the distance and a gunshot. Somewhere near the back of the Chamber there was a flare, like a fireball being thrown. The sound was coming from everywhere, from beside and below and behind and above, and it was the sound of a battle being fought.

Dark figures were visible now, around the edge of the room, and they were struggling, running and leaping. Some of them carried weapons and Valkyrie recognised the silhouettes of Cleavers.

There was a shadow in the steam in front of them, throwing Cleavers back like they were little more than an annoyance.

Valkyrie backed up until she was beside Skulduggery. "What are we seeing?"

"The future," he said slowly.

The images cleared and a new figure drifted into being. Valkyrie saw *herself*, a few years older than she was now.

The Valkyrie in the steam was taller, and her bare arms were lean and muscled, like Tanith's. A tattoo swirled from her left shoulder to her elbow and she wore a black metal gauntlet on her right hand. Her legs were strong, the black trousers clinging to them. Her boots were scuffed, splattered with blood.

"I've seen this," the Valkyrie in the steam said, her dark hair whipping across her face. "I was watching from..." She turned her head and looked straight at where Valkyrie was standing. "...there."

Valkyrie couldn't move.

"This is where it happens," her older self continued, sadness in her voice.

"Stephanie!"

Two people, in the distance, sprinting this way. The older Valkyrie shook her head slowly. "Please don't make me watch it again."

As if her prayer was answered, the older Valkyrie disappeared, the two people came closer and Valkyrie's heart plummeted. Desmond and Melissa Edgley ran through the steam.

Skulduggery held her back against the wall. "This hasn't happened yet," he reminded her quietly.

Her parents stopped running and looked around, and the dark figure Valkyrie had glimpsed earlier stepped out behind them.

"No!" Valkyrie screamed and Skulduggery held her tighter as they watched her parents turn.

"Darquesse," Finbar whispered.

The shadow called Darquesse raised her arm and black flame engulfed the steam images of Valkyrie's parents, turning them to ash before they could even scream their agony.

Valkyrie went cold as a fresh billow of steam took away the image. The sound faded and the steam became clouds. Valkyrie looked down and saw a city below her.

A wave of vertigo hit and she staggered, standing on nothing but air, miles above the ground, but beneath the city she glimpsed the metal grille of the Chamber. She took a breath and willed herself not to throw up. They were in the same room. They hadn't moved. They were not standing in mid-air.

There was a blackness spreading across the city and engulfing the surrounding countryside, as if the grass and the trees were suddenly dying, as if all life was being snuffed out in a wave that spread out and just kept on spreading. Within seconds the land beneath them was dead.

Then the city went away and they were in the Chamber, and the steam was quickly dispersing. Valkyrie realised for the first time that her face was wet with sweat and her hair clung to her scalp.

Cassandra walked forward, shaking the water off the yellow umbrella. "This is the future as I have seen it," she said. "But the future can be changed. Come. You look like you could do with a glass of water."

They followed her up the stairs and Finbar, who hadn't said anything for the past few minutes, wandered into the other room. While Cassandra went to the kitchen, Valkyrie looked at Skulduggery. Her headache pounded. It hurt to even move her eyes.

"My parents were there," she said quietly.

"We can change it."

Her voice shook. "My *parents*, Skulduggery."

He laid a hand on her shoulder and his voice was soft. "You'll save them."

"You saw what I did. I let them die."

"No. *She* let them die. Not you."

"She *is* me."

"Not yet."

"There's no use. She saw what we saw, she knew it was coming and she still just stood there and let Darquesse kill them. *That's* what's going to happen."

"No, Valkyrie. You'll find a way to save them. I have faith."

"My head hurts."

Cassandra came back, handed her a glass of water that she only took a sip from, and a folded leaf, the kind Kenspeckle had, to numb the pain of the headache.

"I can only imagine how hard that was to watch," Cassandra said. "But this is about more than you, and more than your parents. This is about everything."

"The end of the world," Finbar said, rejoining them. He looked tired. "That's the bit I saw in my vision – the darkness spreading across the planet. I didn't see the other stuff." He looked at Valkyrie. "I didn't see you and your folks. I'm sorry."

"We're not dead yet," Skulduggery interjected. "Well, I am, but the rest of you have a bit to go."

"You know as well as anyone," Cassandra said, "that visions of the future are subject to change *and* to interpretation."

Skulduggery turned to Cassandra. "Do you have any idea of a time frame? When is all this going to happen?"

"I don't know. Valkyrie looked three or four years older than she is now, but we can't be sure. The only thing we know for certain is that Darquesse *is* coming, and she's coming to kill us all."

Skulduggery put on his hat, dipping it over his eye sockets. "Not if we kill her first."

19

THE NEW PET

Valkyrie had to go home. The moment they left Cassandra's cottage, she knew she had to go home, to see her parents, to make sure they were OK. She was trying so hard not to let Skulduggery see how badly she was hurting, or how much she wanted to cry. She barely said anything on the drive back to Haggard.

She called the reflection's phone and arranged to pick it up as it made its way home from school. It got in the back seat and didn't ask any questions. They pulled in a few miles later and Skulduggery got out of the car while Valkyrie and her reflection switched clothes. Ten minutes later they arrived in Haggard. The reflection sneaked around back to hide in the bushes while Valkyrie walked in the front door. It was an unusual sensation she realised, not to be coming in through her bedroom window.

"Mum," she called, dumping her schoolbag in the hall, "I'm home."

For three long seconds there was nothing but a dreadful, heavy silence, and then her mother appeared in the doorway to the kitchen. Smiling. Safe. Alive.

"How was school?" she asked and Valkyrie bounded forward and hugged her. Her mum laughed. "That bad, huh?"

Valkyrie laughed in return and hoped it was convincing. She hugged tight and then forced herself to break it off, moving immediately to the fridge to hide the tears that threatened to spill on to her cheeks. "School was fine," she said, as brashly as she could. "School is always fine. Nothing interesting ever happens there."

She opened the fridge, took a breath, and when she was composed, she shut the fridge door and turned. "How was *your* day?"

"Full of adventure and drama," her mum said. "I just got back myself. I'm expecting your father home any minute."

"He's finishing work early? He *never* finishes early."

Her mum shrugged and they heard the front door open.

"Is she back yet?" Valkyrie's dad asked from the hall, as he stumbled over something, probably her schoolbag. "Yes, she's home," she heard him mutter. He walked into the kitchen and Valkyrie hugged him.

"You told her?" he asked.

"Nope," her mum said. "She's just in a hugging mood."

Valkyrie stepped back. "Told me what?"

Her father looked down at her. "You grow taller every day, you know that?"

She made herself keep the smile. Suddenly she didn't want to get any taller. She didn't want to grow any older. Being taller and older and stronger meant being closer to the time when Darquesse would come for them. She wanted to stay the same height and age forever.

"We have news," her mother said, wrapping her arm around her husband's waist.

Valkyrie frowned. "What?"

"We've decided to get a pet," her dad announced.

Valkyrie laughed, and it was a real and genuine laugh. After everything that she'd had to deal with over the past few months, having something so gloriously normal and fun as a new pet took on unimaginable levels of comfort. Plus, she'd always wanted a pet.

"Can we have a dog?" she asked. "And not one of those annoying yappy dogs. Hannah Foley has a Chinese Crested dog that doesn't have any hair, and it looks like the little guy who hangs out of Jabba the Hutt's ceiling. I don't want one of those. I wouldn't be able to take it for walks without being embarrassed for it."

Her dad frowned. "You've seen *Star Wars*? When did you see *Star Wars*? I've been trying to get you to watch it for *years*."

Valkyrie hesitated. Tanith had made her sit down and watch the movies over the course of one weekend. It had been an educational experience.

"I like the lightsabres," she said.

"We're not getting a dog," her mother told her, bringing the conversation back to where it started.

"We can't get a cat," Valkyrie argued. "They don't do anything except plot against you and multiply like Gremlins."

"We're not getting a cat either."

"Can we get a snake?"

"No."

"Please? I can keep it in my room and I'll feed it mice and things and I won't kill it."

"No snakes, no hamsters, no rats, no guinea pigs."

Valkyrie smiled hopefully. "A horse?"

"How about something a little smaller?" her dad said. "Like, I don't know, a brother or a sister?"

Valkyrie looked at them. "*What?*"

Her mother's smile widened. "I'm pregnant, sweetheart."

It took a moment, and when that moment was over, Valkyrie found herself leaping across the room and hugging her mother and screaming "Oh my God!" over and over. Then she thought that she might damage the baby, so she jumped back and leaped for her father and hugged him, and he laughed.

And later, in her room, tears came to her eyes when she thought of what kind of danger this child would be born into.

20

THE ZOMBIE HORDE

There is a very particular process one goes through to become a zombie. Scapegrace didn't go through it because he was raised from the dead by magic, but after a little bit of trial and error he finally figured out what the process entailed. The person he was recruiting needed to be bitten while still alive, so that the infection had time to spread through the system. Scapegrace was hesitant to bite at first, as he was worried how it might look. He had initially planned to just go after attractive females, but quickly realised that this wouldn't be too time-efficient.

His first successful recruitment had been in Phoenix Park. The recruit was a middle-aged man out for a stroll. Scapegrace had waited until there was no one else around and then slipped out from his hiding place. He leaped on the man and dragged him into the bushes, where he bit him. The man tried struggling, but the infection was surprisingly fast acting, and within sixty seconds, the man was dead. After a few moments, however, his eyes opened again and he was looking up at Scapegrace.

"Am I in heaven?" he had asked.

"Don't be stupid," Scapegrace snapped.

"Sorry," the man said and got up.

Scapegrace had looked at his first recruit. A shabby specimen if ever there was one, who seemed to wear a permanently dazed expression on his face.

"What's your name?" Scapegrace asked.

"Gerald," said the man.

Scapegrace pondered. Gerald the zombie just didn't have that fear-inducing ring to it. "I'm going to call you Thrasher," he said.

Thrasher blinked. "All right," he said uncertainly.

Scapegrace nodded. Thrasher was a good name. Thrasher would be his right-hand man in the new zombie army he was building for his Master.

"Come with me, Thrasher," Scapegrace said, leading the way and liking the sound of it.

He had done a lot more recruiting that afternoon. In Phoenix Park alone he recruited Slasher, Crasher, Dasher and Basher, then they all took Crasher's van and he recruited Slicer, Dicer, Wrecker and Boiler. Boiler signified the end of Scapegrace's new name strategy, and from then on he just called them

Zombie One and Zombie Two, things like that. He had more on his mind than thinking up stupid names for his zombies.

He had brought them back to his Master's castle, and the first problem to arise was that none of the other zombies seemed to respect Thrasher's authority. It was too late to demote him now though. Such an act would be seen as weak leadership. The recruits needed to see Scapegrace as infallible, much like a pope or a politician. Scapegrace couldn't admit that appointing Thrasher as his second-in-command had been a mistake, and instead hoped that Thrasher's head would fall off or something.

The second problem was that Scapegrace was starting to smell, but he was confident that new plans he had set in motion would take care of it. There might even be a cream out there that would help. He had taken to wearing car fresheners around his neck, tucked beneath his shirt.

Scapegrace walked the stone corridors, heading for the room which housed his new zombie army. He put on a fierce expression, opened the door and walked in.

They were chatting among themselves, telling jokes and laughing. Thrasher was standing at the edge, trying to laugh along with them, but seemed unsettlingly happy to see Scapegrace when he walked in. He went up to him and stood to attention.

"Good evening, sir!" he said. Idiot. "We're all here, sir!"

"Of course you're all here," Scapegrace responded, annoyed.

"Sir, one of the men was asking about food, sir."

Scapegrace made a mental note not to refer to the zombies as an army *again. Thrasher was letting it go to his head and it wasn't very scary at all. Horde would be better. His zombie horde. Much better.*

"What about food?" Scapegrace grumbled.

"He was wondering what it is we eat, sir."

"We don't eat anything," Scapegrace answered. "We're sustained by magic. We don't need food."

"I shall inform the men, sir!" Thrasher turned on his heel and faced the zombies. "May I have your attention!" he shouted.

A zombie from the back said, "Go to hell, Gerald."

Thrasher looked like he was about to cry. Scapegrace was now seriously regretting his recruitment process.

"We don't eat anything," Thrasher said, trying to keep a brave face while his lower lip quivered. The zombie horde stopped talking among themselves and looked at Scapegrace.

"We don't eat?" Slicer asked. "What, nothing?"

"Not even brains?" Zombie Eleven asked.

"Nothing!" Scapegrace told them. "Under no circumstances are you to eat! Not even one tiny little bite! Is that understood?"

They nodded sullenly and Scapegrace turned to the door. Before he'd even reached it, they started bickering among themselves about what would taste better, brains or flesh. These were not the slavering, mindless creatures of the undead he had hoped for. These were not fearsome in the slightest. His zombies bickered. Scapegrace left the room quickly, closing the door lest the sound of bickering drift to his Master's ears. He hurried back the way he had come, trying his best not to panic.

He didn't want to disappoint his Master. He had been so looking forward to presenting his zombie horde and getting the recognition he sought, the praise he longed for. Maybe even a hug. But it wasn't going to happen. His Master would take one look at the horde and recognise instantly what a petty bunch of failures they were, and what a grotesque disappointment Scapegrace himself was.

Scapegrace reached the small room that served as his personal quarters, hearing the low gentle hum. He opened the rotten door and quickly stepped in, closing it behind him. One advantage of the new recruits was that their credit cards could still be used, and Scapegrace had ordered Thrasher to buy him a place to rest.

"Like a coffin?" Thrasher had asked, wide-eyed and stupid-looking. Scapegrace had hit him, told him not to ask insolent questions, to just do what he was told, and Thrasher had scurried off, nearly crying yet again. But now that Scapegrace thought of it, he quite liked the idea of having a coffin of sorts. He reckoned it was actually pretty nifty. He hadn't told his Master about it, and he did feel terrible about that, but he needed this. He didn't want his body to fall apart, and until he figured out a way to stop any decomposition, the giant freezer would just have to do.

Scapegrace opened the lid and climbed in. He had to curl up to fit, but apart from that it was pretty comfortable. He closed the lid and darkness consumed him. Comforted by the darkness and the hum of power, he lay there and thought about all the ways he could kill the girl.

21

THE RAID

've always thought," Skulduggery said as he drove, "that Skulduggery would be an excellent name to give a baby."

"Well," Valkyrie said, nodding slowly, "I'll be sure to pass on the suggestion. But what if it's a girl?"

"Skulduggery," Skulduggery said.

"Boy or girl, the same name?"

"Yes."

"I don't think my parents would go for the name Skulduggery, if I'm being honest. If it's a girl, they might decide on Stephanie Number Two because they'll probably never see *me* again."

"You're such a pessimist."

"We're about to walk into the Sanctuary, where they all want to arrest me."

"You *did* break the law."

"I was rescuing *you*."

He shrugged. "I was happy where I was."

"Don't talk to me any more."

"I still haven't thanked you properly for rescuing me, have I?"

"Nope."

"I will," he said and nodded.

They parked at the rear of the Waxworks Museum and got out.

"They're not going to arrest you," Skulduggery said as they walked through the door. "They might glare at you and say angry words, but they won't arrest you. Well, they *might* arrest you. There's a good chance they will. But the important thing is that *I've* done nothing wrong."

"For once."

Skulduggery led the way through the darkness and Valkyrie frowned. Her Necromancer ring was cold. Skulduggery murmured something and took out his gun. The Sanctuary door was open and the Phil Lynott figure was lying motionless on the ground. It didn't look up as they crept by. Skulduggery headed down the stairs first, Valkyrie right behind him. There was blood smeared on the wall.

They stepped out into the Foyer. Cleavers lay dead. Valkyrie couldn't tell how many there were. They'd been torn to pieces.

Skulduggery motioned to the open door ahead and they moved to it quietly. A sorcerer was crumpled in the corridor beyond, a gaping hole in his chest. They went through, sticking to the walls, not making a sound. The Sanctuary was eerily, unnaturally quiet.

There was a dead vampire around the next corner. Its bone-white body had almost been cut in half by a Cleaver's scythe. Valkyrie had never had the opportunity to study one of these animals close up before – not without fighting for her life at the same time. It was male, and bald, and its wide mouth was open, a red pointed tongue lolling out over its jagged teeth. Its black eyes stared sightlessly at the ceiling.

They moved on and saw another vampire, its head cut off. Beside it lay a sorcerer Valkyrie had once chatted with. His face had been ripped apart by a swipe of the vampire's claw. He was dead too.

Skulduggery motioned to her then pointed down an

adjoining corridor, towards the holding cells. She nodded and they changed course. Her mouth was dry. She realised she was terrified. Every new corridor held more dead bodies. An army of vampires had come through here – for all they knew, an army of vampires was *still* down here.

They turned a corner and Davina Marr spun towards them, her eyes wild. Skulduggery waved and her gun flew from her hand. He pushed and she shot back off her feet and hit the wall. He kept his hand splayed, holding her there.

"What happened?" he whispered.

Marr opened her mouth to shout and Skulduggery whipped his hand to the side. Marr hit the opposite wall and fell to the ground, unconscious.

Valkyrie resisted the urge to kick her as they passed, and they continued on to the holding cells. Skulduggery stood guard while Valkyrie released Ghastly and Tanith. Moving quietly, Tanith hugged Skulduggery and Ghastly shook his hand.

"Welcome back," Ghastly said, speaking softly. "Now *what* is going on?"

"Vampires."

"*What?*"

"We don't know how many are still here, so move out and keep it quiet."

They moved quickly back the way they had come then broke right. Tanith picked up a Cleaver's fallen scythe. They passed the open doors into the Repository, the closed door into the Gaol and turned left. In the corridor ahead of them, Thurid Guild was propped up against the wall. He was clutching his arm, which was obviously broken. Blood ran from a cut above his eye.

He saw them and shook his head sharply. They froze. His eyes twitched left.

A vampire padded into view, its mouth smeared with the blood of others. It approached Guild and he shrank back. It sniffed him and growled. Guild raised his hand to push the air and the vampire swiped, almost lazily, and the Grand Mage's fingers fell to the floor. Guild screamed and the vampire moved in. Skulduggery whistled through his teeth.

The vampire swivelled its head, its black eyes widening when it saw all the fresh meat on offer. It forgot about Guild and bounded towards them.

Valkyrie, Skulduggery and Ghastly pressed against the air and the vampire hit an invisible wall. It snapped and clawed and roared, but there were no gaps to get through. Skulduggery held out his other hand and Valkyrie felt the air shift, as another invisible wall closed in on the vampire from behind.

Skulduggery closed his hand gently, trapping the creature. The vampire lifted off the ground, squirming and flailing, but unable to free itself.

"Stay here," Skulduggery muttered, tossing his revolver to Ghastly before moving back to the holding cells, taking the vampire with him.

They crossed to Guild and Tanith helped him to his feet. He was sweating and his teeth were chattering. Valkyrie knew well the signs of someone going into shock.

"Get his fingers," Tanith told her as she helped Guild hobble down the corridor, Ghastly leading the way.

Valkyrie blanched. Doing her best not to gag, she picked up the three pale fingers and held them away from her as she followed the others. She dropped one and stepped on it.

"Damn," she said.

"Why is she saying damn?" Guild muttered, too weak to look around. "What is she doing?"

Tanith glanced back to see Valkyrie hopping on one foot, trying to work the finger out from the grooves on the bottom of her boot.

"Nothing," Tanith said, shooting her a glare before turning back.

Once again holding all three fingers, Valkyrie hurried after them.

The Cleavers were on their third sweep of the Sanctuary by the time Guild's fingers were reattached. The final tally was fourteen dead vampires, plus one live vampire in a holding cell, and seventeen dead sorcerers. Nine Cleavers had died. The injured were brought in and quarantined as the Sanctuary doctors worked to rid their systems of the infections brought on by vampire bites. Three more died on the operating tables while Valkyrie was standing there.

Against the doctor's orders, Guild left the Medical Bay as soon as he was able. His broken arm was in a sling and his damaged hand was wrapped in a glove designed to speed up the healing process.

"It was Dusk," he told them as they walked the blood-splattered corridors. "We thought he was still imprisoned in Russia. They didn't bother to tell us he'd escaped two weeks ago. Billy-Ray Sanguine burrowed into his cell apparently, and they fought their way out. The Russians didn't bother to tell us *that* either."

"So Sanguine and Dusk are working together again," Skulduggery said. "But why? What happened here?"

"Dusk planted explosives on the door and led the way in. I've never seen so many vampires. They came like a wave, swarmed over everyone and just kept coming."

"Dusk hadn't shed his skin?" Skulduggery asked.

Guild shook his head. "He was still human. He let the vampires come at us, but he broke off to the north wing, to the Repository. I have people down there now, trying to ascertain what he was after."

There was a curse and they turned to see Davina Marr pointing her gun at them, fury in her eyes. "Step away from the Grand Mage," she demanded.

Guild shook his head. "Put down the gun, Detective."

"Sir, these people are fugitives! Pleasant and Cain were working with the vampires! They assaulted me!"

"They were not working with the vampires," Guild said, "and as much as it pains me to admit it, they saved my life. They're free to go, Detective Marr. Put down the gun. That is an order."

Marr blinked and lowered the weapon. "The Desolation Engine," she said dully.

"What?"

"Dusk took the Desolation Engine. We're doing a visual search now, but it appears to be the only item that's missing."

"What's the Desolation Engine?" Valkyrie asked.

"Essentially, it's a bomb," Ghastly said. "It obliterates everything within its radius, wipes it all out. These days it would be called a Weapon of Mass Destruction."

"It was only ever used once," Tanith said. "Back in, when was it, 1498? A town outside of Naples. Every living thing, every building, tree and stone, was obliterated."

Valkyrie frowned. "Why is there a bomb in the Repository?"

"That's a very good question."

"It's been made safe," Guild said. "It can't be activated. It was kept here because it's the only one of its kind. The Engine is useless to whoever has it."

"You're sure about that?" Skulduggery asked.

"Positive. It's a paperweight now."

"That may be so, but there's a reason Dusk went after it."

"Then get it back," Guild said. "Do what you need to do to find them and stop them. You will have access to every resource we have for the duration of the investigation." He sighed. "Pleasant, I don't like you and the idea that you were going to spend the rest of your existence on a world of Faceless Ones really warmed my heart these past few months. My wife was saying to me just the other day how she's noticed a spring in my step lately. That was because I thought you were gone forever."

"I missed you too, Thurid."

"But it's time to set my personal loathing of you to one side. We've just witnessed a massacre, and we need to catch those responsible and make them pay."

"You seek revenge," said Skulduggery.

"I seek retribution."

Skulduggery looked at him and nodded. Valkyrie and the others followed him as he walked away. Marr glared at them with fury in her eyes and they left her to whatever argument she was about to have with her boss.

"I'm only going to be telling you the absolute minimum about what I've been doing these past eleven months," Skulduggery said to Ghastly and Tanith as they reached the Foyer and climbed the stairs, "so don't bother prying."

"Fine with me," Ghastly said.

"A *little* prying would have been nice," Skulduggery mumbled. They passed through the Waxworks Museum and emerged into the chill night air to find Fletcher standing beside the Bentley. His arms were folded.

"You abandoning me?" he asked crossly as they neared. "Is that what's happening? I do what you need me to do and then you discard me, yeah?"

"This really isn't the time to be petty," Valkyrie said, frowning at him.

"On the contrary," Skulduggery said, "this is an excellent time to be petty. Fletcher, we didn't bring you with us because we didn't want to risk you."

Fletcher narrowed his eyes. "So... I'm still on the team?"

"Of course you are," Skulduggery said happily. "Apart from anything else, you're the only one who can *guarantee* that we escape any more vampires that we come across. You're going to prolong all our lives, my boy."

"I am?"

"You are. You, Fletcher Renn, are good for our health."

Fletcher beamed.

"You're like our own little vegetable," Skulduggery continued and Fletcher's smile disappeared.

"I need my sword," said Tanith.

"I'll take you to it," Skulduggery said. "Valkyrie, take Fletcher and go and see China."

Fletcher frowned. "I'm not a *bus*."

Skulduggery ignored him. "If anyone has heard rumours abut Sanguine or Dusk, she has. The fact of the matter is that Sanguine doesn't do anything for free, so if there is someone paying his bills, we need to find out who that is, and what he wants with both the Desolation Engine *and* the Soul Catcher."

"Or what *she* wants," Valkyrie added.

"That's a good point," Skulduggery said. "This might be the first move Darquesse makes on her road to destruction. If it is, then we're in a lot of trouble."

"And if it isn't?"

"Let's face it," he admitted, "we're probably still in a lot of trouble."

22

THE MAN WHO KILLED
ESRYN VANGUARD

Valkyrie and Fletcher appeared in China's library. It was late at night and there was nobody around. Fletcher didn't say anything as they walked and she knew he was thinking about Skulduggery's dismissive attitude towards him. Fletcher didn't talk much about his parents. She knew his mother was dead, but he rarely mentioned his father. Was that why he could be so insecure and intimidated by Skulduggery? Was Fletcher harbouring a secret need for a father figure's approval?

She led the way across the hall and knocked on the apartment door. China bid them enter. Valkyrie turned to Fletcher.

"You stay out here," she said.

He frowned. "Why?"

"Because China's probably still weak after being shot and she doesn't need the both of us in there. Also every time you're around her you make a fool of yourself."

"Not *every* time."

"You're staying out here."

"I think you're confusing me with a dog."

"Stay."

He looked annoyed so she left him to it and stepped in, closing the door behind her.

China walked in from the bedroom and Valkyrie stared. China looked awful. She was too pale and her eyes looked bruised. She moved stiffly and wore a silk robe tied with a sash. Still beautiful, unnaturally so, but sick. For the first time Valkyrie saw China in a moment of weakness and she didn't know what to say.

"Your silence says it all," China said, a faint smile on her bloodless lips.

"I'm sorry."

"Nonsense." She sank into a chair with an audible sigh. "Take a seat, Valkyrie. You reaction is refreshing. Most people do their best not to catch my eye and prattle on like nothing is different. Now then, you were at the Sanctuary?"

Valkyrie sat. "Yes."

"It was raided I hear. By vampires."

"News travels fast. It was Dusk who led them."

"Him again."

"He stole the Desolation Engine."

"I thought that had been made safe."

"It *has* been, so we don't know why he took it."

China shifted in her seat and grimaced.

Valkyrie hesitated. "Are you... OK?"

"I'll survive. This is what happens when you invest all your magic into healing a bullet wound. It's not pretty. Tomorrow I should be back to normal."

"Should?"

China waved a delicate hand. "You worry too much about people who mean nothing to you."

Valkyrie's eyes widened a fraction, but China still noticed.

"Oh, I'm sorry," she continued. "I didn't mean to sound so cold. What I meant was there are others who would deserve your sympathy much more than I. Fletcher, for instance. That boy is always getting himself into trouble. How is he?"

"He's fine I suppose. He's out in the hall."

"My, you have him well trained."

"China, do you think I don't like you?"

China's smile was gentle. "No, my dear, I'm sure you do. You shouldn't, but I'm sure you do. You've got a big heart. That's not a compliment by the way. That's a flaw in your character."

"I'll work on it."

"That's all I ask."

"Sanguine is back. He stole a Soul Catcher from the Necromancer Temple and he's working with Dusk."

"That *is* interesting, but I'm afraid I can't help you with Dusk. My ongoing inquiries about Sanguine, on the other hand, have finally borne fruit. What do you know of the assassination of Esryn Vanguard during the war?"

"Just that he was a pacifist and the guy who killed him got out of prison a few days ago."

"At the time of his death support for Vanguard and his ideas was coming from soldiers on both sides of the war. I'd always despised the man – this was when I was a supporter of Mevolent's, you understand, and I know that Mevolent did not appreciate Vanguard's attempts to broker peace.

"He suspected that Vanguard was working for Eachan

Meritorious, in an effort to rob Mevolent's troops of the will to die for him. A reasonable suspicion, I think you would agree."

"So he sent Dreylan Scarab to kill Vanguard."

"I had turned my back on the Faceless Ones by this stage, but yes, from what I can gather, Scarab was dispatched to eliminate the problem. An arrow, dipped in poison, while Vanguard was addressing a hall full of supporters. It happened so fast nobody had time to do anything. Vanguard was dead within seconds. The crowd, and bear in mind these were all sorcerers, swarmed the area, hunting for the killer, but Scarab was gone. Skulduggery found him a few days later, and with Guild's help, he arrested him."

Valkyrie frowned. "Guild?"

"Guild was one of Meritorious's most trusted men. He oversaw certain departments within the Sanctuary and his duties included direct interaction with the investigators."

"I didn't think Skulduggery and Guild were ever friends."

"Oh, they weren't," China smiled. "They hated each other from the very start, for reasons I won't go into here. But they worked together on occasion."

"So they arrested Scarab and he was sent to an American prison. Where does Sanguine come into this?"

"It took a long time for me to come across this little piece of information, so I hope you understand how much of a sacrifice it is to part with it for free."

"It wouldn't be for free," Valkyrie said. "You'd have my undying gratitude."

"Free then," China sighed. "Scarab had a son, Valkyrie. You are trying to find out who is pulling Sanguine's strings? I'd look no further than his father."

"Scarab is Sanguine's *dad*?" Valkyrie stood. "This is... This is *huge*."

"Quite."

"China, I'm really sorry, I have to go. If I have some spare time, maybe I can stop by later to see how you are."

"By this time tomorrow I'll be back to my usual self. But your concern – while pointless – is noted. Of course, if our positions were reversed..."

"I know," Valkyrie smiled. "You'd do the same for me."

China arched an eyebrow. "I'm sorry? Do I *look* like I make house calls? You may leave me now."

"Thank you, China," Valkyrie said and turned to go. "Oh, one more thing. Ghastly's façade. It's great."

China smiled. "He seems to like it, doesn't he? It took me long enough to devise, but I think it's worth it."

"Me too," smiled Valkyrie then hurried out to the corridor.

"Well?" Fletcher asked grumpily.

"We have the connection," she told him, and immediately his grumpiness vanished and he took her hand.

They appeared in Ghastly's shop. It was dark, so they turned on the lights and waited for Skulduggery and the others to get there. Valkyrie crossed her arms and looked at Fletcher.

"What?" he asked innocently.

"You're dying to say it."

"Don't know what you mean."

"They're still on their way back from the Sanctuary. We've been to China's, found a very large piece of the puzzle and we're here before them. Say it."

"I'm sorry, Valkyrie, I really don't know what you want me to say."

She waited.

"Although," he began.

"Here it comes."

"Teleportation is clearly the best power to have and you should all be really grateful that I'm on your side. Why anyone would still be using cars, I have no idea. Is it pride? Is it because Skulduggery doesn't want to admit how useful I am? I don't think I'm appreciated as much as I should be, that's all."

"Right."

"We were getting on fine without him, you know."

"We really weren't."

"We were doing OK. It wasn't a *disaster*. No one got killed."

"A few people got killed."

"But not any of *us*," he said, exasperated.

"Anything else you want to complain about before he gets here?"

Fletcher laughed. "What, do you really think I'm scared of him? I'm *not* scared of him. But since you brought it up, yes, there is one thing. I'm older than you. I should be the one giving *you* orders."

"Yeah, no. That's not going to happen."

"I have more world experience."

"At doing your hair."

"What is everyone's problem with my hair? My hair's *cool*."

He kept talking about his hair until Valkyrie told him to shut up. A few minutes later Skulduggery and the others got back and Valkyrie told them what she'd learned.

"It's too neat to be a coincidence," Skulduggery agreed. "Well, all right then. That means we have our big boss. Scarab is released, he has an emotional father-son reunion with his psychopathic offspring and they recruit Dusk, maybe Remus Crux, and whoever else happens to be around and holding a grudge against society."

"So what does Scarab *want?*" Tanith asked as she lovingly cleaned her sword.

"My guess is he wants revenge," Skulduggery said.

"For what? He committed a crime and he was punished for it. If he was going to take these things personally, he shouldn't have killed Vanguard in the first place."

"Ah," Skulduggery said, "that's the thing. You see, I don't think he *did* kill Vanguard. It's something I've suspected for a while now."

Ghastly stared. "But… you arrested him."

"Because all the evidence pointed his way," Skulduggery nodded. "It was only later than I began to suspect that the evidence was rather too easy to come by."

"Scarab was framed?" asked Valkyrie. "He's innocent?"

"Not *entirely* innocent. Or even *remotely* innocent. He *was* Mevolent's top assassin, remember. But, as regards this particular crime, yes, I believe he was innocent."

"You have a theory then?"

"Naturally."

"So who framed Scarab? Who killed Vanguard?"

Skulduggery hesitated. "I actually have a horrible feeling that *we* did."

23

CRUX

Remus Crux dreamed of gods without faces and girls without heads. He dreamed of a vast forest of dead trees, of screaming things hunting him. He saw things in his dream that he recognised as pieces from his old life. They passed him by and he watched them go and didn't miss them.

He woke.

He had told Dusk how to breach the Sanctuary's defences, and where to go to get what they were after, and now the vampire was back, mission accomplished, and Crux felt not one shred of remorse. People that had once been his colleagues had just been killed and he didn't care. They were heathens, unbelievers, enemies of the Faceless Ones.

Dreylan Scarab was a heathen too, but he was a useful heathen. He served a purpose. Crux viewed Scarab and his little Revengers' Club as a conduit to get him where he needed to be. Once they had fulfilled their usefulness, Crux would either abandon them or kill them, whichever was easier. But for now, they wanted the Sanctuary to fall almost as much as he did, and so he was content to go along with their plan.

He could be patient. He could wait. He'd get his chance. The girl had killed two of his Dark Gods after all. The girl had to pay for that and she had to pay for the legacy she had inherited.

Crux knew the legend well. The Faceless Ones had ruled this world until the first sorcerers, the Ancients, constructed the Sceptre to kill them and drive them out. Once the Faceless Ones had been banished, the Ancients fought among themselves like the petty insects they were, until only one of them was left alive. Valkyrie Cain was descended from the last of them.

It was now time for her to pay for the crimes of her ancestors.

24

THE PLOT THICKENS...

"Vanguard had noble intentions," Skulduggery said, his voice filling the space between them all. "His dream of peace was a dream that inspired a great many people who were sick of the war, people on both sides. Someone once said about him that he had seen what he was capable of, what we all were capable of, and it frightened him. So he tried to save us.

"He believed the answer was to allow Mevolent and his lot to worship the Faceless Ones openly, as a religion. He was certain that, given time, they would learn to curb their ruthlessness and to behave with... civility.

"Meritorious didn't agree. He didn't trust Mevolent or any who stood with him. And while Vanguard had started out as a lone voice, preaching understanding and acceptance, it was a voice that echoed and carried. Soon it was a roar.

"The dream of peace, you understand, is a dream that comforts everyone except the soldier on the battlefield. He can't think about peace. He can't hesitate. The soldier lives *in* the war. In combat, war is his mother, his friend and his god. To believe in anything else is suicide.

"I think Meritorious came to the conclusion that the voice that started it all had to be silenced. It was getting too dangerous. Too many people were starting to believe that there was an easy way out. Too many soldiers were starting to have doubts. Meritorious needed them fighting Mevolent, not dreaming of peace."

"But this is all guesswork," Ghastly said. "Skulduggery, I had my issues with Meritorious, but he was a good man. What you're suggesting here is cold-blooded murder."

"I know," Skulduggery said. "And something like that, if it got out, would tear the Sanctuary apart. Which is why he would have assigned the job to Thurid Guild."

Ghastly took a seat – heavily. "Of course. Guild headed the Exigency Programme."

"What's that?" Fletcher asked.

"Exigency Mages are highly trained individuals used for covert strikes against the enemy," Skulduggery said. "Assassination. Sabotage. Dirty tricks. It's not pretty, what they do, but it is necessary."

"They tried to recruit us," Ghastly said. "Skulduggery, me, a few others. We were an independent unit in the war. Guild tried to recruit us, but we didn't like what he was asking us to do." He looked up. "So you think Guild assigned the job to one of his guys?"

Skulduggery nodded. "It makes sense. Meritorious needed an assassin who could completely disappear afterwards and Guild would have volunteered his people. He's always been brave like that."

"Do you know who it was?" Valkyrie asked.

"No. Every single shred of evidence pointed to Mevolent's men and Scarab in particular. By the time it registered that this was all too neat, too easy, we'd already captured Scarab and thrown him in prison."

"You could have said something."

Skulduggery didn't answer.

"Let's say you're right," Tanith said. "Let's say Meritorious and Guild orchestrated Vanguard's assassination and framed

Scarab. For 200 years Scarab's been sitting in his cell. After being cut off from his magic for so long, he would have started to age again, right? So he's an old man, he's out and he's angry. He has his psycho son and their nutball gang, and they're looking for revenge. So they steal a Desolation Engine that won't go off and a Soul Catcher. How does this help them get their revenge?"

"And who are they going to get revenge on?" Fletcher added. "Meritorious is dead."

"They'll be going after Guild," said Skulduggery, "so we should warn him. They'll probably be after me too, but you don't have to warn *me*. I already know. As for what they want with the things they've stolen, I haven't worked that out yet. But I will.

"On the plus side, the more people Scarab has, the greater our chances are of finding one of them. Crux was last seen in Haggard – maybe he's still there, trying to find a way through China's perimeter."

"I know the area," Tanith said. "I'll take my bike, have a look around."

"And I know of a couple of bars Sanguine used to frequent when he was here last," Ghastly said. "They'll still be open, even this late. I can ask if he's been in recently."

Skulduggery nodded. "Take Fletcher with you – you'll get through it faster. Unfortunately, we know next to nothing about Dusk. The vampire I took to the holding cell isn't co-operating, which isn't much of a surprise, and his kind are impervious to most kinds of psychic reading."

"Then just get Valkyrie to ask her vampire mate," Fletcher said.

Skulduggery turned sharply. "Her *what?*"

Valkyrie glared at Fletcher and he blushed.

"Uh, didn't she... She didn't tell you?"

"I didn't tell him," Valkyrie said, her jaw tight.

Skulduggery looked at her. "You have a vampire friend?"

"He set up the meeting with Chabon," she explained. "I was never alone with him. Tanith or Ghastly were always—"

Skulduggery whirled on them. "You *knew* about this? You knew she was meeting with a vampire and you *allowed* it?"

"We had it under control," Tanith said.

"*You never have a vampire under control!*" Skulduggery roared. "It could have killed her! For what? For a chance to get me back? *You should have left me there!*"

Tanith looked away and Valkyrie lowered her eyes, her face burning. Only Ghastly kept his gaze level.

"It was a risk," Ghastly said, as calm as ever, "but it was a risk we decided to take. And now that she *has* made contact with this vampire, we should consider using him to try and find Dusk. It's only logical."

Skulduggery didn't move for a moment.

"Agreed," he said at last, all anger gone from his voice. "Valkyrie, would you be able to arrange that?"

She nodded slowly. These abrupt changes of mood were becoming unsettling.

"Excellent. If we're lucky, one of those three possibilities will lead to Scarab. Call if you find anything out. Valkyrie?"

She led the way out of the shop. The night was cold, but at least it hadn't started to rain yet. They walked to the Bentley.

"I *could* have said something," Skulduggery told her.

"What?"

"You said I could have said something, once I realised Scarab had been framed. I was agreeing with you."

"So why didn't you?"

They reached the car. He unlocked it, but they didn't get in.

"When the war started," he said, "I was flesh and blood. I was a father and a husband first, and a soldier second. When Serpine killed my family, killed me, that changed. I came back a soldier. The war was all I had.

"I didn't like Esryn Vanguard and I didn't agree with him. I saw him as a weakening influence that we couldn't afford to tolerate. If he continued to make his speeches, to try to negotiate with Mevolent, I truly felt we would have lost the war.

"I found out, a few years later, that Meritorious's suspicions had been correct. Mevolent planned to accept the peace that Vanguard was preaching then move his people into position and strike against his enemies in one bloody night. I happen to take some comfort from that – the knowledge that what Meritorious did was, essentially, the right thing to do."

"So you approved of him ordering the murder of an innocent man?"

"We were fighting a war," Skulduggery said. "Harsh decisions had to be made every day. This was one of them."

The first raindrops of the night fell. Valkyrie didn't move.

"I have done terrible things in my life, Valkyrie. Things that haunt me. Some of those things I had to do. Some... I didn't. But I did them anyway. For my sins I should have stayed on the other side of that portal, where I belonged. I should have been hunted and tortured until my bones turned to dust. But you came into hell and you brought me back. I may disappoint you, but you have *never* disappointed me. And you never will."

He got in the car. A few seconds later she did too. They drove.

She slept in the Bentley, seat back and using her coat as a blanket. When she woke, just after dawn, her dream slipped away from her and she sat up.

"Bad dream?" Skulduggery asked.

"Was it? I can't remember."

"Sounded like a nightmare from all that muttering. Not that you could be blamed for having nightmares."

Valkyrie frowned, the dream too far gone now, dispersing even as she grasped for it. "Don't know," she said. "It was an odd one though, I can remember that much. Did I say anything embarrassing?"

"Nothing that could be used against you."

She smiled thinly and looked across the street to the storage facility. "Any movement?"

"Not yet, but it takes a few minutes for a vampire's human skin and hair to grow back. He should be out soon, if he's even in there at all."

Valkyrie readjusted her seat. "This is where he's got his cage set up."

"Why did he help you? Vampires aren't known for being nice."

"He hates Dusk. He won't tell me why, but he hates him. He helped us because we put Dusk in prison. Dusk's stay didn't last too long, but Caelan still appreciated it."

The door of the facility opened and Caelan stepped out. For a moment Valkyrie didn't make a sound. She hadn't realised he was so good-looking. His new skin was so fresh it practically glowed with health and his black hair shone. She watched him walk to a car parked nearby, then stop. He turned his head and looked directly at her. Skulduggery got out and she followed.

"Be nice," she muttered as they walked over.

"I'm always nice," Skulduggery responded.

"Don't point your gun at his head."

"Oh," he said, "*that* kind of nice."

Caelan greeted them with a nod. He didn't waste time mentioning the obvious – that she had got Skulduggery back. Neither did he waste time looking for an introduction. He just stood there and waited for them to start speaking.

"I don't like you," Skulduggery said.

"OK," Caelan said with a single nod.

"I don't like vampires as a rule," Skulduggery continued. "I don't trust them. I don't trust you."

Valkyrie sighed. "I told you to be nice."

"Well, I haven't shot him yet."

She rolled her eyes and said to Caelan, "We need your help finding Dusk."

"I'm sorry. I wouldn't know where to find him even if I wanted to."

"But you'd know people who *would* know, yes?" Skulduggery asked. "Other vampires, like the ones who stormed the Sanctuary last night and slaughtered twenty-nine people. I wonder, were you locked up in your cage the *entire* night, Caelan? Or did you slip out for a snack?"

Caelan looked at him slowly. "My cage is time-locked, programmed to open only at dawn."

"You're a vampire with a conscience, is that it?"

"No, sir," Caelan said. "I'm a monster, just like you say I am. I lock myself up at night because if I don't, someone like you will come and hunt me down. And someone like you will eventually find a way to kill me."

Valkyrie stepped between them and Caelan's eyes came back to her. They were as dark as her own. Maybe darker. "Caelan, I know you helped me out with Chabon, and I know you don't owe me anything, but we need to find Dusk and stop him."

"I keep to myself."

"I know."

His eyes flickered away, to her shoulder. "I can ask Moloch. But I can't go alone."

"We'll come with you."

He nodded. "I can't promise that he'll have anything useful for you, or even that he'll agree to see us. But really, he's the only one who might talk to me."

"The other vampires don't like you?" Skulduggery asked. "Why is that?"

Caelan hesitated. "In our culture it's forbidden for one vampire to kill another."

"You killed another vampire?"

"Yes, sir. I did."

"Why?

Caelan shrugged. "He had it coming."

25

LAST VAMPIRE STANDING

The tower blocks rose from the cement like dreary canyon walls, oppressive in stature and depressing in structure. Built in the 1960s, most of the towers had been demolished decades later in an attempt to get rid of the drugs and crime that had seeped through, permeating everything. Six of the seven Ballymun Flats had been flattened, the Sheriff Street Flats had been torn down, the Flats at Fatima Mansions redeveloped and replaced. By the time Dublin City Council got round to the Faircourt Flats, however, they had run out of money.

Towers, thirteen stories high, of tiny apartments stacked side by side. No grass. No trees. One little shop, defaced by graffiti. Rusted shopping trolleys and old mattresses.

The gleaming Bentley parked beside a burnt-out husk of a car and Skulduggery, Valkyrie and Caelan got out. Skulduggery clicked on the car alarm and they followed Caelan through a rubbish-strewn tunnel, as grey as the sky it was blocking. They emerged on the other side and walked across a concrete square to a stairwell that stank of human waste. They passed no one.

The elevator was broken and the climb to the top burned the muscles of Valkyrie's legs. Skulduggery and Caelan didn't even notice it.

Still they passed no one.

They reached the top, where every second door was paint-flecked steel, with the locks and the bolts on the outside. Heavy bars criss-crossed the windows.

Caelan hammered his fist against one of the steel doors and they waited. There was the click of a lock being undone on the other side and the door cracked open. A young woman looked out. She was pale and sweating, her eyes red-rimmed and jittery.

"We're here to see Moloch," Caelan said and the woman licked her lips, glanced behind her and slipped out. Valkyrie watched her hurry away, arms wrapped around herself.

Valkyrie followed the others into the apartment. It was unfurnished. There were grooves in the walls, long and deep, and more scratches on the back of the steel door. This was where a vampire lived – where a vampire raged and fought to leave. There was another steel door in the living room, leading into the next apartment. In much the same way as China had knocked down the walls in her building to accommodate her library, the vampire Moloch had expanded his living space to accommodate both sides of his nature.

In this furnished apartment they found Moloch. He may have been handsome once, but the years had turned his sharp features cruel. His hair was thinning and his eyes burned with intelligence. He wore tracksuit bottoms and a white T-shirt, despite the cold, and he sat on the couch, hands laced behind his head, master of his domain.

"You scared away my breakfast," he said in a thick Dublin accent. His eyes drank in Valkyrie. "But it looks like you've come with a healthier option. There's a syringe on the table beside you, love. One pint of your blood is all I'll be needing."

"It's an interesting set-up you've got here," Skulduggery said, ignoring his comment. "Let me guess. The other tenants provide you and your brethren with nourishment, while you protect them from the drug dealers and petty criminals. Am I about right?"

"You sound like you disapprove," Moloch said. "But isn't it better than vampires going around killing mortals? This way we don't have to be the hunters and they don't have to be afraid."

"Someone should have probably told that to the girl who ran out of here."

"The first time is daunting," Moloch shrugged. "But enough about our situation. I'd heard you were gone. The story I heard, you were pulled into hell and you were gone for good."

"I was," Skulduggery said. "I'm not any more."

Moloch cracked a smile. "The skeleton detective, standing here in my own home. Imagine that. All this time we've managed to keep a non-existent profile. You didn't even know we were here, did you? So what's next I wonder? You send the Cleavers in?"

"They're looking for Dusk," Caelan said.

Moloch blurred from the couch and then Caelan was gone from Valkyrie's side. There was a crash and she whirled. Moloch had Caelan by the throat, pressing him up against the far wall.

"*You led them here*," Moloch snarled. "You led them to my *home*, you ignorant pup. I should rip your head off right *now*."

Skulduggery had his hands in his pockets, seemingly unperturbed by the possibility.

"We forced him to bring us here," Valkyrie tried.

Moloch tightened his grip and Caelan kicked uselessly, but then he released him. Moloch turned.

"Valkyrie Cain," he said, wiping the spittle from his lips. "Two years ago you killed my Infected brothers. You led them into the sea, so I hear."

"I *jumped* into the sea," Valkyrie responded. "It's not my fault they jumped in after me."

"You misunderstand, young one. I'm thanking you. If they'd been allowed to turn, one of them would probably have gone on a rampage through the city, or been caught on camera, or been seen doing *something*. It would have been disastrous for us.

"Creating new vampires is an art form. The Infected have to be contained, trained, taught how to behave. They're not *zombies*, for God's sake. But Dusk views them as an army, not family."

"He sent fourteen fresh vampires into the Sanctuary last night," Skulduggery said.

"Is that so?"

"You didn't hear?"

"I sleep late. What makes you think I'll help you anyway? We're not all tortured souls like Caelan here pretends to be. I don't work with sorcerers. And I sure don't work with Sanctuary agents."

"You've been wondering how to solve a problem like Dusk for a long time. Every morning you've been waiting for an opportunity to come knocking on your door. Well, we knocked."

Moloch considered. Behind him, Caelan stayed flat against the wall, staring at the back of Moloch's head like he was boring a hole through it.

Moloch pulled back the rug, revealing a steel trapdoor. It was big and round, and looked heavy, but Moloch opened it without difficulty. Valkyrie and Skulduggery stepped to the edge and peered into the gloom.

"It's where we keep them," Moloch said. "You'd be surprised how many people living in these buildings want to be like us. Strength, speed, long life and no magic required. Just a bite. Or maybe you wouldn't be surprised. Poverty, unemployment, no prospects, no self-respect – what else is there to aim for? The point is, being a vampire is just like any other attractive employment opportunity – there are a lot of people applying for a small number of places.

"So whenever we need more, we gather the applicants together, take a little bite and dump them down this hole. For two days they fight among themselves. Whoever is left at the end, once the infection is complete, joins the family."

"And the rest are slaughtered along the way," Skulduggery said.

"Darwinian in its simplicity, don't you think?"

"How does this help us find Dusk?" Valkyrie asked.

"One of my potential brothers down there was not infected by us – he was infected by one of Dusk's vampires. He saw their lair before he managed to escape and come here."

She frowned. "How do we ask him?"

"You're going to have to do that in person," Moloch said, and moved. He crashed into Skulduggery, sending him hurtling off his feet. Caelan came forward and Moloch threw him across the room, then he grabbed Valkyrie.

"By killing those Infected," he snarled, "you did us a favour. Thanks for that. But I can't let that crime go unpunished."

She raised her arm, but he was already pushing her and she cried out as she fell into the hole. She twisted as she fell, hands out against the darkness, dropping through another hole in the next apartment. She felt pressure on her palms as the floor rushed to meet her and she pushed against the air. Her descent slowed and she got her feet under her, landing in a crouch.

Dim light drifted from low-wattage bulbs, illuminating faded wallpaper, ratty carpet and not much else. She'd fallen from the thirteenth floor, through the twelfth, and now she was in the eleventh. Moloch had already closed the trapdoor above her, sealing her in. Valkyrie focused and tested the air, feeling movement around her. She was not alone.

She stepped back against the wall, saw a gap that had been knocked out of it and slipped through. There was another gap ahead, and through the murk she saw yet another beyond that. Every apartment on this floor was clumsily linked together, and by the looks of it, every door and window was bricked over.

No, she told herself, not *every* door. There would be one door, undoubtedly steel and locked from the other side, that allowed the last vampire standing to get out of here.

She just had to find it.

There was a snarl, somewhere to her left. A flurry of movement and a man darted into the light, and she pushed at the air and caught him just as he jumped at her. She spun, gripping the shadows and punching them into the chest of the woman coming up behind her. Then she ran.

She jumped through a hole in the next wall, straight into the arms of another Infected. His mouth was open, sharpened teeth diving for her throat. She slammed her forehead into his face and he howled in pain and dropped her. She staggered, dazed, knocking against a small table. Her hand found a lamp and she swung it into his head. The light exploded and darkness swarmed around them, but she was already pushing by him.

There were three Infected waiting for her. She clicked her fingers and set fire to a sofa, then sent it hurtling towards them. The Infected dodged out of the way and she ran by, through a door into a dark kitchen, out through the wall, tripping over herself and stumbling into the next apartment's bedroom.

Something rushed her and for a moment she flew through empty space. The wall smacked into her and as she fell, she saw the man lunging at her again. She tried to push at the air, but he grabbed her wrist. He squeezed and the pain brought her to her knees. His other hand lifted her and he whirled, sending her through into the living room. She landed on a table, scattering whatever junk had been piled on top of it, and rolled off.

Another one grabbed her. Valkyrie jammed her forearm into his mouth as he tried to bite her, forcing his head back, and with her free hand she sent a half-fist into his throat. He gagged and fell away, and a weight landed on her. She went down and a fist cracked against her cheek and the world spun. She covered up as the Infected sent punches raining down on top of her, her coat sleeves absorbing much of the punishment. The others would be coming. If she stayed down for any length of time, they'd be all over her.

She clicked her fingers and thrust a handful of flame into the

Infected's face. He screeched and recoiled. She pushed at the air and he was flung back, crashing his head into the wall. She got up. Through the gloom she saw more of them running in. This wasn't going to work. Skulduggery could have battled his way to the door, but she wasn't Skulduggery. She needed a new plan.

"Stop!" she shouted.

Amazingly, the Infected stopped.

"I'm not here to fight you," Valkyrie said loudly and clearly. "I'm not here to hurt you or compete with you. Moloch sent me down here to talk. He wants one of you to help me. Do you understand?"

They looked at her like she was food, but they stayed where they were. Somewhere in the darkness an Infected growled.

"I need to find Dusk. One of *his* vampires infected one of *you*. You were brought to his lair. I need to know where that is."

Somewhere to her right, there was another growl.

"If you don't help me," she continued, glaring at them, "you're all going to *burn*. Do you hear me? Moloch has no time for vampires who disobey him."

She figured about half of them were growling now and she was seriously regretting this plan. Her back was to the wall and they were gathered in front of her, ready to rip her apart the moment she said the wrong thing.

"My name is Valkyrie Cain," she shouted over the noise. "You may have heard of me. I killed *twenty* of you two years ago and I'll kill twenty more today and I won't think it too many."

The growling stopped.

"I'm not down here for the good of my health, so I'm going to ask just one more time – which one of you knows where Dusk is?"

She saw them glance at each other, and then one of them, a girl with a shaved head, stepped forward. She pointed at the unconscious Infected on the floor, the one Valkyrie had burned.

"He does," she said.

Valkyrie's shoulders sagged. "You're kidding me."

"He was talking about it earlier, before we were thrown down here."

"Did he happen to mention where he was brought?"

"Not that I heard."

"Anyone? Did he mention it to anyone?"

No one answered. One of them started to growl again.

"Where's the door?" she asked quickly, before she lost them completely. "The steel door out of here, Moloch told me to find it. Where is it?"

The skinhead's eyes were once again locked on to her, but she managed to nod her head to the next apartment over.

215

"OK," Valkyrie said, preparing herself. "OK."

The first Infected came at her like a bullet, and she sidestepped and slapped her fist into his back, sending him into the wall behind her. The skinhead girl charged and Valkyrie kicked her knee then kneed her face. She whipped the shadows at the next Infected who came close and sent a wave of darkness into another. She clicked her fingers and threw fireballs and manoeuvred over to the unconscious man.

The moment there was a break in the attacks, she squatted down and lifted him by his collar. She snapped her palms, sending his ragdoll body across the room, knocking down the Infected like bowling pins.

Hands reached for her as she ran after him. The air shimmered and she cleared a path, reaching him and dragging him through the hole in the wall. She glanced over her shoulder and saw the outline of a door in the darkness. Now all she had to do was hold them off until Skulduggery did what he tended to do – arrive in the nick of time.

The unconscious Infected murmured.

"Hey," she said into his ear. "Moloch wants to know where Dusk is."

He groaned. She slapped him across the face, hard.

"Where is Dusk? Where were you taken?"

"A castle," he muttered, as a dark shape came through the hole and collided with her.

They went sprawling in the mess on the floor. She grabbed a chunk of debris and smacked it into the face of her attacker. She rolled, now she was on top, and punched him with her left, and it felt like her hand had broken. She got up and he kicked her legs from under her.

Light flooded the room as the door opened behind her and hands grabbed her. Suddenly she was being hauled out.

"No!" she cried. "That one knows where they are!"

She was outside now, pressed against the concrete railing, looking out at the other tower blocks and the grey sky and the eleven-storey drop beneath her. She spun round to tell Skulduggery to get the Infected man she'd burned. But it wasn't Skulduggery.

Dusk lifted her and threw her over the railing.

26

KIDNAPPED

The tower tilted away from her, and then there was nothing but the grey sky and the sound of wind rushing in her ears.

The other towers veered into view then the ground swept in and out again, and Valkyrie was turning over as she fell. There was the sky and heavy clouds and her hair, and a shape, Skulduggery, dropping towards her. She turned again and saw the ground and his arms wrapped around her.

Their plummet slowed and now they were merely drifting. Then they stopped and Skulduggery let her put her feet on the ground.

"Are you OK?" he asked.

She couldn't answer. She could barely breathe. She just gripped his shoulder to make sure she didn't fall over.

There were people looking at them. The ordinary tenants of the building had stepped out of their apartments and they were looking down at them silently.

"Dusk," she managed to say. "He's up there."

The only floors that didn't have a line of people at the balconies were the eleventh and the thirteenth, but now she could see movement on the uppermost floor. People were climbing over the railing. Eight of them.

They let themselves go.

They fell gracefully, three stories at a time, balcony to balcony, pausing only momentarily before allowing themselves to continue down. Then half of them sprang, propelling themselves away from the building, and the others waited a heartbeat and then dived. All eight vampires flipped and landed in a perfect circle surrounding Skulduggery and Valkyrie.

The vampires smiled at them, not even out of breath.

Moloch came down last, carrying something big over his shoulder. He got to the fourth-floor balcony and let it drop. It tumbled and spun as it fell, and she saw that it was Caelan. He hit the ground hard and lay there, unconscious and bleeding.

Moloch landed. The ring of vampires parted and he walked through.

"Give Dusk to us," Skulduggery said.

"He's already gone," Moloch responded.

Skulduggery nodded, considering what he was going to say next, and then his gun flashed from his jacket and Moloch batted it from his hand. Another vampire caught it. One of them laughed.

"You won't kill us," Skulduggery told Moloch.

"Really?" Moloch said. "Why not?"

"Because you won't be able to. And then we will come back with an army of Cleavers and tear these towers down around you. We want Dusk."

"I've helped you all I can," Moloch shrugged.

"Helped us? You tried to *kill* Valkyrie."

"No, I didn't. I put her in a situation where she might die, yeah, but I didn't try to kill her. Did you get what you needed, young one?"

Valkyrie met his eyes. "He just said a castle."

"There you go then. He was brought to a castle. That's a clue, isn't it? I mean, how many castles are there around here? Not that many, I'd wager."

"When we take down Dusk," Skulduggery said, "we're going

to take down everyone who stands with him."

The amusement left Moloch's face. "We don't stand with him, skeleton. He made us an offer and if certain things go certain ways, we'll be considering it. If you happen to take him down before that, so be it."

"Then what was he doing here?"

"Requesting some of the Infected to bring home, to replace the lads lost in the Sanctuary raid. Apparently, he can't afford to be waiting the two nights it takes to turn vampires on his own."

"And did you give him your Infected?"

"Of course not. He wasn't exactly happy about it, but there you go."

Skulduggery held out his hand to the vampire with his gun. Moloch nodded assent and the gun was returned. Skulduggery slid it into his holster.

"We're going to be watching you," he said.

"Of course you are," Moloch replied, bitterness in his voice. At an unseen signal, the eight vampires left them, walking silently from the square. "Take Caelan with you when you leave," Moloch continued. "He's used up any good grace I have left. Tell him never to come back here."

Skulduggery nodded and they watched him go.

*

They'd left Caelan at the storage facility, and he had limped from the car without looking back. Valkyrie felt bad – he'd been hurt because of them after all. But they couldn't bring him with them to see Kenspeckle Grouse, not with the Professor's vampire phobia at an all-time high lately.

They parked at the back of the old Hibernian Cinema and walked in. Now that the adrenaline had worn off, the pain from the hand Valkyrie had broken while punching was shooting through her. She cradled her arm as she followed Skulduggery up on to the stage and through the door projected on to the screen.

They took the first corridor to their right, almost bumping into Clarabelle. She held two long test tubes, one in each hand, both filled with a clear liquid.

"Hi, Clarabelle," Valkyrie said. "Is the Professor in?"

Clarabelle's eyes were moving between the test tubes. "Safe, unsafe. Safe, unsafe. Left one safe, right one unsafe. Left safe, right unsafe." She looked up and smiled brightly. "Hello, Valkyrie! Hello, Skulduggery! I haven't seen *you* in ages!"

"Well," Skulduggery said, "I've been—"

"It's been weeks, hasn't it?" Clarabelle continued and laughed. "It's probably only been a few days, but it *feels* like it's been weeks! I'd take that as a compliment if I were you!"

"I'll try," Skulduggery murmured.

Clarabelle looked back at the tubes. "Left safe, right unsafe. Safe, unsafe."

"What's that you're holding?" Valkyrie asked because she had to – there was really no way around it.

"Oh, these?" beamed Clarabelle. "They're nothing."

"Oh."

"They're not *really* nothing though. It's just another of the Professor's experiments – you know how he is. But the important thing to remember is not to drink either of them. That's what he told me. He said above all else, do *not* drink. So I asked him, if I *did* drink, which one would be worse for me? And the Professor said *don't* drink. And I said yes, but if I *did*, and he said why *would* I, since he's just told me *not* to? But I said yes, I know that, but just say I *did* drink one of them, which one would be worse for me? And he said the one in my left hand."

"But that's the safe one," Valkyrie said.

"Sorry?"

"You were saying left safe, right unsafe, just a moment ago."

"Are you sure? Are you sure it wasn't the other way around?"

"The left one is the safe one," Skulduggery said. "That's what you were chanting."

Clarabelle frowned. "I don't really know my right hand from my left hand though."

Skulduggery pointed. "That's your left hand."

"But this is the unsafe one."

"Are you sure?"

"Practically. I'll check."

Before they could stop her, Clarabelle sipped from the tube in her right hand. She sloshed it around in her mouth, swallowed and nodded. "Yes," she said happily.

"Was that the safe one?" Valkyrie asked.

"No idea," Clarabelle said and walked on.

Kenspeckle Grouse hurried into the Emergency Room ahead of them. They walked in after him. He was brushing his white hair, his back to them. He saw them enter in the mirror he was using.

"I don't know why I bother," he grumbled. "I never neaten my hair. I just move it around on my head."

"Hello, Professor," Skulduggery said.

"I heard you were back." Kenspeckle turned. He was wearing slacks, a blazer and a yellow bow tie. "I said to myself, it's only a matter of time before he arrives in here, Valkyrie beside him, with another injury for me to fix. What is it this time, Valkyrie? Broken arm?"

"Just the hand."

"Oh, that's much better," he said scornfully. He picked a leaf from a bowl on the table and folded it. "Open," he ordered. She opened her mouth and he popped it in. He examined her hand while she chewed and immediately the pain lessened. Pleasingly, it also blocked off another headache that was threatening to emerge.

"We passed Clarabelle," Skulduggery said. "She drank from one of the test tubes she was holding."

Kenspeckle's head drooped. "That girl," he said. "One of these days she'll learn. I don't know *what* she'll learn, but she'll learn and it will be a good day."

"Is she in any danger?"

He started searching drawers. "Not really. Both tubes contain mineral water. You'd be astonished how many times I've given her water and told her it was something else and not to drink it. She always drinks it though. Always. It's a compulsion." He showed them a huge uneven bowl that looked like it was made in an idiot's pottery class. "She made this for me, as a token of her appreciation for employing her when nobody else would."

"It's nice," Valkyrie lied. "Colourful."

"It was meant to be a mug," Kenspeckle told her. "How big does she think my mouth is? I could fit my whole *head* in there, for God's sake. It doesn't even have a handle. And look at this." He put the bowl on the table and it tilted drastically. "It's so off balance it's in danger of falling off a flat surface."

He poured various liquids and powders into the bowl and checked his watch.

Valkyrie frowned. "Are you going out?" she asked.

Kenspeckle started stirring. The bowl rocked rhythmically. "I am."

"You're all dressed up. You *never* get dressed up. Are you...? Do you have a *date*?"

"Why do you sound so surprised? Because I'm old, is that it? Because I'm an old man and old people shouldn't go out on dates? Because we don't need love or companionship, and we don't get lonely? Is that it? Is that why you're so surprised I have a date?"

"No," she said. "It's because you're really grumpy."

"Ah. Yes. I *am* rather grumpy. But what can I say? Some women like that."

"What women?"

"Women with low expectations."

"So you have a date now? It's not even lunchtime. Where are you going?"

"Bingo."

"Bingo?"

"Bingo. Everyone's playing it apparently." He motioned Valkyrie over and nodded to the bowl, which was now full of brown sludge. "Put your hand in," he said.

She did so. It was cold and gritty sludge.

"Keep it there for three or four minutes, until the tingling stops. Do not flex your fingers, do you hear me? Once you're done, wash your hand in the sink. And wash it *well* – I don't want you ruining the towel. There will be some mild bruising, but by this afternoon you won't even know it was broken."

"You're going?"

"I have a date, Valkyrie."

"Right. Yes. Sorry. You go on, I'll be fine."

"Your medical opinion means so much to me, you have no idea. Detective Pleasant, please make sure she doesn't break anything else while she's standing there."

"I'll do my best."

"That's all I can ask."

He bowed to them both and swept from the room.

"He's in a good mood," she said.

"He is," Skulduggery agreed. "It's disconcerting."

"And a little gross."

"That too."

Her phone rang and she answered with her free hand. It was Fletcher. She told him where they were and Fletcher said he was going to get Tanith. A minute later Fletcher and Tanith appeared beside them.

Tanith arched an eyebrow at Valkyrie's sludge-covered hand that she was washing in the sink. "What happened?"

"Vampires," Valkyrie said. "We learned that Dusk's lair is a castle."

"How did you do?" Skulduggery asked.

"I couldn't find Remus Crux anywhere near Haggard," Tanith told them, "and none of the seals had been broken, so he hasn't been trying to break through."

"Myself and Ghastly went looking for friends of Sanguine," said Fletcher. "Turns out he doesn't have any. Can't say I'm surprised."

"So our only lead is a castle," Skulduggery said. "Well, at least it *is* a lead."

Then they heard Clarabelle shouting for help. She ran in.

"They've taken the Professor!" she cried.

Valkyrie and Tanith gripped Fletcher's arms and Skulduggery put a hand on his shoulder.

"Outside, Fletcher," he said and then they were standing in the rain beside the Bentley as Billy-Ray Sanguine threw Kenspeckle into the back of his car.

Something moved overhead and Skulduggery grunted and went flying over the bonnet of the Bentley. A man landed in front of them and immediately flipped, catching Tanith with a kick that sent her crashing back into Fletcher.

Springheeled Jack whirled to Valkyrie, smiling. He doffed his hat and leaped backwards when she pushed at the air. He dropped on to the top of Sanguine's car and slid in through the open window, and the car sped out of sight.

The Bentley beeped as the alarm deactivated and the locks sprang open. Fletcher and Tanith got in the back seat and Valkyrie clicked her seatbelt into place. Skulduggery turned the key and stomped on the accelerator. The Bentley roared out on to the road.

They followed Sanguine's car round the corner, swerving to avoid an oncoming van. The roads were slick with rain and the back of the Bentley swung wildly, but Skulduggery kept it under control. They overtook a car on the inside and then overtook another by crossing to the opposite lane. Half a dozen drivers blasted their horns as Skulduggery nudged the Bentley back into their own lane, and now there was nothing between them and Sanguine except a whole lot of road.

"Fletcher," Skulduggery said, "can you teleport over? Grab the Professor?"

Fletcher stared at the car in front, gripping the headrest of Valkyrie's seat.

"It's moving too fast," he said. "A moving target's too hard."

The speed piled on. Valkyrie never had any idea that the Bentley could *go* this fast. They were gaining and they were gaining easily.

The car in front took a right and took it hard. The tyres squealed as the car drifted sideways, but Sanguine was good and with a sudden burst of speed it leaped onward.

Skulduggery turned the wheel and tapped the brake, his hand working the gear stick, and the Bentley growled in appreciation. He straightened the car out and brought it to a roar again and Valkyrie felt herself being pressed back into her seat. The streets whipped by. She saw Springheeled Jack open the passenger door of the car in front and move out slightly. He looked down at the road passing beneath him, like he was judging their speed.

Fletcher leaned forward. "What the hell's he doing? He's not going to jump, is he?"

But he didn't jump. Defying all laws of inertia and velocity, Jack planted his foot on the ground and simply stepped out, and now he was standing on the road as they hurtled towards him.

"This is not good," Skulduggery murmured.

Jack leaped before the Bentley hit him, landing on the bonnet without even swaying. He looked down at them, his ragged coat flapping in the wind and his hat staying on.

"If there is one thing I cannot abide," Skulduggery said, pointing his gun out of the window, "it's hood ornaments."

Before he could fire, Jack stepped up on to the roof.

"I've got him," Tanith said, handing her sword to Fletcher and opening the window. Moving with unerring grace, she slid out of the car.

"We can't do this," Valkyrie said, glimpsing the astonished faces of people they passed. "We're in public, for God's sake! People can see us!"

But Skulduggery's attention had returned to closing the gap on the car in front. They swerved on to a side street and the Bentley roared. They were gaining again.

Jack crashed on to the bonnet and Skulduggery muttered a curse, craning his neck to see around him. Valkyrie watched Tanith step off the roof. She kicked Jack and he rolled off the side of the car, but as he fell, his fingers found purchase, and for a moment he clung on to the door, his malformed face pressed against Valkyrie's window.

And then he hauled himself up out of sight and Tanith joined him, their feet heavy on the roof.

"Please stop standing on my car," Skulduggery said softly.

There was a moment of sudden silence and then Tanith's boots passed over the windscreen, kicking. Jack followed. He stepped from the roof to the bonnet, his right hand closed around Tanith's throat, lifting her up and holding her out before him.

Valkyrie watched in horror as Jack held Tanith over the side of the car, the ground rushing beneath her. He looked down at Valkyrie and as he did so, he let go.

Valkyrie screamed Tanith's name as Tanith dropped, but the Bentley sped on and she didn't see Tanith hit the road.

Skulduggery put his hand out of the window, his fingers moving, and ahead of them the air started to ripple. Jack turned, realised what was happening, but was unable to prevent it. The Bentley passed through the wall of air, but Jack slammed into it and it knocked him back.

Valkyrie spun in her seat, and managed to see him land on both feet in the middle of the road, but the Bentley was already rounding another corner.

"She'll be all right," Skulduggery said, not even waiting for Valkyrie to ask. "Tanith Low has fallen off more cars than you've ridden in."

He wrenched the wheel to the right and the Bentley fishtailed a little, then the tyres found their grip again.

The car in front wasn't doing so well. It veered off the road and pedestrians jumped from its path as it mounted the kerb and crashed through an iron gate. The car jolted and spun, and the gate pinwheeled over it and hit the ground. Skulduggery slammed on the brakes.

The car ahead had stopped, its bonnet crumpled and thick grey smoke billowed from its engine. Valkyrie saw movement.

"He's getting out," she said, unbuckling her seatbelt and kicking open the door. Instantly she heard the siren.

She ran by a teenage boy, his eyes wide and his mouth open, raising his phone to take a picture, and she snatched the phone from his hand and leaped over the mangled gate. She ran to the ruined car, pushing at the air to clear the smoke from her sight, but the car was empty. She glimpsed Sanguine, dragging Kenspeckle around the corner of a building.

She grabbed Fletcher's hand and pointed. "There!"

And then a Garda squad car braked sharply behind them.

They froze. She could tell that Fletcher was fighting his natural instinct to teleport. Her eyes flickered to Skulduggery. They all had their backs to the Gardaí, but Skulduggery had lost his scarf. If he turned, they'd see what he was.

"Get down on the ground!" one of the cops shouted. She

watched them out of the corner of her eye as they advanced cautiously. They weren't armed.

"Put down any weapons you are carrying and get down on the ground!" the second cop ordered.

Valkyrie didn't move. Skulduggery raised his hands above his head. She heard the clink of handcuffs. She saw the first cop reach for Skulduggery and Skulduggery spun, grabbing the cop's hand and twisting it. The one behind Valkyrie suddenly had a baton in his hand, but she whirled, kicking his feet from under him as he went to help his colleague.

Skulduggery wrapped an arm around the first Garda's throat and applied the choke. Valkyrie pushed the air and the second Garda went skidding along the ground. He hit Sanguine's car and groaned.

There were more sirens, getting louder.

Skulduggery laid the unconscious cop on the ground and all three of them walked quickly to the car. Valkyrie took the battery from the teenage boy's phone and tossed the phone back to him. They got in the car and sped away – pulling in sharply to the side of the road as three squad cars passed. They got back to where they had last seen Tanith and slowed. The street was empty.

Valkyrie pulled her phone from her pocket and called

Tanith's number. After a few rings, the call was answered.

"'Ello, my lovely," Springheeled Jack said, a smile in his voice. "Tanith can't come to the phone right now, on account of her bein' so unconscious. If you'd like to leave a message—"

"Let her go," Valkyrie snapped.

"—I'll make sure she gets it. 'Ave a nice day."

The phone went dead.

27

WHEN KENSPECKLE
MET SCARAB

Scarab laid the Desolation Engine on the worktable in front of Kenspeckle Grouse. It was relatively small for such a destructive weapon, resembling a stone hourglass about the length of Scarab's hand. There were two glass vials within the stone frame, both of them half-full of a calm green liquid.

Professor Grouse's voice was strained when he spoke. "And what do you expect me to do with this?"

"I want you to fix it," Scarab said.

"So you can use it to kill thousands of innocent people? No."

"Professor, I'm not going to waste our time. I'm not going to tell you that I was framed and imprisoned for a crime I didn't commit. I'm not going to tell you how I watched my youth slip away from me while I was in that cell. I'm not going to tell you about the anger or the need to see my enemies suffer. I'm not going to tell you any of that."

"Really?" Grouse asked. "Because it sounds like you just did."

"You'd die before you'd help me, Professor. I know that full well. But you have the skills, the talent and the knowledge I need, and the only thing that's stopping you from doing what I ask... is you."

"And so your plan is...?"

"It's quite simple. If you won't change you mind, I'm going to change it for you."

28

THE MIDNIGHT HOTEL

uild narrowed his eyes at their approach. "I'm starting to regret my decision," he said. "A car chase? In broad daylight? Maybe Marr was right. Maybe you *should* all be locked up."

"Maybe you should give Detective Marr something worthwhile to do," Skulduggery said. "Right now Ghastly is checking out every castle within a two-hour drive of here. I'm sure he'd appreciate the help."

"Oh, yes, because a source you will not divulge told you that Scarab's base is *probably* a castle. That's all you have to go on?"

"We work with what we have, Thurid."

"Well, do you have anything *else?*"

"We have motive," Valkyrie said. "Scarab wants revenge on the people who framed him."

Guild looked at her. "What are you talking about?" he said at last.

"You guys killed this Esryn Vanguard bloke," Fletcher told him. "You didn't want him weakening your side or stopping the war or whatever it was you were scared he was going to do."

"That's ridiculous."

Valkyrie held his gaze. "You had one of your Exigency Mages assassinate Vanguard, and then you framed Scarab for it and locked him away without a proper trial."

Guild snarled at Skulduggery. "You're supposed to be investigating *Scarab*, not me. You're wasting valuable—"

"If we want to anticipate Scarab's moves," Skulduggery interrupted, "we need to know the truth. Is he coming after you, or both of us, or everyone? If he *did* kill Vanguard, then all we have to do is put you in protective custody for a year or so. He'll get bored, or die, and it'll all be over.

"But if he *didn't* kill Vanguard, we have bigger problems. And we need to know what they are now."

"Well, why don't you work on the assumption that we *have*

bigger problems and take it from there?" said Guild.

"Did Scarab kill Vanguard?"

"This is not—"

"Did Scarab kill Vanguard?"

"*No,*" Guild snapped.

"Meritorious ordered the assassination," Valkyrie pressed.

"It was a necessary move to make," Guild said.

"Vanguard was on *your own side.*"

"Vanguard was on no one's side but his own."

"That didn't make him an enemy."

"I'm not going to stand here and explain our actions to *you.* We did what had to be done and if there are ramifications, I'll deal with them when this particular crisis is over. Are we agreed? Excellent. So now that you know all of Scarab's grievances, you're going to catch him, yes?"

"It brings us a step closer," Skulduggery said. "But our main concern is that Desolation Engine."

"It's deactivated," Guild said. "Useless. Why would that be of concern to us?"

"Because there's only one man alive who could possibly fix it and Scarab's just kidnapped him."

Guild paled. "Grouse could repair the Engine?"

"The man's a scientific genius. He could do anything. The

question becomes, of course, *will* he repair it? And I really don't think he will. I think he'd rather die than be responsible for hurting people."

"You had better be right."

"But we don't *want* him to die," Valkyrie said angrily. "If anyone dies, it should be..."

Guild looked at her and she shut up.

"Will he be tortured?" Fletcher asked, his voice quiet. "I know you people do a lot of that kind of stuff... But the Professor's an old man. He won't be able to take it. It was bad enough he was in a car crash."

Valkyrie frowned, the thought suddenly striking her. "Why *was* he in a car crash? Why were they in a *car* at all? Sanguine could have just grabbed him and tunnelled away with him. Why did they take a car?"

"I was wondering that myself," Skulduggery said. "The only explanation I can think of is that maybe he was trying to lead us somewhere."

"A trap?"

"That's the only thing that makes sense."

"Then it's a good thing he crashed."

"It has been reported on the news," Guild snapped. "It is in no way a good thing *any* of this happened. If the worst comes to pass, if Grouse *does* repair that Engine, what will Scarab use it for? To kill me?"

"If he just wanted to just kill you, he could have done it when Dusk came in with his vampires. He might see the Sanctuary, as a whole, as being responsible for his imprisonment."

"Then that is why he wants the Engine. He wants to destroy this place."

"Maybe," Skulduggery said, then looked up suddenly. "I know why they stole the Soul Catcher."

"You do?"

"I know how they'll make Professor Grouse help them. I even know where at least one of them will be tonight."

"And you figured all that out while we were standing here talking?"

"I *am* a detective."

"So what do they want with the Desolation Engine?"

"It's probably what we think – they want to destroy this place. But I don't know that for sure."

"When you *do* know something for sure," Guild sighed, "would you be kind enough to tell me? I'm quite looking forward to the day when you become useful."

*

They walked to the Bentley.

"Fletcher," Skulduggery said, "I want you to help Ghastly find the castle we're looking for."

"What are you two going to do?"

"Never mind that," Valkyrie said. "Why did Sanguine steal the Soul Catcher?"

Skulduggery unlocked the car. "Have you ever heard of Remnants?"

"Are they a band?" Fletcher asked.

"Remnants are dark spirits, beings infused with absolute evil. They lost their bodies long ago, so when they're able, they possess the living – sharing their memories, absorbing their personalities and hijacking their bodies. They are a plague. The last time they struck, in 1892, they took over an entire town in Kerry and burned it to the ground. The Sanctuary asked the Necromancers for help in constructing what would basically be a giant Soul Catcher inside a mountain in the MacGillycuddy's Reeks. The Necromancers didn't want to help so the Sanctuary did the best they could. The townspeople were led there, the giant Soul Catcher somehow, *miraculously*, worked and the Remnants were torn out of them."

"Where are the Remnants now?"

"Trapped. Hundreds of them, it's impossible to say exactly

how many, were then transferred to a room they can't escape from. If they ever got out, they would ravage this world, moving from host body to host body, building up their strength, building up their army."

"If Sanguine traps one of them in the Soul Catcher," Valkyrie said, "could he put it in Kenspeckle, use it to take over his mind?"

"I think that's his plan," Skulduggery said. "The Remnant will have all the Professor's memories and skills, but it wouldn't *be* him— not really. It certainly wouldn't have his conscience."

"Where's this room then?" Fletcher asked. "I can probably get you there faster."

"Not this time, Fletcher. You can only teleport to places you've already been, and this room in particular has a tendency to move around a lot."

Valkyrie frowned. "What does *that* mean?"

Fletcher went off to help Ghastly, and Skulduggery and Valkyrie drove out of the city. As they drove, he told her all about the Midnight Hotel.

It was run by a sorcerer named Anton Shudder, an old friend of Skulduggery's who fought alongside him during the war with Mevolent. Dissatisfied with the various Sanctuaries around the world, which he felt had grown too powerful and bureaucratic, he had built the hotel as a refuge for those who operated outside of official boundaries. His guests were often outcasts or outlaws or sometimes even out-and-out criminals, but as long as they obeyed the primary rule of the hotel, all were welcome.

The primary rule, Skulduggery said, was simple: no violence against any guest. If a fight *did* break out, Shudder himself would fight on behalf of the victim, whoever it happened to be. And no one, apparently, wanted to go up against Shudder.

"He must be pretty good," Valkyrie said, "if everyone's afraid of him. Is he Elemental or Adept?"

"Adept," Skulduggery said. "If you're lucky, you'll never have to see what he can do."

They drove on and Valkyrie tried to pin down something that had been bugging her for the past few hours – a nagging feeling in the back of her mind that wouldn't go away. They arrived at a clearing in woodland, but she still had no idea what this stray thought might be. Skulduggery parked the car and they got out.

"You had better hold on to me," Skulduggery said.

She clung to him and they rose up off the ground, away from the road and into the air. They passed over the tops of the trees, her feet rustling the branches lightly. Skulduggery kept them on course, and every so often she thought she heard him talking to himself, words that the wind whipped from his lipless mouth before they reached her ears.

They drifted down to a clearing, landing gently.

"What are we doing?" Valkyrie asked. "Where's the hotel?"

"Any second now," he answered, checking his pocket watch. He put it away.

A moment later the ground in the clearing rumbled and a building grew.

Wooden beams sprang from the earth and concrete seeped from the grass and hardened. The walls blossomed around the foundations, and inside Valkyrie saw rooms being born and tables flowering. A second storey grew and then a third, and the walls sprouted a roof that joined in the middle. Glass dripped from the tops of windows and formed panes, and doorways grew doors. The last thing to grow was a sign that said The Midnight Hotel.

"Every twelve hours it grows in another location around the world," Skulduggery said, "and everyone inside is transported with it. He could have called it the Midday Hotel, I suppose, but Midnight sounds so much better, don't you think?"

"I do," Valkyrie said, a little stunned. She followed him inside.

There was a reception desk and maybe two dozen hooks on a board behind it for the room keys to hang from. Beside the board there was an open door that led to a backroom. There was a lamp and a ledger on the desk, and a single pen.

They walked through into the common room. A couple of old chairs, a sofa and a low table were arranged around the fireplace, for guests to come down to in the evening and relax. There was a bookshelf along one wall and a door that led somewhere, possibly the kitchen or the dining area. A woman came down the stairs, ignored them and walked out. They went back to the reception desk. A man stood there now – tall, with long black hair, dressed like a funeral director. He smiled gently.

"Hello, my friend," he said to Skulduggery. "Providing you are not here to bother my guests, it is good to see you."

"Likewise. Valkyrie Cain, this is Anton Shudder, the owner and manager of the Midnight Hotel."

Shudder bowed his head to her. "It pleases me to meet you, Valkyrie. I've heard stories."

"Good stories or bad stories?"

"All stories are good stories," he smiled, "even the bad ones. What can I do for you?"

"We're here to check on the Remnants," Skulduggery said.

Shudder took a moment to react. "I see," he said eventually. "Are you here to count them?"

"We just want to make sure they're still where they're supposed to be."

"You have reason to believe they wouldn't be?" Shudder asked, stepping out from behind the desk.

"Dreylan Scarab is out of prison," Skulduggery said as they followed him up the stairs. "He's got himself a little gang of like-minded killers and we think they want to set a Remnant free."

"And you think they have managed this without my knowing?"

"I don't underestimate my enemies."

"And yet you seem to underestimate your friends." Shudder looked back at Valkyrie. "Twenty-four rooms, the walls, doors and windows reinforced physically and magically. There are seals around the perimeter, guarding against certain types of undesirables. I make it a point of offering the best protection to my guests. There is one room, however, that is different from all the others."

They stopped outside a door on the second floor, marked 24.

"This is where I keep the Remnants," Shudder said. "They've been here for over a hundred years and they've never managed to escape. This door hasn't been opened in a century and it won't be opened for a century more. They're not going anywhere."

Skulduggery took off his hat and brushed imaginary lint

from the brim. "These are some very resourceful people we're talking about, Anton."

"In that case they will try and they will fail. I would offer you the room across the hall, to make sure nobody gets in, but I am fully booked and expecting another guest at any time."

"If it's all the same to you though, we'll stick around for a few hours."

"By all means."

Shudder led them back down and into the reception area, where they found Billy-Ray Sanguine standing at the desk.

Skulduggery's gun leaped into his hand, and Sanguine laughed and backed away, hands up.

"Don't shoot!" he cried in mock horror. "I'm unarmed!"

Skulduggery didn't say anything. The gun didn't waver.

Sanguine lost the laugh. "Hey, I'm serious now. Don't you shoot me."

"You're under arrest," Skulduggery said.

"Sanctuary agents have no jurisdiction in the Midnight Hotel," Sanguine said. "Ain't that right? I checked the rules before I came."

"That is correct," said Shudder.

"Makes no difference to me," Skulduggery said coldly. "I can throw you out of here and arrest you *then* just as easily."

"You can't lay a finger on me," Sanguine smiled. "You're Shudder, right? Mr Shudder, I believe I have a reservation at this fine establishment for one whole night. The name's William-Raymond Sanguine. Billy-Ray to my friends."

Shudder went to his desk and looked in the book, then raised his eyes to Valkyrie and Skulduggery. "He is a guest," he confirmed.

"Not yet he isn't," Skulduggery said, moving to Sanguine. Shudder stepped between them.

"Skulduggery, this man is a guest of the Midnight Hotel. As such he is under my protection. Please put away your gun."

Skulduggery didn't move for a moment then, slowly, his gun slid back into its holster.

Shudder turned to Sanguine. "Do you have any bags, Mr Sanguine?"

"Just this one," the Texan answered, nudging a small case at his feet.

"Is that where you're keeping the Soul Catcher?" Valkyrie asked.

"Valkyrie, I'm sure I don't know what you mean. All I've got in my case is a change of underwear and a good book to read." He turned to Shudder. "Now then, let's make this official. Where do I sign in?"

29

THE SIT-DOWN

The common room was empty except for Valkyrie and Skulduggery, who were sitting at the round table. Most of the hotel's guests were gone for the day, leaving the place quiet. That changed when Sanguine came downstairs, whistling a tune. He saw them, waved and came over.

"May I?" he asked, indicating one of the empty chairs. When they didn't object, he sat. Valkyrie saw her darkened reflection in his sunglasses.

"Well, now that we're sittin' here," he said with a flash of white teeth, "I can't think of anythin' interestin' to say."

"How about you tell us where you're keeping Kenspeckle Grouse and Tanith Low?" Skulduggery suggested. "And then where exactly you plan to detonate the Desolation Engine, assuming you manage to get it repaired? After that, we can go wherever the conversation takes us."

"And if I don't? Will you beat it out of me?"

"With pleasure."

"The proprietor will not stand for violence in his hotel," Sanguine reminded them happily. "I checked with him and he is a stickler about this. If you go after me, he'll go after you. Ain't that great? Ain't that just the greatest rule you ever heard?"

"I'm sure my friend will make an exception in this case," Skulduggery said.

"Maybe. Maybe not."

"Where's Tanith?" Valkyrie asked.

"She's safe," Sanguine answered. "Relatively unharmed – though I feel I must state for the record, I voted to have her killed immediately. Good thing for her our little Revengers' Club is a democracy. By the people, for the people."

"That's what you're calling yourselves?" Skulduggery asked. "The Revengers' Club?"

"It has a ring to it, don't you think? It's not as sinister as the

Diablerie, but heck, we don't want to bring back gods or destroy the world. We just want a little payback."

Valkyrie sat forward. "What do *you* want? Scarab is doing this because he thinks he was framed. Crux is doing this because he's insane. Dusk is holding a grudge against me because of his scar. Why are *you* doing this?"

Sanguine inspected his fingernails. "I got my reasons."

"Oh," Skulduggery murmured. "Of course."

Valkyrie looked at him, but his attention was focused on Sanguine.

"A few weeks ago, you burrowed in and out of the Necromancer Temple," he said, "but later, when you broke Dusk out of prison, you only burrowed *in*. You had to fight your way out. You could have snatched Professor Grouse without a fuss, but you didn't. You bundled him into a car and you *drove*. What's wrong with you, Billy-Ray?"

Sanguine grinned. "You can't expect me to reveal all my secrets before the—"

"You're hurt," Skulduggery interrupted and Sanguine's jaw clenched. "My guess is the wound Valkyrie inflicted on you at Aranmore Farm last year is causing you more trouble than you'd anticipated. You hurt yourself when you stole the Soul Catcher, didn't you? Maybe you tore something up inside. Is that what happened? You tried breaking Dusk out quietly, but you just couldn't face using your power for the return journey. That's why you're looking for revenge – because Valkyrie stole your magic from you."

Sanguine lunged at Valkyrie, but Skulduggery caught his wrist and kicked the chair from under him. Sanguine went sprawling and Shudder walked into the room.

"Is everything all right here?" he asked in his quiet voice.

"Billy-Ray fell off his chair," Skulduggery said. "Billy-Ray, are you OK down there?"

Sanguine stood, his face tight. He brought his chair back to the table. "I'm good," he said. "Just clumsy, is all."

Shudder looked at them all for a moment then came forward and sat. "You may continue your conversation," he said.

Sanguine turned sideways in his chair, resting one elbow on the table. "Is there a rule against threats?" he asked.

"No," said Shudder.

"There a rule against the promise of a violent death?"

"There is not."

"Well, OK then." Sanguine's eyeless gaze fell upon Valkyrie. "I'm goin' to kill you. You cut me right across the belly with that damned sword, an' I couldn't go to no big-shot professor to get stitched up. I had to go to some back-alley moron who talked the talk, but when it came to walkin' the walk, he barely got faster than a shuffle. I'm fairly certain he made things worse. He said give it a few weeks to heal and I gave it a month, but when I went burrowin', it was like my guts were on fire and the smoke was collectin' in my lungs. Now, I can't go back and demand he fix me up on account of the fact that he's already dead, an' so the only person I have left to blame is the little brat who cut me in the first place."

"It was self-defence," Valkyrie said.

"That ain't no excuse. Fact is that makes it worse. If you'd just let me kill you when I wanted to kill you, we wouldn't be in this situation. This whole thing is your fault."

"Your logic is impeccable," Skulduggery said. "Then what about Springheeled Jack? What is his motivation for revenge?"

Sanguine gave a shrug. "Jack is doin' what Jack does – causin' mischief. He just wants to cause *more* of it, on a wider scale, and he wants to get rid of anyone who'd try an' stop him."

"But why the Engine? Why go to the trouble of working to repair a bomb of that magnitude if all you want is revenge on a few select individuals?"

"Now that," Sanguine said, his smile returning, "is the *secret* part of our secret plan."

"Why are you here, Mr Sanguine?" interrupted Shudder.

"I make it a point not to pry into my guest's private lives, but Skulduggery has indicated that you're here for a Remnant. If that's true, we may have a problem."

"Well," Sanguine said, "it *is* true, so what kind of a problem do we have?"

Shudder sighed. "I have twenty-three rooms in this hotel that people are free to use. The twenty-fourth room, however, is off-limits to everybody."

"I had heard this, yeah."

"Even if you were able to use your powers," Shudder continued, "you wouldn't be able to enter. The twenty-fourth room is more secure than any prison cell. It's why I was asked to keep the Remnants here in the first place."

"I'm sure that is true," Sanguine nodded.

"There is no window and only one door into the twenty-fourth room and there is only one key for that door."

"I get it, yeah."

"And I keep it on me at all times."

"I guessed you would."

"And yet you still plan to take a Remnant with you when you leave."

"I have to be honest here – yeah, I do. It's a nice subtle little plan. You'll like it. Without goin' into specifics, when the time comes, I'm fully expectin' to either be given the key or to take it from your cold, dead hand and just let myself in."

"I see," Shudder murmured. "You should know that's very unlikely."

"It's unlikely *now*. When the time comes, it'll be pretty likely, believe me." He glanced at his watch. "An' the time's approachin'..."

Valkyrie detected movement outside the window. She went to it and looked out. "There are people out there," she said.

Skulduggery and Shudder joined her. People were approaching from all directions – dozens of them. Valkyrie saw dried blood on their clothes. They got closer and she realised how pale they were, how dishevelled. Some of them stumbled as they walked. Their faces were expressionless.

"Zombies," Skulduggery said. "Zombies at the door. This is your version of subtle, is it?"

Sanguine stood up from the table and grinned.

"The dead can't pass through," Shudder said. "They can stay out there until they rot and this hotel will move on at midnight. I fail to see how any of this would make me open the door to the Remnants."

"Well," said Sanguine, "that's because you don't have all the facts. You got your security mojo workin', keepin' out undesirables like the walkin' dead, and all that's great. But see, the problem with security symbols is that there's always a way round them. And that whole magical alphabet thing has always been a bit of a hobby for my daddy. He's no expert, but he knows *which* symbol cancels out *what* symbol, y'know? All those zombies out there? They're all got this symbol carved into their smelly, rottin' skin." He handed a crumpled piece of paper to Shudder. "What d'you think? Think it'll do the job?"

Shudder examined the paper and his eyes narrowed. He didn't respond.

"You know it's enough for those pesky critters to come stormin' in here, don't you?" Sanguine continued. "So here's my offer, Anton. You open that door for me, you let me get what I came here to get and I'll call off the zombie horde."

Shudder looked at him then out of the window. He shook his head. "No."

Sanguine sighed. "That's the wrong move, buddy. It'll be a bloodbath once they get started."

"We can hold them off," Shudder said. "What do you think, Skulduggery?"

"Should be fun," Skulduggery responded. "Valkyrie here has never held off a horde of zombies before. It'll be good experience for her."

"Oh, joy," she muttered.

"You people," Sanguine said. "Always so eager to die heroic deaths. I don't want any blood on this suit, so if you don't mind, I'll be headin' outside now. Wouldn't want to be caught in here when the carnage starts."

He turned to go and Shudder punched him. Sanguine spun and fell back, nearly tumbling over a chair.

"What about your no violence rule?" he said, rubbing his jaw.

"No violence towards guests," Shudder clarified. "You are no longer considered a guest."

Skulduggery walked towards him and Sanguine straightened up.

"You can punch me all you like," he began and Skulduggery said, "Oh, good," and hit him. Sanguine tripped over the coffee table and fell backwards to the ground.

"It won't do no good!" he barked. "Them zombies are comin' in an' there's nothin' you can do to stop it!"

"Call them off," Skulduggery said.

Sanguine spat blood and grinned up at him. "Shan't."

"Call them off or I'll hurt you."

"How much hurt can you deliver in thirty seconds? Because that's how long you have. They're goin' to come in here and you're goin' to fight 'em off, and can you guess which one of you's goin' to fall first? My money's on the girl. They're goin' to tear her apart. They're goin' to eat her alive and I'm goin' to watch and it'll be a show I ain't never goin' to forget."

A tune filled the air – a terrible, shrill version of Patsy Cline's 'Crazy'.

"That'll be them now," Sanguine said, taking out his phone. He moved slowly, like he expected Skulduggery to start kicking him. Instead, Skulduggery gestured and the phone flew from Sanguine's hand towards Valkyrie. She caught it, pressed the answer button and held it to her ear.

"Uh, hi," said a man. She knew the voice from somewhere. "Uh, we may have a slight problem." It was Vaurien Scapegrace. Of course. It stood to reason *he'd* be involved in this. "The others kind of, they ate someone. And I know you said not to, but they did it without me knowing so... Basically, they're acting kind of weird and I'm wondering what I should do."

Valkyrie covered the mouthpiece and looked at Skulduggery. "It's Scapegrace," she said. "He's outside with the zombies and he says they're acting strangely. He says they ate someone."

Sanguine sat up, all colour gone from his face. "They *what?*"

Skulduggery tilted his head. "Eating people is what zombies tend to do."

"Not these guys," Sanguine said. "Let me talk to him."

"Not a chance," Valkyrie said.

Sanguine got to his knees. "You have to let me talk to him. I swear to God, you have to. If I tell 'em to attack, you can shoot me, OK? But I *need* to talk to him."

There was panic in his voice, a real fear, and Skulduggery hesitated then gave a nod. Valkyrie tossed Sanguine his phone.

"What do you mean they ate someone?" he said into it. "Who'd they eat? No, I don't want to know his damn name. I just want to know if it was someone livin'. Oh, you idiot. Oh, you moron. My father told you. He said one thing above all else – do *not* let them taste human flesh and what did you do? What did you do? Exactly. You're a moron. You're lucky you're already dead."

Sanguine hung up, put his phone away and looked at them.

"Slight change of plans," he said. "I ain't goin' outside."

"And why is that?" Skulduggery asked.

Sanguine got to his feet, both hands held open in front of him. "You keep those zombies from eatin' people an' they're fine. They rot, an' they smell, an' they get dumber an' dumber as they go on, but they do what they're told. But you let 'em get one mouthful of human flesh, from a *livin'* human, and they go native. The only thing on their minds right now is killin' an' eatin' a whole lot of people. Now obviously, that was the threat

I was plannin' on usin' against you, but I kind of figured I'd be well out of the way before any of this flesh-eatin' actually took place."

"So you're stuck in here," Shudder said, "with us."

Sanguine tried a smile. "Ain't it ironic?"

30

MID-AFTRNOON
OF THE DEAD

"They're coming closer," Valkyrie said, backing away
from the window.

Skulduggery took his gun from its holster and
looked at Shudder. "How many guests do you have here right
now?"

"Five," he said, "all upstairs in their rooms."

"You should go tell them to prepare. Any of them who want
to help us, they're welcome. Anyone else should barricade their
door."

Shudder nodded and disappeared up the stairs.

There were hands on the window, pressing and knocking against the glass. Valkyrie saw a face, wide-eyed and uncomprehending. The zombie saw her and snarled. Skulduggery swept his hand slowly and the bookcase slid in front of the window.

They turned the table on its side and laid it against the door in the reception area, then jammed the couch against it to hold it in place. The hotel didn't have a back door, and there wasn't much they could do to barricade every window on the ground floor except pull the curtains shut. At least now the zombies couldn't see their movements. Shudder came down the stairs with a small, thin woman and a balding man.

"We have two volunteers," he said. "Mr Jib is an Elemental and Miss Nuncio is an Adept."

"Glad to have another Elemental in the mix," Skulduggery said to them. "Miss Nuncio, what Adept discipline have you studied?"

"Linguistics and etymology," she said.

Skulduggery paused. "Languages?"

Miss Nuncio nodded. "I can speak every mortal language ever spoken."

"Well, pardon me," Sanguine said, "but how in tarnation is

that goin' to help us fight off a pack of bloodthirsty zombies? You goin' to throw dictionaries at 'em or just talk 'em to death?"

"Mr Shudder said you could use all the help you could get," Miss Nuncio said rather primly. "Just because I decided *not* to devote my life to the study of hurting people does *not* mean I can't be useful."

"You're a pacifist," Sanguine groaned.

"I'm a realist, sir. And if a pack of bloodthirsty zombies, as you put it, want to eat me, I *will* defend myself, you can be certain of that."

"Goin' to get stuck in a zombie's throat – that your big plan?"

"Sanguine," said Valkyrie, "shut up. You're the only one down here who *can't* use any magic, so you really can't afford to dismiss those who can."

He looked at her. "I hate you."

A window broke. Then another. They moved into the common room. There were two windows in here. One was blocked by the bookcase, the other by nothing more than a curtain. A zombie was trying to crawl through the second one. They watched the curtain writhe like it was alive, and then it parted. The zombie was halfway through and it looked up. It growled and reached for them, so Skulduggery shot it.

"Go for the head if you can," he said. "Burning them works,

but it takes a lot longer. Break their legs to slow them down. Don't let them bite you."

"I've never fought zombies before," Mr Jib said. "I've fought every other kind of creature, but not zombies. Always wanted to, though."

"Here at the Midnight Hotel," Shudder said quietly, "we aim to please."

Two more zombies were struggling through the window and Skulduggery shot them both. The bookcase was shaking now. Another window broke, somewhere at the back of the hotel.

"I'll take care of it," Shudder said grimly, and moved out of the common room. The hotel door was being given a pounding.

Sanguine picked up a table and smashed it against a wall. He pulled one of the legs from the resulting mess and threw it to Miss Nuncio, who hefted it in both hands. The second leg he threw to Mr Jib, and the third he kept for himself.

Glaring at Sanguine, Valkyrie clicked her fingers and summoned a flame. Sanguine muttered something and gave her the fourth leg.

"Come on," Mr Jib called to the zombies outside. "I don't have all night."

"Don't taunt the zombies," Skulduggery said disapprovingly.

Mr Jib laughed and moved up to the window. "These guys

are harmless," he said. "The stench'll kill us faster than they will."

A hand reached in, closed around Mr Jib's wrist, and he was jerked forward.

"Hey, no, wait," he said and then he was yanked out through the window before Skulduggery or Valkyrie could reach him. He didn't even have time to scream.

"Oh my God," Miss Nuncio said.

"Do you get many of your linguistics sorcerers eaten alive then?" Sanguine asked lazily.

The hotel door burst open, shoving the sofa and the table back, and the zombies came spilling through.

Skulduggery's gun roared, again and again. Zombies stumbled and fell, and Skulduggery reloaded while Valkyrie hurled fireballs. A flaming zombie came stumbling and Valkyrie cracked the table leg against its head. It hit the ground and tried to get up, but the other zombies trampled over it.

The bookcase toppled and Miss Nuncio was at the window, battering the zombies who were trying to crawl through. One got past Skulduggery and Valkyrie then charged at Sanguine. Sanguine cursed and lost the table leg, and the zombie pushed him back against the wall. Sanguine swung punches to no effect, then his hand closed around its throat.

He pushed with all his strength, keeping those biting jaws away from him. He twisted and the zombie was forced up against the wall. The wall crumbled and its head sank through. Sanguine stepped away, leaving the puzzled zombie stuck there.

Skulduggery was out of bullets. He dropped the revolver and curled his hands. The air closed around the nearest zombie and it froze, gurgling slightly, before Skulduggery swept his arms wide and its head flew from its body.

Valkyrie punched a hole through a zombie's chest with her shadows. It staggered forward and she ducked under it, bringing the shadows back and turning them sharp. They sliced through the zombie's ankle and it toppled over. She hefted the table leg in both hands and used it like a baseball bat on the next one to get near. It stumbled over its fallen friend and knocked a third one down. They weren't too bright, these zombies.

A big zombie rushed her and wrapped its arms around her. Its mouth was on her shoulder, trying to bite through. The table leg fell from Valkyrie's hand as she was taken off her feet and carried backwards. She hit the wall beside the door to the kitchen, and the big zombie tried to take a bite out of her face. She raised her arms sharply, loosening its hold on her, and dropped to the ground. It moaned something, pitiful and disappointed, and she pushed at the air and launched it away from her.

She got up and Sanguine came crashing into her. They both went sprawling into the kitchen, the zombie who had thrown him following them in.

Valkyrie was the first up. She grabbed a massive meat cleaver from the worktop and hurled it. The back of the cleaver smacked into the zombie's head and bounced off. She hurled another knife and this time it was the handle that hit. Sanguine stood, fixed his sunglasses, looked around for his straight razor and saw the zombie reaching for him. He yelped and ducked, but it grabbed his jacket.

Valkyrie ran up behind it, whacking a frying pan into the back of its knee. It went down and Sanguine pushed the hand that had grabbed him into the wall. The wall solidified and the zombie moaned, trapped there.

Valkyrie and Sanguine stepped away, well out of its reach, and looked at each other, and for a moment it was merely in appreciation of a job well done. And then it turned to something else.

Sanguine swung a punch and Valkyrie ducked under it and thrust her shoulder into his gut. He grunted and fell back, but grabbed her as he went, throwing her to the floor. She rolled and hit the wall as he stooped for the straight razor, but a flick of her hand sent it spinning away from him. He growled and kicked her as she lay there. She folded her body around the kick and lashed out with one of her own, catching him in the side of the knee. He yelled as he went down. She got up and jumped over him, but he snagged her ankle and she fell.

Valkyrie rolled and came up and Sanguine sprang at her. She tried flipping him over her hip, but he was too big and too heavy. She turned into him and his hands gripped her throat. Her elbow shot up between his arms and found his chin. His head rocketed back and his mouth hung open and his grip loosened. She punched a fistful of shadows into his chest and Sanguine was flung backwards. He hit the wall and dropped to the floor. The trapped zombie reached out for him, but it was just too far away. It moaned again.

Valkyrie heard Miss Nuncio scream and she ran out of the kitchen.

31

BILLY-RAY

anguine lay there for a bit, waiting for his brain to kick back into gear.

Moving slowly, he picked himself up. He figured two, maybe three ribs were broken, thanks to the girl and that damned ring of hers. He tried not to dwell on the fact that he'd had his hands around her throat, but had failed to kill her. He was already angry enough as it was.

He found his razor beneath the stove. His ribs bit into his side when he bent to retrieve it, but when it was in his hand again, he felt better.

He left the kitchen, stepping over the bodies of zombies. He made sure the girl and the skeleton were otherwise occupied, then hurried to the back of the hotel. A zombie reared up before him, but he shoved it back against the wall. The wall crumbled and he pushed the zombie halfway through and the wall grew solid around it. This was what his magic was reduced to — the magical equivalent of opening a door, but being unable to pass through it. He snarled and continued on. Speaking of doors...

Anton Shudder had been busy holding off the zombies at the back of the hotel. He was on his knees on the floor, head down, exhausted, and all around him were pieces of the dead.

"Did we do it?" Shudder asked weakly.

Sanguine approached without speaking and kicked Shudder in the face. The kick lifted Shudder off his knees and threw him backwards. Sanguine howled and clutched his ribs. Every move he made sent bullets of hot pain ricocheting around his body. Gritting his teeth, Sanguine staggered over, dropped to his knees and searched for the key.

32

THINGS GET WORSE

Skulduggery took a long splinter of wood from the ruined table and impaled the last zombie's head with it. He looked across the room at Valkyrie. Between them was a sea of body parts. Some of it moaned and some of it writhed, but most of it lay still and didn't make much of a fuss.

Miss Nuncio was dead. She had been holding four of them back and had slipped in the gore. The zombies had descended on her, biting off chunks as she struggled and screamed, cursing them in twenty different languages before falling silent. The only good thing about her death was that there wasn't enough left of her to come back to life.

Valkyrie was covered in blood. Her arms were so tired she couldn't lift them, and her legs were so tired it was all she could do to stand without falling over.

"I'm going to check on Anton," Skulduggery said and left the room.

Every chair or sofa or seat in the place was in pieces. There was nowhere to sit down. Dragging her heavy feet, Valkyrie crossed the common room, heading for the chair behind the reception desk. All she wanted in this world was a shower and a lie-down. That, she reasoned, wasn't too much to ask.

She got to the reception area and two more zombies barged in. Valkyrie dropped back and clicked her fingers, summoning a flame into her hand. She was about to call for help, but stopped when she saw who it was.

Vaurien Scapegrace glared at her, and the middle-aged zombie beside him did his best to look annoyed.

"My arch-enemy," Scapegrace snarled.

Valkyrie frowned. "Me?"

"You may have killed my savage brethren," he continued, "but you're facing the Killer Supreme now, and I'm new and improved."

"Scapegrace, I'm *really* tired."

"I don't feel pain," Scapegrace said, ignoring her, "I don't feel pity and I don't feel..." He hesitated. "Bad. I *won't* feel bad, I mean, about killing you, which is what's going to happen very, very soon indeed."

"Do you want to, like, go away and rehearse that a little more?"

"How dare you speak to the Killer Supreme in such a manner!" the middle-aged zombie screeched in a sudden and dramatic fury.

"Listen to me," she said to them, "you don't want to be involved in this. Scapegrace, look at what they've done to you, for God's sake. They've turned you into a monster."

"I've always been a monster," Scapegrace told her, "but now, finally, my physical form reflects my inner darkness."

"You smell terrible."

"That's the smell of evil."

"It's like rancid meat and bad eggs."

"Evil," Scapegrace insisted.

"Where are they holding Tanith and the Professor?" she asked. "You have a chance to help us end this. Maybe we can help you – maybe there's a cure for... being a zombie."

"We don't need a cure," the other zombie said.

"That's right," Scapegrace nodded.

"We're happy the way we are."

"Happy with the power," Scapegrace clarified.

"Very happy, just the two of us, and there's nothing wrong with us either. It's very natural in fact. Nothing to be ashamed of—"

"Thrasher," said Scapegrace, "shut up."

"Okey-dokey."

"We are not going to betray our Master," Scapegrace said. "I joined the Vengeance Brigade for one reason and one—"

"I'm sorry?"

"You're sorry what?"

"The Vengeance Brigade? That's what you're calling it?"

"What's wrong with that?"

"It's... Nothing. It's grand. Sanguine called it the Revengers' Club, that's all."

"Club sounds stupid," Scapegrace said defensively. "Brigade sounds better."

"Actually," said Thrasher, "a brigade usually consists of two to five army regiments, so maybe it isn't really *that* accurate."

Scapegrace glowered. "But the Vengeance *Regiment* doesn't have the same ring to it."

"Well, that wouldn't be accurate either," Thrasher told him, "seeing as how a regiment is composed of a number of battalions. It *could* be the Vengeance *Battalion*, I suppose, but really a battalion usually has around a thousand soldiers in it, and there aren't a thousand people in your group."

"How about the Vengeance Squad?" suggested Valkyrie.

"That might work," Thrasher nodded.

"I prefer *Brigade*," Scapegrace snapped. "And now I've lost my train of thought."

"You were about to tell me where Tanith and the Professor are being held," said Valkyrie.

"No," Scapegrace said, "I'm pretty sure I was about to start killing you."

"Don't even try it."

"I've dreamed about nothing else for the last two years."

"You need better things to dream about."

"Valkyrie Cain, welcome to death."

"That is such a stupid thing to say."

Scapegrace ran at her and Valkyrie threw the ball of fire she'd been holding for the past few minutes. Scapegrace was instantly enveloped in flame. He wheeled around, screaming.

"Master Scapegrace!" Thrasher yelled, horrified.

Valkyrie frowned. "I thought he couldn't feel pain."

Scapegrace immediately stopped screaming and running about. He just stood there and continued to burn.

"You're burning quite easily," she said. "Is that a zombie thing or something?"

"He has been using an awful lot of skin creams lately," Thrasher mused. "Maybe the mixture is especially flammable."

Valkyrie waved her hand and the fire went out.

"You haven't seen the last of me," Scapegrace said without enthusiasm, as he turned and walked out of the hotel, leaving a trail of smoke behind him. Thrasher gave her a parting growl and quickly followed the trail out of the door.

The aroma of charred flesh forced Valkyrie to go looking for Skulduggery. She found him in the back room, helping Shudder to his feet. The walls were decorated with bits of zombie.

"Shudder did this?" she said, stunned at the sheer violence of what she saw. "Alone? Without a weapon?"

"Technically," Skulduggery said, "Anton *is* a weapon. Or at least his gist is."

"What's a gist?"

"It's the bad part of me," Shudder said, speaking like every word was painful. "When I need it, I let it come out. Every time I do, however, it takes me a little longer to recover." He frowned. "Sanguine was here. He came in and..." He grasped his sleeve and yanked it up. There was a metal band on his forearm, and hanging from it was a short link of a cut chain. "He has the key."

Valkyrie followed Skulduggery up the two flights of stairs. They got to the twenty-fourth room. The door was closed and the key was in the lock.

"He has it," Skulduggery said.

"How do you know? He might still be in there."

Skulduggery shook his head. "He didn't set one foot inside that room. He opened the door less than a centimetre and the nearest Remnant was sucked into the Soul Catcher. If he'd stepped in, they'd have swarmed him and then they'd have swarmed the hotel. After that, they'd have gone on and swarmed the country. We failed."

"So now what?"

"Now we find Scarab's castle before Kenspeckle repairs the Desolation Engine. I know someone who might be able to help us — it's a long shot, but what isn't these days? We've run out of options." Skulduggery turned the key until they heard the lock clicking into place, then he withdrew it. "And we kick the living daylights out of anyone who stands in our way."

33

POSSESSED

Scarab released the Remnant, then quickly stepped back and shut the door. He went to the next room, where Billy-Ray had set up the monitor, and watched Professor Grouse. He could see the anger in his face as the Remnant, little more than a sliver of shadow, flitted about from corner to corner. The Professor knew what was coming, but he didn't cry out or start to plead. Scarab respected that.

Once it had satisfied its curiosity about its surroundings, the Remnant turned its attention to the old man chained to the wall. The Professor kept his eyes on the Remnant as it darted in and out of his line of sight. It came close and the Professor jerked away instinctively. It was playing with him.

It whipped by him again and the Professor cursed at it. Then it struck. It darted to his open mouth and the Professor's eyes widened in panic as the Remnant forced its way down. His throat bulged, then the bulge moved and disappeared. Kenspeckle Grouse went limp.

Billy-Ray shook his head. "Hate those things," he muttered.

Scarab walked back into the room and Professor Grouse looked up.

"You know why you're here," Scarab said. "We went to a whole lot of trouble to get you out of that room you were stuck in. If you do what we want, we'll release you after. If you don't, we'll put you back where we found you and collect one of your brethren. I'm sure the next one we bring here will welcome a chance for freedom. What do you say?"

"I don't trust you," Grouse said in a voice that picked over the words like a carrion bird picking at meat. The Remnant inside him was unused to speaking aloud.

"Well," said Scarab, "I don't trust you either. But we are in a situation where we can help each other. As you know by now, we're hoping that the old man you're wearing like a bad suit has the all the knowledge and know-how we need. Does he?"

"Oh, he does," Grouse said. "Oh, I do. And I have so much more."

"Then do we have a deal?"

The old man looked at him and a smile drifted across his face like a seeping wound. "We have a deal, Mr Scarab."

34

THE MEETING

Davina Marr went up to the counter and told the dim-looking boy what kind of sandwich she wanted, then repeated her order slowly, using smaller words. He finally nodded and went away, and she just knew he was going to get it wrong. That's what she despised about mortals – their ineptitude. Their casual ignorance. Their downright stupidity.

She couldn't say any of this out loud, however, not as an agent of the Sanctuary, and certainly not as its Prime Detective. It was part of her job to protect the mortals, to keep them safe from the dangers posed by the magical community. But was she *still* the Sanctuary's Prime Detective now that Skulduggery Pleasant was back? Instead of doing her job, tracking down the vampire that had led the raid on the Sanctuary, Marr had been relegated to checking out *castles* as per the skeleton detective's request. Such a task was so far beneath her it would have been almost laughable if it wasn't so humiliating.

She became aware of the man standing beside her, but she didn't look at him. "You're late."

"I had to make sure you weren't leading me into a trap," the man responded, his golden eyes scanning the menu above them. "Forgive me if I'm sceptical, but you have already turned us down twice. Why the change of heart?"

"I'm seeing things clearer."

The dim-looking boy came back, checked her order and went away again.

"Guild isn't fit to run the Sanctuary," she said. "He's making stupid mistakes. Shirking his responsibility."

"We heard he demoted you."

The heat rose in her face, but Marr kept her voice even. "Temporary reassignment," she said. "Just one of his recent errors of judgement."

"So you'll help us then?"

"Yes."

"We had Mr Bliss in line to take over," the man told her. "His death has meant a drastic change in our plans. I hope you realise that."

"How drastic?" she asked.

"We're going to destroy the Sanctuary," he said, "and take over what's left."

The dim-looking boy returned with her sandwich. It was completely wrong, but she wasn't hungry anyway. She paid for it and collected her change, catching the man's eye as she turned.

"Suits me," she said and walked out.

35

MYRON STRAY

The house had a face.

The two large windows on the first floor peered down at the Bentley as it drew to a halt. The paint was like dried skin, cracked and peeling back, and the front door was open like a great gaping mouth. It would have been creepy, Valkyrie reflected, were it not for the drawn blinds that gave the face a half-asleep expression. As it was, it looked as if it was caught in the middle of a giant yawn.

"Once upon a time," Skulduggery said, "Myron Stray was an information broker, much like China is today. He was respected too. Until it all fell apart for him."

"What happened?" Valkyrie asked.

"Mr Bliss found out Myron's true name. Myron and Bliss never got on – always at each other's throats. One night, in a pub in Belfast where they were supposed to be planning how to take down Mevolent, they got into an argument. I wasn't there, but the way I heard it, Myron was taunting him, goading him, and Bliss just sat back in his chair and then very calmly, very quietly, said, '*Laudigan, leave.*' Myron went white as a sheet, apparently, and walked out. Mr Bliss just smiled."

"Laudigan is his true name?"

"Indeed it is. Something like that spreads like nothing you've ever seen. And just like that, Myron's life, the life he had built up for himself, was over. He dealt in information and now anyone could use that name to control him, make him give up his secrets or lie to their enemies. His friends left. The woman he was living with walked out the very next day. His life fell apart."

"That's terrible."

"I suppose it is. But taunting Mr Bliss – that was Myron's mistake."

"But *you* stayed friends with him, right? With Myron? When everyone else abandoned him?"

"To be honest, we were never really friends. And even if we

had been, I wasn't around in those days. I was sick of the whole thing. I was sick of the war and I just wanted it to be over. By the time I came back, and I heard what had happened, there wasn't a whole lot I could do to help him out, even if I had wanted to."

"But you're hoping that he still hears things, aren't you?"

"China is still recovering – she could have missed something important. We don't have the luxury of waiting for her to get better, so yes, we're forced to scrape the bottom of the barrel. And if there's one place where Myron is at home these days, it's the bottom of the barrel."

They got out of the car and Valkyrie followed Skulduggery through the broken gate and up the cracked path to the house. They peered in through the open door. The damp walls were covered with faded green wallpaper, bleached in places by the sun. The floor was bare, but the stairs were carpeted. Whoever had owned this house in the 1970s had obviously tried to match the stairs with the wallpaper, but the best they could manage was an ugly carpet the colour of bile. Skulduggery rapped his knuckles on the doorframe and Valkyrie heard movement from deep within the house.

A moment later, Myron Stray appeared. He wasn't too tall, wasn't too slim, and wasn't too good-looking. In fact, he wasn't too anything. He was pretty average in a pale, unshaven kind of way.

"Skulduggery," he said. "You haven't darkened my door in an age."

"I've been away."

"I heard. This must be Valkyrie Cain then."

Valkyrie smiled and held out her hand. Myron turned away.

"Come on in," he said.

Valkyrie took an instant dislike to the man. They followed him into the kitchen. The table was a mass of pizza boxes and wine bottles, and dishes were piled up in the sink. Substances that may once have been food had long since dried and hardened to the plates, and each and every cup Valkyrie saw had fuzzy mould creeping over the brim. The air was stale, and flies tapped and buzzed against the grimy windows.

"I like what you've done to the place," Skulduggery said eventually.

Myron took a can of beer from the fridge and cracked it open. "I always wanted someone to come up with a Mary Poppins trick, didn't you? You know, just click your fingers and dishes wash themselves and the floor mops itself and all that stuff? It'd save me a bundle on housekeeping."

Valkyrie frowned. "You have a housekeeper?"

"I was making a joke. This one's not too smart is she, Skulduggery?"

All pretence at being civil left Valkyrie's face, to be replaced by open and obvious hostility.

"Not like your last partner," Myron continued, sitting at the table, "the one who died. How did he die again? I can't quite remember."

"Horribly," Skulduggery said.

"He died screaming your name, didn't he? Now here's where things get a little fuzzy. When he was screaming your name, was he calling for help, or was he cursing you?"

"A little bit of both I would imagine. Myron, I don't appreciate you insulting my partner. I would have leaped to her defence, but Valkyrie is more than capable of fighting her own battles. Valkyrie? You can respond however you wish."

"Thank you," Valkyrie said, smiling thinly. "In that case, we came here to ask you a few questions, Myron, and that's what we're going to do. You don't mind if I call you Myron, do you?" He opened his mouth to utter a lazy reply, but she cut him off. "Thank you. I didn't think you would. We need to know anything you've heard concerning Dreylan Scarab and any possible base of operations."

Myron looked at her for a long time. "I'm afraid I can't help you."

"And I'm afraid I'm going to have to insist. I could continue calling you Myron, you see, or I could switch to your other name. What was it again? The name that makes you do anything you're told?"

Myron's eyes turned hard and he looked at Skulduggery. "You promised me you would never use my true name against me."

"Yes, I did," Skulduggery said, crossing his arms and leaning back against the wall. "And I won't. Unfortunately, you were rude to my partner and friend, and she made you no such promise."

Valkyrie pulled a chair from beneath the table, wiped the seat and sat. "I read somewhere," she said, "that you can protect your true name. Isn't that right? There's a way to seal it so it can't be used against you? Why didn't you do that?"

Myron licked his lips. "It was too late," he said stiffly. "That only works if you seal the name before it's used."

"I see," she nodded. "But you didn't even know what it was, did you? And Mr Bliss did. And you annoyed him. I can't possibly imagine *how*, seeing as you're just *so* nice and polite, and such fun to be around."

Myron put his beer can on the cluttered tabletop and glared. "You want to know if I've heard anything? I heard about *you*. Both of you. Sensitives are talking and they're saying that some freak called Darquesse is going to kill you. I for one can't wait. Skulduggery, we've never really liked each other, and girl, I have certainly not taken a shine to you, either. If you ask me, the sooner this freak gets to you, the better."

"We heard about those visions," Skulduggery said calmly. "But I wouldn't sound too pleased about it, if I were you. Darquesse kills *us*, yes, but she kills everyone *else* while she's at it. You may have missed that bit."

Myron rubbed the bristles on his jaw and didn't respond.

"We want to know where Scarab is hiding," said Valkyrie.

"I don't *know* where. *No one* knows where. That bunch of psychos he has with him don't let things slip to friends, because they don't *have* any friends. Nobody knows where they are."

"We know that they're in a castle somewhere," Valkyrie said.

"Well, why didn't you say that at the start?" Myron snapped. "I didn't pay this any attention when I heard it, but there's been a lot of activity around Serpine's old place recently."

"Serpine's castle has been sealed off," Skulduggery said.

"Well, they must have found a way to unseal it then."

Skulduggery stood and put on his hat. He took a roll of cash from his coat pocket and left it on top of an upturned fried chicken bucket on the table. "Thanks for your help," he said.

"My pleasure," grunted Myron.

Skulduggery tipped his hat and walked out. Valkyrie got up to follow him.

"Interesting people you hang around with," Myron said, and she looked back at him. "Couple of bad habits you're picking up too. Got a pretty smart mouth on you, don't you?"

"I suppose I do."

"Word of warning though. There might not be many people out there who trust me, but there are even fewer who trust your friend. Just something to think about."

He took a swig from his beer can and Valkyrie walked out to the car.

36

PLAYTIME

Scarab and Billy-Ray walked over to inspect the bomb on the table.

"That was quick," Scarab murmured. "We had all the materials ready for you, but still, how did you do it so fast?"

"This one has secrets," Professor Grouse said. The chains that kept him on his side of the room weren't bound, but they were enough to slow him down. "Who cares? I did the job, didn't I? Didn't I do the job? Now the job is done. Now you release me, yes?"

"You added the specifications I asked for?"

"Yes, yes, yes," the Professor replied. "It was no problem, not for someone like me. This mind is a wonderful thing. I'd be sorry to leave it, if the body wasn't so decrepit."

Scarab didn't know a whole lot about Desolation Engines, but everything seemed to be where it should be.

"We're not releasing you," he said. "You're too mischievous. You might tell our enemies where we are."

Grouse's smile dropped, very slowly, from his face. "Your enemies are my enemies. My enemies are everywhere. Everyone is my enemy. You release me now!"

"Not goin' to happen," said Billy-Ray. "But we sure do appreciate the work you've put into this. Assumin' our plan goes well, we'll release you after."

"You said now!"

"Calm down, Professor. We understand how upset you must be, so we have a gift we'd like to give to you."

Grouse cocked his head curiously. "A gift?"

"A lovely gift," Billy-Ray said, smiling. "One for you to play with to your little heart's content."

The door opened and, with a clang of shackles, Tanith Low was led in.

"Our gift," said Scarab, "to you."

Grouse clapped his hands and laughed.

37

CHINA'S DARK SECRET

ver the bed there was a sigil painted on to the ceiling and it glowed gently, its power drifting down into China's body. She lay with her eyes closed, hands folded on her stomach, her mind attuned to the sigil, manipulating its properties. The ebb and flow of magic raged like a storm-tossed sea, and yet none of that was evident from outward appearances. Instead of a storm-tossed sea there seemed to be a still lake, not even a ripple on the water's surface, exactly the way China preferred it to be.

The sigil stopped glowing and her eyes opened. She sat up

smoothly, without hurry. As she dressed, she observed herself in the mirror. She looked pale and weak. Her body was still tired, her magic still exhausted. She wasn't strong enough to do what she needed to do, but it had to be done.

China left the bedroom, took the gun from her desk drawer and put it in her purse. She couldn't risk taking one of her own cars, so she called a taxi and endured forty-five minutes of the taxi driver telling her how much he loved her before they arrived at their destination. The driver wept as he drove away.

China stepped off the cracked pavement and followed a thin trail between a tall rotten fence and a high crumbling wall. The trail was overgrown with weeds and grasses, and it led to a small house, tucked away from prying eyes and passing cars. She knocked on the door and a small man in a three-piece suit answered. His face was a catalogue of disappointments, of cohesion attempted but never achieved. His name was Prave, and his bulbous eyes grew so wide they practically erupted from their sockets and rolled down his cheeks.

"China Sorrows," he said in a hushed tone. She had forgotten how nasal his voice was. "I knew this day would come. I knew it. You've come to kill me, haven't you?"

"Now why would I want to do something like that?" China

asked. She didn't smile at him. He wasn't worthy of her smile. "May I come in?"

"I've done nothing wrong," he said quickly.

"That must make a nice change. Stand aside, please."

Prave did as he was told and China walked in. The house was a hundred years old and she knew it well, for upon completion it had been converted into a church for the followers of the Faceless Ones. Its existence was one of the best-kept secrets in the city, mainly because the man who ran it, Prave himself, was an ineffectual fool who posed no serious threat to anyone. The walls were decorated with the paintings and iconography of the Dark Gods, and the main room contained an altar and a well-worn carpet, where a handful of desperate disciples had kneeled and worshipped and prayed for the end of humanity.

"Where is he?" China asked, flicking through the book on the altar. It was a particularly battered edition of the Gospel of the Faceless, a moronic book written by a moron in an attempt to rationalise the behaviour of his ilk.

Prave shook his head. "I don't know who you're talking about, but even if I did, I wouldn't tell you. You are a traitor and a blasphemer and a heretic."

"I seem to be a lot of things. I'm looking for Remus Crux."

Prave adopted a look he probably thought was aloof. "I don't know who that is. A lot has changed since you started your blaspheming ways, Miss Sorrows. We are a respectable religion now, and should be treated as such. We are tired of this persecution we have been subjected to. We have our rights, you know."

"No, you don't."

"Well, we *should*. We're not hurting anyone, nor do we condone the use of violence *towards* anyone."

"So eleven months ago, when the Faceless Ones stopped by for a visit and all those people were killed..."

"That's different," Prave said. "Those people were asking for it."

"You're annoying me now, Prave, so you'd better answer. Where is Remus Crux?"

Prave remained defiant for two or three seconds then wilted. "I don't know," he said. "He's been here a few times, but not with any regularity. He likes to sit around and talk in clichés about how the Faceless Ones are going to smite humanity and turn the world to ash, that kind of thing. He doesn't understand the beauty of what they do – he's just interested in the end result. I thought talking to him would be a revelation – his mind has been touched by the Dark Gods, after all. But no. He holds no insights, no startling truths. He's just... insane."

"I need to find him."

"I can't help you. I don't know where he's living. I don't even know the people he knows. From what I can see, I'm the only one he talks to, and even then, most of what he says is gibberish."

"It must make you question your religion."

Prave glared. "Our gods will reward our faith when they return and wipe the heretics from the face of the world."

He didn't know anything of use, and even if he did, she didn't have the strength to get it out of him. China left him standing by the altar and let herself out. She started back down the trail, and noticed a man walking in off the street. His head was down and his hands were in his pockets. He walked quickly. He was ten steps away from her when he looked up.

"Hello, Remus," said China.

He didn't bolt as she had expected. He just stood there and looked at her, a deer caught in the headlights, a thief caught in the act.

"You've been a very naughty boy," she said. "You tried to kill Valkyrie Cain, and I actually *like* Valkyrie. You got yourself caught up with Scarab and his plans to change the way things are and I *like* the way things are. I don't like change – not when I'm not prepared for it."

"I know about you," Crux said, his voice tight.

"You shouldn't have got involved in this. You should have stayed hidden and as far away from me as possible."

"I know your secret," he said quickly. "And now you're scared. Scared of what he'll do to you when he finds out."

"Did you tell my secret to anyone else, Remus?"

"Everyone."

China smiled. "Now that's a lie. I don't think you told a soul."

He shook his head. "I did. I did. You don't know."

Her hand slipped into her purse. "The last eleven months have been hard on you, haven't they? You've had nowhere to go to for help. No friends. No colleagues. Just you and your scrambled little mind. All you needed was to have one lucid moment... but you didn't get it, did you?"

Crux licked his lips. "Everyone knows what you did. I told them. They're all talking about you. They're all whispering. *China Sorrows, China Sorrows, she's the one,* they're saying. *She's the one. Nefarian Serpine killed Skulduggery Pleasant, but China Sorrows led his family into the trap.*"

She stepped towards him. Crux clicked his fingers and fire flared in his hands. China pulled the trigger. The bullet ruined a perfectly good purse and then made a mess of Remus Crux's chest. He fell backwards, fire extinguished, and was already dead when China stepped over his body and walked away.

38

THE CASTLE

The last time Valkyrie had seen this castle she had been running from it. They had just rescued Skulduggery and Serpine's Hollow Men had been closing in from all sides.

"I rescue you a lot," she muttered.

"Sorry?" Skulduggery said, looking back.

"Nothing."

Every ground floor entrance had been bricked up, so they got in through a window on the first floor and worked their way down. It was quiet and cold. Skulduggery went first down the stone stairs, then Fletcher and Anton Shudder. Valkyrie and Ghastly brought up the rear.

The stairs to the basement level were cemented over.

"Spread out," said Skulduggery. "We're looking for any sign of recent activity."

They split up. Valkyrie went to the back of the castle. Here and there were items of old furniture, dust-covered, standing alone in otherwise empty rooms. She stepped into a drawing room with an ornate fireplace, turned to go, then stopped. She looked at the way the light caught the grooves that had been scraped into the floor in front of the fireplace. She knelt by them, running her fingers along the worn edges. Valkyrie was no expert, but she reckoned that these shallow grooves that curved in a uniform pattern had been here for about as long as the castle had been standing. Something heavy had been repeatedly moved across this area over the years – but had it happened recently?

Valkyrie stepped on to the fireplace's base and ran her hands along the mantle. The right corner was the only spot free of dust and her fingers drifted lightly over the stone. She felt something give and the fireplace rotated silently, swinging her around and through the wall into a cold corridor. The fireplace completed its rotation with a soft *click*. Valkyrie didn't move. The corridor was dark and made of stone, lit by torches in brackets along the walls. To her left was a thick chain, trundling up from a large gap in the floor through a big hole in the ceiling, like it was part of some huge pulley system.

And no more than two metres away, standing with its back to her, was a Hollow Man.

The torchlight flickered off its papery skin, catching the stitches and the strains where its arms were pulled down by its heavy fists.

Valkyrie tried activating the switch again, but the mechanism was locked. The Hollow Man twitched its head as if it had heard something. Valkyrie reached out to the thick chain and gripped it with both hands. It carried her off her feet and up through the gap in the ceiling. As she looked down, the Hollow Man turned, too late to catch sight of her.

She passed up through the gap and checked around quickly before letting go of the chain. She took out her phone and checked the bars. The signal was blocked. She'd pretty much expected that. She hurried down to the end of the corridor, keeping tight to the wall, doing her best to make sure that her shadow wasn't going to give her away. She reached an intersection and peeked out and saw Springheeled Jack.

Valkyrie dropped back and hunkered down. Three strides

took him abreast of her, but he passed without glancing down. Once she started thinking again she counted to ten then added another five before getting up. She peeked out, but he was gone, moving along some other corridor. She crept in the opposite direction, putting as much distance between them as possible. If she had to run from Hollow Men, she figured she could do it, but running from him? She wouldn't get three steps.

She heard a man talking. There was a laugh and it wasn't nice. The further she crept, the clearer the voice became. She still couldn't make out the words. The voice reached its clearest as she passed a door, but when she put her ear to it, she couldn't hear any better. Valkyrie frowned and stepped back, following the sound, her eyes dropping. On the ground beside the door was an opening. A ventilation shaft. She heard Kenspeckle's voice, but still couldn't hear what was being said.

Valkyrie got to her hands and knees and peered in. It was dark. Very dark. She flattened herself to the floor and crawled into the shaft. She let her eyes adjust, feeling the thick layer of dust under her hands. She moved forward on her elbows, banging her head against the roof of the shaft and gritting her teeth against the pain. She could hear the words now.

"...nice of them to give me a plaything, don't you think? So thoughtful. They don't want me getting bored, you see."

Valkyrie moved on, feeling a cobweb break against her face. With a controlled franticness she cleared it away, trying to dam her mind against the images of spiders scuttling in her hair. Ahead of her was a junction, a break in the darkness, where the ventilation shaft opened into the room where the voice was coming from. Valkyrie squirmed up, laid her face against the cold stone and peered in.

Tanith wasn't chained up or shackled to a wall, as Valkyrie had expected. Instead she was sitting in an armchair, hands flat on the armrests, legs crossed. An old man sat opposite in an identical armchair. His white hair stood out in clumps and he had dark rings under his eyes. It took her a moment to recognise Kenspeckle.

Beside both chairs was a small table. On Tanith's table were a cup and saucer, and on the table beside Kenspeckle was a teapot and a bowl of sugar cubes. The room was stone, but the armchairs were on a rug and there was a frayed tapestry hanging on the wall. There was a lamp, minus a lampshade, in the far corner of the room. The bulb was broken. It was a feeble attempt at introducing warmth and normality to the stark and bizarre, and it was even more unsettling for it.

Kenspeckle drank his tea and returned the cup to its saucer with a delicate *plink*.

Tanith's face was strained and wet with sweat. Her eyes were unfocused and her body rigid. Valkyrie searched for a shackle or a sign that Tanith's powers were being bound, but she couldn't see anything.

There was a small pool of dried blood beside the armrest closest to the ventilation shaft. Valkyrie followed the course the blood would have had to have taken, and noticed for the first time Tanith's hands. On first glance nothing was out of the ordinary, but it was as if someone had taken a cloth to them and wiped them quickly and without care, not bothering to clean away all the blood.

Valkyrie saw the way the light hit something metal on the back of Tanith's hand, and she realised with a lurch in her stomach that Tanith's hands had been nailed to the armrests.

She wanted to cry out and tears came to her eyes. She saw two more nails. They were thick and looked long and old, and had been hammered through Tanith's collarbones to keep her upright in the chair. A fifth nail entered Tanith's right leg just above the knee and drove down and through her left, pinning them together.

Kenspeckle was talking again, but Valkyrie wasn't listening to the words. She stared at her friend. She couldn't breathe. She was suddenly too hot in the ventilation shaft and it was tight, far too tight, and close. She had to get out. She had to back out the way she had come, and she had to smash down that door and rip that Remnant out of Kenspeckle's body. It was the only thing to do. It was the only thing that mattered.

Valkyrie tried moving backwards, the anger churning. It was bubbling, boiling, rising in her throat. She wasn't moving. She couldn't move backwards. Panic mixed with anger and fuelled it, and a small voice somewhere in Valkyrie's mind told her to calm down, but she wasn't listening.

She moved on, crawling, moving quickly, grunting, not caring if that thing that was not Kenspeckle Grouse could hear her or not. And then there was no more ground and Valkyrie was suddenly sliding downwards. She cursed as she went, trying to snag an intersecting crawlspace, but only succeeded in taking a rat's nest with her. The rats squealed beneath and beside her and she lashed out, trying to throw them off. Her head struck stone. Her body twisted.

Below her, brightness and heat.

She tumbled through the gap and fell about a metre. There was another gap directly below it and she reached out instinctively, spreading her arms and legs and jamming herself over the opening, stopping herself from falling through to the room below.

Valkyrie looked down on to a large wooden table, and the partially inflated skin of the Hollow Man that lay upon it.

Another Hollow Man lumbered into view, carrying a bucket of slop and what looked like entrails. It didn't look up and Valkyrie didn't make a sound. It went to the furnace built into the wall, the only source of light in the room, and opened the metal grille above the flames. Spilling some and not caring, the Hollow Man poured the slop into the furnace. Valkyrie's muscles were beginning to ache.

The Hollow Man picked up a large pair of bellows, its heavy hands clumsy and awkward, and poked the tip through the hole at the top of the furnace. It pulled the handles apart, sucking in the foul gases, and Valkyrie watched it shuffle over to the table. It jammed the tip into the skin and the bellows wheezed, and the skin inflated a little more. The Hollow Man picked up a large needle and sewed, making sure the gases wouldn't escape.

Valkyrie's arms were trembling. Her legs wouldn't betray her, but her arms were about to go. She looked back down at the Hollow Man as it picked up the bellows and returned to the furnace. She felt something heavy move in her hair and she flinched, her arms giving way. She fell through the opening and hit the table.

She heard the bellows drop and lay flat on her back, holding her breath. The partially inflated Hollow Man lay beside her, blocking her from view. She didn't know how good a Hollow Man's eyesight was, but in this gloom she hoped it wasn't any better than hers.

Valkyrie gritted her teeth when she felt the rat in her hair again. Every ounce of her wanted to tear it away, but she stayed still, even when it crawled out on to her chest. It sat for a moment and then leaped on to the Hollow Man's skin. She heard it jump to the ground and scamper away. A second later she heard the bellows being picked up. She let out her breath and raised herself up a bit, just enough to make sure that she wasn't being tricked.

And then the Hollow Man skin turned its half-inflated head to her.

39

HOLLOW MAN

Valkyrie grabbed the thick thread that was holding the Hollow Man together and yanked. The sewing came undone and the gas hissed at her as the skin deflated. She tasted the stench and gagged as she rolled off the table, the gas making the bile rise in her throat. She threw up, her eyes stinging and streaming tears.

She felt rough hands on her and then she was hauled off her knees and thrown against the wall. A fist crunched into her ribs and she cried out. Something crashed into the side of her head and she went stumbling, tripping over a discarded chair and falling painfully to the hard ground.

Her eyes wouldn't open. She tried crawling away, but her ankle was grabbed and she was pulled back. She knocked her chin against the floor and tasted blood. She turned over, lashing out a kick at knee-height. Her boot hit the Hollow Man's leg and it was soft, but there was no knee to break. The grip on her ankle was released and she covered up, waiting in the darkness for the next blow. It found its way above her raised knees and below her elbows, dropping straight down on to her belly, and the breath left her. She tried to roll over, but those hands were on her again, those coarse, clumsy fingers, and she was yanked to her feet and sent stumbling blindly. Her hip struck something, the edge of the table, and Valkyrie folded and sank to her knees.

Her eyes opened a crack. All she could see was a blurred murkiness. She closed them. She couldn't breathe. She heard the whispering of papery skin behind her and she launched herself backwards. She collided with the Hollow Man, but she'd misjudged the angle and she felt it stagger but not fall. She tucked her head in as she rolled, came up in a crouch, her stomach muscles still not allowing her to straighten. She felt tears on her face and tasted blood and vomit.

She moved, staying low, stepping away from the Hollow Man's footsteps. Her hands were held out in front and she concentrated on feeling the air against her skin. Immediately, she felt the draughts, the heat from the furnace pushing through the room, rising up through the gap from which she had fallen. She stood on something and nearly tripped. The bellows maybe. The furnace was behind her. A blast of heat, uncomfortable on her back.

The air shifted and she felt the Hollow Man's movements, felt it lurching through the streams of clogging warmth, disrupting them as it came. It was close and unsubtle, coming head-on, and she used the air, drawing it in to her and then pushing, hard. It collided with the Hollow Man and drove it back, out of her sensory range. She heard it crash against the table.

Valkyrie rubbed her eyes before attempting to open them. They still stung, but it was bearable. The tears turned everything to a blur. She wiped her face with her sleeve and blinked rapidly. The Hollow Man came into focus. It was on the ground, crawling towards her, its own sewing needle sticking out of its lower back. Its legs were already half-deflated, the green gas slowly escaping through the puncture wound.

Valkyrie stepped sideways to avoid its grab. She went to the chair, righted it and sat with a groan. She worked at getting her breathing under control as she watched the Hollow Man change direction and crawl over. By the time she was taking deep breaths again and her eyes had stopped watering, the Hollow Man's flat, outstretched fingers were centimetres away from her foot. It had stopped moving.

Valkyrie stood and spat, trying to get rid of the foul taste in her mouth. She crossed to the door and opened it, making sure there was no one around, and eased out. As she hurried down the flame-licked corridor, she felt the pain, but ignored it, just like she ignored the part of herself that wanted to hunker down and cry. She focused on the *other* part, the part that revelled in her triumph. Another fight that she'd won. Another battle where she hadn't died.

She moved through the junction and found stairs leading up. She listened for a few seconds, made sure no one was going to surprise her, and ascended. The stairs curled around a thick column of stone like a vine around a sapling. Valkyrie reached the top and kept moving in what she decided was a southerly direction. She came to a corner and Billy-Ray Sanguine rounded it.

He looked at her for a moment, a little surprised, like he couldn't quite place her, and then that white-toothed grin came, but by then she was running the other way. She heard him laugh as she barrelled through a door.

There were shouts now, from all over, and she heard running footsteps, the echoes rebounding along the stone. Valkyrie came to another set of stairs leading up and took them three at a time. There were two Hollow Men at the top. They reached for her, but she slipped by them. She reached a corridor with a window at the end and piled on the speed, hearing someone behind her. Beyond the window was a room, its light spilling through into the darkness. The walls of this room had tapestries. She saw a chandelier. It was the castle's main hall. Which meant that this wasn't a window – it was a mirror.

Valkyrie jumped, curling into a ball as she hit the glass. The world fragmented with a crash that filled her head. The main hall was lower than the corridor and she fell through the air, shards of mirror falling with her. She slammed to the floor and rolled, crunching the glass beneath her. She caught a glimpse of Skulduggery and then he was beside her, helping her up, and Ghastly, Fletcher and Shudder were running in.

Somebody cleared his throat. Loudly. They all looked up at the broken mirror. Billy-Ray Sanguine stood in the corridor above them, hands in his pockets. "How is everyone?" he asked. "How's everyone doin'? We should catch up later, all of us, talk about old times and have a laugh. Can't do it now, I'm afraid. Bit pressed for time, what with our ultimate masterplan and all."

"Come down here, Sanguine," Skulduggery said

"Why, so you can arrest me?"

"No," said Ghastly, "so we can kick the hell out of you."

An elderly man appeared beside Sanguine and Valkyrie knew she was looking at Scarab.

"We have guests?" Scarab asked.

"Yes, we do, Pops," Sanguine replied. "I'm afraid the girl broke a mirror though."

"Well, that's OK," smiled Scarab. "I don't believe any of that *seven years' bad luck* stuff anyhow. Heck, even if I did, it wouldn't matter – they're all going to be dead by tomorrow anyway. Hello there, Detective Pleasant. Been a while."

"We want Tanith Low and Kenspeckle Grouse returned to us," Skulduggery said. "And then we want you and the others to give yourselves up."

Scarab laughed and Sanguine shook his head, amused.

"I like you guys," Sanguine said. "I do. You know why I like you? Because you're *funny*. You look all weird and you say all these silly things. Funny, y'know?"

"You act as if you're not hopelessly outnumbered," said Scarab, "which, by the way, you *are*. You act like you'd stand a chance against the fellas we have with us *and* all the Hollow Men we've been stitching together – which, by the way, you *don't*. That's impressive."

Sanguine nodded. "That, and I don't mind sayin' this because I know it'll stay in this room, is a beautiful thing."

It was a psycho double act they were watching – father and son lunatics. But even so, they were talking too much. Skulduggery felt it too.

"I take it you're not going to surrender," he said.

"The last time you arrested me," Scarab responded, all humour gone from his voice, "you locked me away without a trial. If it's all the same to you, I'm not going to repeat my mistakes. There will be no prison cells this time. There will be no cover-ups. There will be justice."

"That's why you had Professor Grouse repair the Desolation Engine? You think setting it off will be justice?"

"Depends who I kill, now doesn't it?"

Skulduggery tilted his head. "What's to stop us from putting an end to all of this right *now*, and kicking the hell out of the both of you while we're at it?"

Sanguine frowned. "Well, we're, we're up so *high*..." He brightened. "Oh, yeah *and* we've got reinforcements."

"See," Scarab said, "we *were* planning to use the Hollow Men in our grand finale, but seeing as how you found our base here, we'll just have to improvise a little. So we're going to head off now and no doubt we'll meet again to, you know, hit each other or whatever it is people like us do nowadays."

"It's still hit each other," Sanguine told him.

"Well, there you go. You can't beat the classics."

"You can try and stop us," Sanguine said, "but I have a feelin' you'll be just a *tad* busy fending off the army of Hollow Men that are about jump out at you."

At that, a section of wall opened up and a single Hollow Man stumbled out and stood there. Sanguine pursed his lips. A moment passed.

"Awkward," he murmured.

Another wall slid open and Hollow Men poured out, dozens of them, and Sanguine clapped his hands in delight and then disappeared from view with his father.

Valkyrie stood beside Skulduggery and Ghastly, and they clicked their fingers and threw balls of fire. The flames caught the skin of the Hollow Men, taking a few seconds to burn through, and ignited the gases within. And still they came, dozens of them, swarming into the hall.

"The Cleavers are on their way," Skulduggery said, "but we don't have time for this. Anton, we need them taken down *fast*."

Shudder nodded. He closed his eyes and his fists clenched. Then a head pushed through his chest.

Valkyrie stepped back in shock. The head was hazy, like a ghost, and it was Shudder's head, only different. The hair was longer and it had pointed teeth. It snarled as it pushed its way out. Its shoulders came next, then its arms, then its clawed hands. It was dressed in the same shirt and black jacket as the real Shudder. It stayed where it was for a moment then opened its eyes, which were narrow and black. It saw the Hollow Men, its face contorted with effort and it lunged, trailing a blurred stream of light and darkness from its torso back into Shudder's chest. It flew to the nearest Hollow Man and slashed, its claws solid enough to rip through the papery skin.

It moved on, the stream that connected it to Shudder lengthening, and it screeched as it went, tearing and ripping through the Hollow Men as they swiped at it. It looped and curled, swooped and whirled, the stream crossing over and under itself. This ghostly Shudder, this *gist*, was relentless. With each pass its visage became fiercer, and it was no longer so hazy, so transparent. It looked demonic. It looked evil.

Shudder himself grunted. Valkyrie looked at him and saw the sweat on his face, saw the straining muscles on his neck. The stream that flowed from his chest became tight and taut, and the gist screamed in anger as it began to retract. Like a fish on a hook it twisted and writhed, but it could do nothing to stop itself from being pulled back into Shudder's chest. The last Valkyrie saw of it was a flailing claw.

Shudder took a heavy step back, his face pale, his breathing uneven. The Hollow Men were gone, nothing more than tatters and a foul smell that made her eyes sting again.

"Are you OK?" Valkyrie asked.

"It takes me a few minutes," Shudder said quietly, "to regain my strength."

"What *was* that?" Fletcher asked.

"It's my *gist*," he said. "It's my anger, my hate, my determination. It's the strongest part of me, but it needs to be carefully controlled. Gists can't be allowed too much time out of the host body."

"Why not?"

Shudder looked at them. "It would take over, and then *I'd* be reduced to something that lived inside *it*."

"Fletcher," Skulduggery said, "take Anton outside. Wait there for Marr and the Cleavers. Tell them where we are."

Fletcher nodded, glanced at Valkyrie and disappeared with Shudder.

"Let's go," Skulduggery said to Ghastly and Valkyrie.

They used the air to rise to the broken mirror, then touched down and hurried on. There were more Hollow Men here, but they were dispatched easily.

"Tanith's this way," Valkyrie said, taking the lead. "Kenspeckle's with her. He's been... She's hurt."

They ran on, until Valkyrie pointed at a door and Skulduggery blasted it open.

Kenspeckle Grouse leaped to his feet, snarling. Tanith could barely raise her head. Ghastly moved to Kenspeckle and hit him with a right cross. Kenspeckle laughed. He pushed Ghastly and Ghastly hit the far wall. Kenspeckle threw his chair at Skulduggery and used the distraction to get closer. He laughed again as he yanked Skulduggery's arm from his shoulder. Skulduggery roared in pain and Kenspeckle shoved him away. Valkyrie splayed her hand against the air and Kenspeckle went tumbling backwards.

There were footsteps behind her and Davina Marr burst into the room. "Do not move!" she commanded, gun aimed at Kenspeckle.

Kenspeckle snarled again and turned on his knees, his mouth opening wide. Something bulged in his throat, something that was trying to crawl its way out. If that Remnant got loose in here, it could possess any one of them, or seize its chance to escape, and they'd never get it back. Valkyrie ran forward and kicked, the toe of her boot slamming into Kenspeckle's chin. He lifted slightly with the impact and dropped on to his back.

Marr hurried over, shackles in his hand. She cuffed Kenspeckle's wrists behind him, sealing the Remnant back inside. Valkyrie looked around, realising there were Cleavers over by Tanith, freeing her from the seat.

"This won't hold me for long," Kenspeckle said, spitting blood as Marr hauled him up. "I'll get out. I'll come for you. Every last one of you."

"Cleavers" Marr said, "take him away."

Fletcher came in as Kenspeckle was led out.

"Fletcher," Skulduggery said, stifling a groan as he fixed his arm into place, "take Tanith to the Sanctuary. She needs urgent medical attention."

"You got it," Fletcher said, gently placing his hand on Tanith's arm. They vanished.

"Did you catch Scarab?" Ghastly asked Marr when he'd picked himself up off the floor.

Marr shook her head. "All the major players are gone. All we've come across so far are Hollow Men."

"Look what I found," Detective Pennant said as he walked in. He was smiling triumphantly, a strange stone hourglass in his hand. Green liquid sloshed inside the twin vials. "Looks like they left without their toy."

Valkyrie stared. "*That's* the Desolation Engine?"

"I found a bunch of other stuff," Pennant continued. "Bits and pieces, junk really. One of the Cleavers is taking it to the boffins to make them happy. But this – *this* is the big one."

"That bomb is live," Skulduggery said quietly.

Pennant laughed. "It can't be live. The old man didn't have time to fix it. You're talking days of work and he had, what, a few hours?"

"There are three steps to setting that thing off. Do you see the way the liquid is slightly luminous? That tells us it's live. That's the first step. The second step is arming it. We'll know that happens when the liquid turns red and starts to bubble. The third and final step is when it's triggered. Detective Pennant, you are two steps away from obliterating us all. Maybe you should hand that over to me."

Skulduggery stepped forward, but Marr took it from Pennant before Skulduggery got near. "You may have been granted temporary authority, Mr Pleasant, but I am still Prime Detective and, as such, this is my responsibility. Once it has been declared safe by Sanctuary experts, maybe *then* I will allow you to examine it. But right now, this is ours."

Pennant strained to look professional, even as he backed away from the bomb.

Fletcher appeared beside Valkyrie and she jumped

"Sorry," he said. "The doctors are looking at Tanith now." He saw Pennant and waved. "Hi. Didn't I beat you up once?" Pennant glared, but said nothing.

"You should all return with us to the Sanctuary for a debriefing," said Marr. She hadn't even glanced at the Engine. "Standard operating procedure."

"But as you've just pointed out," Skulduggery said, "we're not official Sanctuary operatives, so I think we'll be skipping that part of things, if it's all right with you."

"It's *not* all right with me."

"And yet we're going to skip it anyway. Please, feel free to tell Thurid Guild that this was all your doing, while we focus on going after Scarab and his lot. And don't worry, when we arrest them, you can tell everyone *you* did it. We don't do what we do for the glory or the fame or the credit; we do it for the quiet satisfaction of making the world a better place, saving the lives of innocents, and being better than you are."

Skulduggery tilted his head to one side and Valkyrie knew he was smiling.

40

WITH GORDON

alkyrie and Fletcher teleported into Gordon's house, arriving in the living room where the sun struggled to come in through the windows.

"I'll be back in a minute," said Valkyrie, making for the stairs.

"I'll come with you," Fletcher said, following.

She turned. "Why?"

"Why what?"

"I'm just going up to the study."

"I'll help you."

"You don't read."

"I read loads. Just not when you're around."

"Read down here."

"Why can't I come up?"

"Because the study is a treasure trove of secrets, and somewhere I like to be alone. It's my uncle's space."

"What's a trove?"

"A trove is a collection of valuable objects."

"How would you know that?"

"It's the kind of thing Skulduggery tells me."

"You must have scintillating conversations."

"They do put this one in the shade. I like the use of scintillating by the way."

"I thought you'd be impressed. So can I see the study?"

"You ask that like you think you've argued your point and won."

"I haven't?"

"Big words don't win arguments."

She left him and climbed the stairs. The study was the same as she'd left it – books on shelves, notes in bundles, awards as paperweights. Valkyrie closed the door and pulled back the false book on the far bookcase, causing the bookcase to swing open. She walked through into the hidden room, the room that contained all of her uncle's most secret magical possessions. The

Echo Stone glowed on the table, and Gordon Edgley shimmered into existence before her.

"Well?" he asked. "How did the rescue mission go? How is Skulduggery?"

"Oh, yes, we got him back."

"You did? Well, that's wonderful news! I'm so happy!"

"Yeah."

Gordon looked around. "I'm always in this room. There are no windows in here." He looked back at her. "What's wrong? You look troubled. Are you feeling OK?"

"I'm fine. I've just got another headache."

"Another…?"

"They've been popping up over the past day or so. It's nothing. I have this thing, just on the edge of my memory, you know that feeling? Every time I reach for it, it scatters."

"I remember the sensation. Highly annoying."

"Highly. But that's not why I'm here. What do you know about Remnants?"

"Lots," he said. "Fetch me my notebook from my desk. The big one."

Valkyrie went to the study and opened the desk. Masses of notebooks. She selected the biggest one.

"I'd like to go for a walk," Gordon announced when she

arrived back. "I haven't gone for a walk since... well, since I was alive really. I've almost forgotten what the outside looks like. Is it still green?"

"It really depends where you are. Can you, like, actually *go* for a walk?"

"Not on my own, but if you put the Echo Stone in your pocket, I can walk beside you. It'll be fun. Do you remember the walks we used to take?"

"Not especially."

"I can't either," he admitted. "I wasn't really a walker when I was alive, was I? I was more of a sitter." He smiled wistfully. "I did love to sit."

"I remember that."

"So? Can we go for a walk? Just around here. Not too far, I promise."

"I... I suppose we could. It can't be for long though – we can only spend a few minutes here."

"We? Someone's downstairs?"

"Yeah, Fletcher."

"Oh! The mysterious Fletcher Renn!"

Valkyrie narrowed her eyes. "Don't say it like that."

"Like what?"

"Like you're teasing me."

Gordon laughed. "If you take me for a walk, I promise I won't tease you. He's a Teleporter, isn't he? Send him away for ten minutes. Or let's just sneak out. I haven't sneaked out of a window in over thirty years!"

"I sneak out every day... OK, but just a short walk and I'm reading as we go."

Her uncle grinned. "Perfect."

They approached the wood on the east side of the house so Fletcher wouldn't see them. It was a surprisingly lovely morning, the rain having taken a break for the day, and warm enough for Valkyrie to have her coat draped over her arm.

"Towards the middle somewhere," Gordon said, peering over her shoulder as she flicked through the notebook. "There! The next few pages contain everything I've ever heard about the Remnants. Some of it is anecdotal, some pure, hard fact. There's more relevant information in those few pages than in any book you're ever likely to read."

"I knew you'd have something useful."

He went back to looking around as they strolled, and took a huge breath and expelled it.

"I don't actually breathe," he said happily, "but it's a nice habit to have."

"I've always thought so," she agreed, then glanced back at the footsteps in the lawn, at the blades of grass that were slowly springing back into shape. There were only her footsteps though. To the blades of grass and the world around then, Gordon was something less than even a ghost.

He started naming the birds they heard in the trees, and she was pretty sure the last four or five were names he'd completely made up. Valkyrie didn't mention it though.

"What are you looking for?" he asked absently.

"There's a Remnant inside Kenspeckle Grouse and we want to get it out."

"Ah. You'll need China Sorrows and her symbols, and a few other bits and pieces. How long has it been inside him? If it's possessed him for more than four days, I'm afraid that means it has permanently grafted itself to its host. It couldn't leave even if it wanted to."

"It hasn't been four days."

"Well then, you should be fine. It's all in those notes." He looked up. "Do you hear that birdsong, the particularly sweet one? That's a Wallowing Twite, if I'm not mistaken."

"Is there anything you don't know, Gordon?" Valkyrie asked as she flicked through.

"Nothing of any importance."

She sighed. "I can see why you and Skulduggery got along so well."

"Planet-sized egos do tend to form an orbit around each other. So what does that make *you*, I wonder?"

"I have no ego."

"Then you'd probably be a moon."

"I'm not a moon."

"Maybe even a gaseous giant."

"And I'm not gaseous. I'm the sun, how about that? The pair of you can orbit around *me* for a change." She closed the notebook. "Thanks for this, Gordon. I'll come back when I actually have time for a chat, OK?"

"I'll look forward to it. Take care of yourself, Niece Number One."

"Always do."

41

THE EXORCISTS

They had Kenspeckle tied to a chair in the middle of the room. His wrists were shackled behind him, and Skulduggery was securing his arms and legs with a thick rope. Kenspeckle was grinning at them.

The Remnant inside him wasn't bothering to hide any more. Dark veins spread beneath Kenspeckle's suddenly pale skin, turning his lips black and his gums grey.

"You'll never get him," Kenspeckle said in a voice that was not his own. "He's mine now and I'm not giving him back."

Skulduggery didn't answer. Kenspeckle's eyes flickered to

Valkyrie and he leered at her. Spittle flecked his chin.

"You'll release me," Kenspeckle said. "Won't you? After everything I've done for you? All the times I've helped you?"

"Kenspeckle helped me," she said. "Not you."

"I *am* Kenspeckle," he said with a little laugh. "I have all of his memories, don't I? I might not be the Kenspeckle you knew, but I *am* Kenspeckle. Valkyrie, please. I'm your friend."

"We're getting rid of you," Valkyrie said. "There was barely enough room in Kenspeckle's head for himself – there's certainly no room for a lodger."

The smile turned to a growl. "I'm going to kill you."

"That's enough," said Skulduggery.

"I'm going to kill all of you."

The door opened and China came in.

"And here comes the witch," Kenspeckle sneered. "Going to draw a little symbol, are you? You think that'll force me out? It'll never happen. I'm too strong. Too powerful."

China didn't respond. She barely looked at him. Her students had been working in the room for hours before they'd even brought Kenspeckle in. Skulduggery nodded to her and she closed her eyes, and the symbols that had been drawn in the room earlier shimmered into view. Ornate signs and complicated sigils appeared on the walls, swept down to join the patterns on the floor and rose upwards and spread along the ceiling. Kenspeckle's arrogance vanished.

"This will kill him," he said quickly. "You hear me? This will kill the old man."

"Don't be ridiculous," China told him. "The Mass Expulsion of 1892 left hundreds of people *unconscious*, not dead. Kenspeckle Grouse will wake up in a few minutes with a sore head and a gap in his memory, but you, my little friend, will be trapped in *this*."

Skulduggery showed him the Soul Catcher. For all its dreadful connotations, it reminded Valkyrie of nothing more threatening than a snowglobe. "You can save yourself a lot of pain by leaving that body willingly," Skulduggery said.

Kenspeckle glared. "I'm not going back to that room."

"This will only take a moment," said China.

The symbols glowed, bathing the room in blue and then red and then green light. Kenspeckle strained against his bonds, cursed all of them and screamed and cried and then cursed them again. China walked around the walls, her fingers touching parts of the sigils, and with each new touch Kenspeckle gave a new scream.

"It's coming," China said.

Kenspeckle arched his spine, his body rigid and his head

thrown back. Valkyrie watched as the Remnant climbed out of his screaming mouth. She thought she saw arms, and white eyes, and it turned sideways and she could see its jaws. It darted to the ceiling and Skulduggery held out the Soul Catcher. The nasty little thing twisted and writhed and screeched as it was dragged into the globe, which instantly turned black and went dead.

And then it was all over.

42

THE NECROMANCERS

reath found them waiting for him in the cemetery above the Temple, dressed simply in their dark robes and talking among themselves. He strode to them, his boots crunching on graveside gravel, his finely tailored coat flapping gently in the breeze. He had never had any time for the false humility the robes represented, a laughable idea that all Necromancers were pure of heart and mind and purpose. He liked nice clothes so he *wore* nice clothes. In his opinion there was nothing as pure and honest as *that*.

The conversation faded as the others watched him approach.

To Wreath's right was Quiver, a tall man who was almost as thin as Skulduggery Pleasant. Quiver's cheeks were sunken hollows and his eyes gleamed from shadowed pockets. He was a man who only spoke when he had something worthwhile to say – quite a rarity in Necromancer circles, Wreath had to admit.

The man on Wreath's left was Quiver's polar opposite. He was blandly good-looking, but a little too pale and a little too weak to be truly memorable. Craven's flattering words had elevated him to an unlikely position of power, but as of yet, Wreath couldn't see how this benefited him in any meaningful way. Because he spent all his time agreeing with everything the High Priest said, he never had a spare moment to exert any influence of his own. Wreath couldn't figure him out, and as such, he trusted him about as much as he liked him. Which was to say, not at all.

The High Priest stood between Quiver and Craven, his robes setting him apart. A little more frayed, but a lot more regal. Wreath wouldn't have been surprised if High Priest Tenebrae wore a brand-new robe every day and had a team of sycophants carefully fraying it overnight, purely for effect. The thought almost made Wreath smile.

Tenebrae folded his long-fingered hands inside his voluminous sleeves and tilted his head on his slender neck. He reminded Wreath of one of those ridiculous birds that stand around in water all day – a crane or possibly a flamingo. Whichever one looked the silliest.

"Your Eminence," Wreath said, bowing with due reverence. "I thought we were going to have this conversation within the Temple walls."

"Walls have ears," Craven announced pompously.

"No, they don't," Wreath reminded him without gracing him with a glance. "You're thinking of people."

Craven glowered and Wreath ignored him.

"I would prefer to discuss this matter outside," Tenebrae said, "where we will not be overheard. I believe the Soul Catcher has been retrieved?"

"Yes," Wreath said. "Valkyrie informs me that they need it to transfer a Remnant back to the Midnight Hotel, but once that is done, it will be returned to us."

"The Soul Catcher is *our* property," Craven said to Tenebrae. "They have no right to dictate to *us* when we can have it *back*. We should demand it be returned to us *immediately*."

"In which case," said Wreath, "they will ignore our demand then we will look weak and ineffectual in their eyes."

"They can't *ignore* us!" Craven spluttered.

"They can and they will. If you were ever to leave the safety of the Temple, you would quickly realise that nobody likes us. They think we're untrustworthy and dangerous."

"Then they should *fear* us!"

"And if we had a history of stepping out into the world, they most assuredly would. But it is widely known that we Necromancers like to stay in our temples with our schemes and our plots, and we really don't like getting our hands dirty. Lord Vile, of course, being the obvious exception."

"Traitor," Quiver said softly, in a tone that almost conveyed emotion.

"Now is not the time to talk of Lord Vile," said Tenebrae. "He was once our Death Bringer, he is not any more and so our search continues. Solomon, you will offer to take the Soul Catcher off their hands once the Remnant is trapped."

"Sir?"

"Tell them you will take it back to the Midnight Hotel yourself, or tell them you want to study the contraption once it has a soul inside it. I don't care what lie you use, just bring me the Soul Catcher and bring me the Remnant. Can you do that?"

"Of course. May I ask why?"

"No, you may not," Craven sneered. Wreath shifted his gaze to him and Craven held that gaze for three whole seconds before crumbling beneath it.

"The Cain girl," Tenebrae said, changing the subject with no need for subtlety. "She knows about the Passage?"

"Pleasant backed me into a corner," Wreath admitted. "It was either tell her or risk losing her."

"I remind you, Cleric Wreath, that we do not all share your conviction that she is the one we're looking for. She's far too young for a start."

"She's a natural, your Eminence. She's taken to Necromancy faster than anyone I've seen since Vile."

"Not auspicious company," muttered Quiver.

"Maybe not," Wreath said, "but she has the potential to surpass even him. She's the one we've been waiting for. I'm sure of it."

"His Eminence is quite correct, however," Craven said, finding his voice again after far too short a time. "She's much too young. Plus, she's entrenched with the skeleton detective. Do you really think you can pry her from *his* side?"

"Not easily," Wreath said, "but it can be done. Skulduggery Pleasant is a fantastically flawed individual."

"Much more than even *you* know," Tenebrae said. "We will need to meet with her, of course. Our encounters in the past few months have been too brief, and we need to accurately form an opinion of her ability."

"Of course, High Priest."

Quiver spoke up. "If she *is* suitable, she will have to be monitored closely to be kept on the right path. History cannot be allowed to repeat itself."

"Agreed," said Wreath, then hesitated. "Your Eminence, if I may return for a moment to the delicate subject of Lord Vile..."

Tenebrae looked displeased, and Craven stood at the High Priest's elbow and copied the look remarkably well. Nevertheless, Wreath continued.

"It seems to me that the closer we get to the Passage, the higher the likelihood of stern opposition from non-believers and enemies alike. News will travel and rumours will spread."

"Are you afraid of rumours, Wreath?" Craven laughed. "Are you afraid of idle chatter? Perhaps you are not the man we thought you were. Perhaps you are unsuited to be our representative outside the Temple."

"Then who will take my place?" Wreath answered icily. "You? If all my post required was a staggering expertise at fawning, then you'd be welcome to it."

"How dare you!" Craven practically screeched.

Wreath took a sudden step towards him and Craven stumbled over his own robe to get away.

"Enough!" growled the High Priest. "Solomon, you're

concerned that these rumours will reach unwelcome ears, yes?"

"Yes, sir."

"Such a concern is reasonable, but I can assure you, you need not worry. The Necromancer Order is stronger now than it was during the war with Mevolent. We are more than capable of dealing with trouble, should it arise."

"With respect, sir, this is more than mere *trouble*. Forgive the melodrama of what I am about to say, but if the news that we are preparing for the Passage were to reach whatever corner of the world he has secluded himself in, Lord Vile *will* return to destroy us all."

"In that case," High Priest Tenebrae said with a patient smile, "we need to be sure that Valkyrie Cain is strong enough to kill him for us, now don't we?"

43

THE ROAD TO
CROKE PARK

Valkyrie walked into a room with a massive tub built into the floor. There was a bouquet of flowers arranged in a delicate vase on a nearby table. The huge tub was filled to the brim with mud, and for a moment Valkyrie thought the mud had eyes, which opened as she came in and blinked up at her.

"Hey, Val," the mud said.

"Hey, Tanith," Valkyrie said back. "You've got something on your face..."

Tanith's mud-covered features broke into a small smile. "Ghastly already made that joke when he brought me the flowers."

"That was nice of him," Valkyrie said. She pulled up the only chair in the room, and sat. "How are your hands?"

Tanith raised them for Valkyrie to see. They were heavily bandaged and wrapped in plastic so that the mud wouldn't get in. "The Professor says they'll be fine in a few days. The doctors in the Sanctuary soaked the bandages in something I never heard of to heal the wounds. The Professor inspected them the moment I was transferred here. He said they'd do the job. All this mud is for the swelling and the, you know, the trauma. I'll be fine, he says. He's doing everything he can to make up for it."

"He blames himself," Valkyrie said. "Even though he couldn't do anything to stop the Remnant, and even though he can't remember one thing about it, he still blames himself."

"I'm not surprised," Tanith said. "I mean, I know it wasn't him that did this to me. But it used his face and it had his voice, and I don't know... I think there's a part of me that hates him for it."

"But you're here," frowned Valkyrie. "If a part of you hates him, wouldn't you have wanted to stay in the Sanctuary, *away* from him?"

"I'm a practical girl, Val, and the practical side of my brain pretty much tells the stupid side what to do. So I'm cool here."

She shrugged and winced and Valkyrie noticed the bandages on her shoulders.

"How are you?" she asked.

"I just told you."

"No, you told me how your *injuries* are."

"All right then, I'm doing OK actually. The pain wasn't really any worse than the White Cleaver stabbing me in the back, but the White Cleaver didn't talk, you know? That Remnant thing in the Professor just would *not* shut up."

"Tanith, you were *tortured*."

"Everyone gets tortured these days. Skulduggery was tortured by Serpine, who then turned around and did that red right-hand thing at *you*. Then Skulduggery was tortured *again* by the Faceless Ones. I figured it was my turn, you know? You're not part of the team if you haven't been tortured – that's what I always say. Well, I'll be saying that from now *on* anyway."

Valkyrie stood there, feeling stupid and awkward. Tanith had been put through hell and Valkyrie didn't have the first idea how to talk to her about it. The pain was evident in her friend's eyes, no matter how hard she tried to hide it. Valkyrie searched clumsily for the words she needed, but they weren't coming to her.

"What are they going to do with the Remnant?" Tanith asked, breaking the silence.

"We've handed it over to Wreath," Valkyrie told her and Tanith's face soured.

"Why does *he* want it?"

"Well, technically, the Soul Catcher is *his* and he asked for it back. He just wants to study it for a while, now that it actually contains something. He'll bring the Remnant back to the Midnight Hotel when he's done."

"I don't know how you can trust that guy, Val."

"He's helped me a lot over the last year. He's helped all of us."

Tanith looked like she was about to argue and then there was a beep from somewhere overhead, and she groaned. "Just when you get comfortable."

Tanith gripped the edges of the tub and rose out of it, moving stiffly. The mud covered her completely as she reached her arm out. Valkyrie grabbed her elbow with both hands to make sure she didn't slip and helped her into a white bathrobe. Tanith wiped her face clean with a towel.

There was a knock on the door. Valkyrie looked over her shoulder to find Skulduggery standing in the doorway.

"Tanith," he said. "You're looking great."

"And I'm ready to go," Tanith said.

"Is that so?"

"You give me my sword back and I'm right behind you."

Before Skulduggery could answer, Tanith's left leg buckled and Valkyrie grabbed her as she fell, guiding her to the chair.

"Bloody hell," Tanith growled. "That hurts."

"Tanith..." Skulduggery began.

"You want to know if I learned anything, right?" she said, pain lending her words an edge. "You want to know if Sanguine or any of them let something slip in all their gloating? They didn't. They kept me shackled in a room and then they gave me to the Professor. Forgive me, but there are patches of the last twelve hours that are a little fuzzy."

"They didn't mention any names? Places? Times?"

"The Remnant in the Professor talked about a lot of stuff. Mainly about how happy he was to have finally found a friend."

Skulduggery nodded slowly. "OK. All right, thank you."

"But what does it matter? We have the Desolation Engine, right?"

"We do, but I'd have liked to have known their target. If they can't take it down with the bomb, they might try some other way."

"Or they're all running," Tanith said. "Let's face it – none of these guys are great team players. They're all in it for their own reasons, so the moment the big plan goes wrong, I think they're going to split."

"That is possible. It's also very likely."

"If you want my opinion, it's over. Now all we have to do is track each one of them down. And I want in on that action, Skulduggery. Springheeled Jack threw me off a moving car. I owe him a few slaps."

"The moment you're fighting fit, we'll call you."

"I'm ready *now*."

"You can't even walk, Tanith."

"An hour or two is all I need."

"A few days' rest – those were your doctor's orders."

"Yeah, well, my doctor's the one who tortured me for God's sake. I don't think his opinion really matters, do you?"

Valkyrie looked at her boots. Skulduggery was silent.

"Fine," Tanith muttered.

"Valkyrie," Skulduggery said as he left, "we have work to do."

She looked at Tanith. "You're really OK, huh?"

"Don't start, Val."

Valkyrie hunkered down until she was looking straight into Tanith's eyes. "You're my sister," she said. "I have another sister or maybe a brother on the way, but you're my sister too. I want you to stay here and get better, and try to accept the fact, with every part of you, that it wasn't Kenspeckle who did this. I want you to be OK. OK?"

"OK," Tanith said softly. Valkyrie hugged her and kissed her cheek.

"You've got mud on your chin," smiled Tanith.

"Yeah, but I make it work."

Ghastly and Anton Shudder were waiting for them in the darkened cinema. Fletcher appeared on the stage, arms crossed and eyes narrowed.

"You have a visitor," he said. "Your friend the vampire's outside. He wants to talk to Valkyrie."

"By all means," Skulduggery said. Then, much to Fletcher's satisfaction, he said, "Fletcher, you go with her. Caelan's been banished from vampire society because of us. He might be cross."

Valkyrie glared. "I don't need protection."

"A vampire's waiting for you outside – of course you need protection. Keep it brief. We'll be waiting for you."

Fletcher grinned. Valkyrie shot him a look and jumped off the stage. He followed her up the aisle and out of the gloom.

Caelan was standing just outside the door. He turned to them as they approached, his dark eyes on Valkyrie. It was as if he didn't even notice Fletcher beside her.

"Hi," she said. "Anything wrong?"

"My home was burned down," Caelan said. "My cage was destroyed. Moloch has lifted his protection – the other vampires see me as fair game now."

"Oh, God," she said. "I'm so sorry."

"That *is* terrible," Fletcher muttered.

"I have no friends left," Caelan continued, "and nowhere to go. I thought you or the skeleton would have a suggestion. I need somewhere secure."

"What about the Midnight Hotel?"

He looked surprised. "That... That would be ideal. You know where it is?"

"I can do better than that – the owner is inside."

A big car pulled in off the street and Thurid Guild got out. He waved his driver away, then strode towards them. By his narrowed eyes, Valkyrie could tell he knew instantly what Caelan was, but he passed them without saying anything and disappeared into the cinema.

"Shudder might not want a vampire as a guest," Fletcher said when Guild was gone. "I mean, let's face it, not many people like vampires. Take me, for instance."

Valkyrie glared at him then softened her gaze for Caelan. "We can ask him," she said. "I'm sure he won't mind."

"Very well," Caelan said. "Thank you."

She walked back into the cinema, Caelan behind her, Fletcher stuck like a limpet at her side. Skulduggery, Ghastly and Shudder stopped talking and watched them approach. Guild didn't look around.

"Anton," she said, "this is Caelan. His home was destroyed and he needs somewhere to stay."

Shudder looked deep into Caelan's eyes. "Over the hotel's history," he said, "I have had two vampires stay as guests. I had to kill one of them."

"Valkyrie and I are responsible for Caelan's situation," Skulduggery said. "I would consider it a personal favour."

Shudder considered this, then inclined his head. "All are welcome, provided they obey the rules. I'll lock you in before dark and unlock the door in the morning. We should have no problems."

Caelan nodded, saying nothing.

"Miss Low could be right," Guild said, resuming their conversation. "It might be over. Scarab and his lackeys may have scuttled back under whatever rocks they choose to call home. It is possible."

"I don't think so," Skulduggery said. "Scarab's an assassin. He never has just one plan, one route to the kill. He has back-ups. I think he has a back up for this too."

"Then the search continues," said Shudder. "But now it could be anything, yes? One route has been blocked for him, but we have no idea what the second route could be."

"We need to figure out what he was planning to do with the Desolation Engine," Ghastly said. "We can work backwards from there."

"The obvious target would have been the Sanctuary," Guild said. "As it is, our work there has been disrupted immensely following the evacuation. We're only just now returning people to their posts."

Kenspeckle came through the door in the screen, walking quickly. Valkyrie hadn't seen much of him since he woke up, on account of the fact that he had immediately thrown himself back into his work. She knew very well what he was doing. He didn't know how to deal with what the Remnant had done when it was in control, so he had retreated to what he *did* know how to deal with – treating injured people and dismantling the Engine.

"There's too many pieces," he said, hurrying across the stage to them. "Do you understand me? The so-called *junk* that was found with the Desolation Engine in the castle, there's too much of it."

He saw Caelan and froze. "Vampire?" he whispered, appalled.

Immediately, Valkyrie grabbed Caelan's arm and led him away. "He has a phobia about people like you," she told him softly. "Would you mind waiting outside?"

"Not at all," Caelan answered smoothly, and left.

"Sorry, Kenspeckle," she said.

Kenspeckle's eyes were wide and his hand was clutching something that hung from his neck. She knew it was the vial of saltwater he wore in case of vampire attack.

"Professor," Skulduggery prompted. "The leftover pieces from the Desolation Engine. Why is that troubling?"

"I-I don't know," Kenspeckle said. "I just... It doesn't make any sense."

"A lot of things don't make any sense," Guild said. "Such as how you were able to restore that Engine to working order so quickly. We thought it would take you days, if you could do it at all."

"Of course I could do it!" Kenspeckle snapped, suddenly back to his old self. "There was never any question of whether I could do it! They didn't know that of course. They just got lucky by picking me."

"I don't care how smart you are," Guild said. "Sanctuary experts have examined that bomb for decades and they still have no idea how it worked, let alone how to fix it in a *single afternoon*"

"Of course they don't, you damn fool. They didn't *build* the thing in the first place, now did they?"

They all stared at Kenspeckle. He was flustered. He rubbed his eyes and took a deep breath.

"You *built* it?" Valkyrie asked.

He looked at her. "What?"

"You... you said you built it. The Desolation Engine."

"I did? I... I suppose I did, yes." For a moment he looked so very old and so very frail, and then the irritation returned to his voice. "Yes, well, I wasn't always who I am now. No one ever is. I've spent my entire lifetime becoming who I am. Finally, I'm here and I'm old. It's depressing, it really is.

"When I was a younger man, I was no less intelligent, but I fear I lacked some basic and fundamental *sense*. My outlook on things was different. My philosophy was different. Different things interested me. The Desolation Engine for instance. I wanted to see if I could build it. It existed in theory, but then it had *always* existed in theory. It was my goal to turn magic-science theory into magic-science *fact*. Which was what I did.

"I don't think I cared about who would use it, or where, or

on whom. These things were immaterial. When I was told about the detonation in Naples, I can't recall being affected by it one way or the other. It worked. I built it, I knew it would work and it did. Project over – start another.

"It was only years later that I understood what I had done and took responsibility for my actions. I didn't take the human equation into account, you see. I was all about the magic and the science. Everything else... slipped by unnoticed."

"And you've been making up for it ever since," Ghastly said.

Kenspeckle looked even more annoyed. "No, no, no, that's not it at all. I merely learned from my mistake and made a decision never to hurt anyone ever again. This isn't about *redemption*. I'm not seeking forgiveness. I did what I did and I will suffer for it for the rest of my life, which is no less than I deserve.

"And I'm not telling you all this because I'm after absolution or your understanding. I'm telling you this because I need you to appreciate just how clever I really am. I took an abstract concept of magic-science theory and I made it real. I am very, *very* clever and I am telling you that something is wrong. There are too many pieces left over."

"So what does it mean?" Skulduggery asked.

"I think there is only one thing it *could* mean," Kenspeckle said, "and it is something that has only occurred to me as I've been speaking. It's not just about the excess parts, it's about the parts that *should* be there, but *aren't*. I don't think I – or the Remnant within me – only repaired the Desolation Engine that Detective Marr has in her possession. I think Scarab got me to build him an entirely new one."

Skulduggery was the first to speak. "Are you *sure?*"

"No," Kenspeckle said at once. "But there is a very big possibility that Scarab has a second Engine."

"I'll alert the Sanctuary," Guild said, taking out his phone.

"Do you have any idea of a kill zone?" Skulduggery asked Kenspeckle while Guild made the call.

"I estimate a lethal radius of 150, maybe 200 square metres," said Kenspeckle.

"I can't get through to Marr," Guild said, putting away his phone, "but the Sanctuary is being evacuated. Again."

Skulduggery cocked his head. "What if the target isn't the Sanctuary? If Scarab's plan was for two bombs all along, he'd have two targets. What's the second target?"

Ghastly said, "Set it off in a crowded street and we're looking at a couple of thousand dead."

Valkyrie frowned. "What would be the point of that? Scarab wants revenge on the Sanctuary, not ordinary people."

"But attacking ordinary people *would* be an attack on the

Sanctuary," Ghastly argued. "That's what it's there for, isn't it? To shield the non-magical population from *us*?"

"So you think Scarab is just going to slaughter thousands of innocent people?" Kenspeckle asked.

Ghastly turned to him. "Why not? The Sanctuary frames Scarab for a crime he didn't commit, and in response, he commits a crime the Sanctuary will never recover from. You think the other Sanctuaries around the world will ignore something like this? They'll descend on us and devour *everything*. They'll tear this country apart and fight over the remains."

"It won't be a street," Skulduggery murmured. "But it *will* be somewhere public. Somewhere densely packed. Like a... sports stadium."

Valkyrie looked at him. "The All-Ireland Championship. My dad was trying to get tickets. But that's *today*. It must have already started by now."

"Good God," Ghastly said in a quiet voice. "He's going to kill 80,000 people live on air."

Skulduggery turned to Fletcher. "Please," he said, "tell me you've been to Croke Park before."

"Of course," Fletcher said. "The VIP area, mostly."

"Perfect. That's where we're going."

"And I'm coming with you," snarled Guild.

44

REVENGE

Valkyrie was eleven years old the last time she'd been to Croke Park. Her father had taken her to the Dublin Kildare game. She had worn her blue jersey and shouted and screamed and cheered along with the thousands of other people in the stands. The sun had been beating down and she remembered it as a day when everyone around her was smiling and laughing. She'd been buzzing with positivity and had talked non-stop all the way home, a rare feat even back then. Her dad had promised to take her again, but they'd never got around to it.

They teleported on to a wide concrete ramp and immediately Valkyrie was hit by the roar of the crowd inside the stadium. Out here though they were alone, high up off the streets and looking out over Dublin. Fletcher led the way down to a set of doors just as they opened and a security guard came out.

"This is the Executive Area," he informed them politely but firmly, in the tone of a man who had already dealt with dozens of people who had strayed from where they were meant to be. "VIPs only."

"We are VIPs," Ghastly smiled. His façade was up, covering his scars. He walked up to the security guard, reaching his hand into his pocket. "I have our tickets here somewhere. Say, you wouldn't have seen some friends of ours, would you? An odd-looking bunch, with an old American man?"

"Haven't seen anyone like that," said the guard, waiting for the tickets to be produced.

"Pity," Ghastly said and hit him, catching the guard as he fell. He laid the unconscious man on the ground then rejoined the others as they walked through the doors.

Cream walls and wooden floors, framed photographs and tasteful art. Everything in the VIP area was clean and new and nice and safe. The door to one of the Executive Boxes was open and Valkyrie could see past the people gathered inside to the huge

windows that overlooked the stadium. It was packed to capacity –
over 82,000 people cheering and singing and waiting to die.

"We're going to need a Sensitive with us," Ghastly said as
they walked on. "We need *someone* with psychic abilities to sort
through this crowd."

"Scarab's gang don't exactly blend in," Skulduggery
responded. "If they're anywhere, they'll be somewhere like this,
away from the masses. We have Caelan coming in on foot. The
rest of us will have to split up and search different areas."

"We shouldn't be trusting a vampire," said Fletcher.

"But you *can* trust vampire nature," Shudder told him. "For
whatever reason, Caelan has a grudge against Dusk. You can
trust him to see that through."

"Fletcher," Skulduggery said, "it's important you understand
this. If you see the enemy, do *not* engage. You might be the
difference between success and mass murder."

"Fine," Fletcher responded grudgingly.

"Guild, you might want to call in some of your operatives –
try to get in touch with Davina Marr again. We could cover a lot
more ground with her and a few Cleavers."

"Let's try to get this done without her," Guild said.

"You'd be willing to risk 80,000 lives just to protect your
secret?" Shudder asked.

"I told Anton the truth about the Vanguard assassination," Skulduggery said.

Anger contorted Guild's features. "You had no right to discuss that matter with *anyone*!"

"Anton's one of us," said Ghastly. "He's not going to use your past indiscretions against you. None of us are. Which is why you trust *us* to go after Scarab's gang and not Davina Marr."

"I knew Vanguard," Shudder said. "He was a good man. And yet I can understand Meritorious's decision. I don't agree with it, and I don't like it, but I understand it. Your secret is safe with me, Grand Mage."

Guild nodded curtly. Valkyrie could see that he didn't like the fact that they now had something to hold over him. From what she knew of the man, he didn't strike her as someone who would be comfortable with trusting other people. By not revealing a secret that could bring him down, each one of them was doing him a favour and he knew it.

They reached the door to the escalators. To their left was a window over the Conference Centre, another Executive Box, an elevator and two wooden doors that stood open wide. Standing in that doorway, a smile on his face, was Dreylan Scarab.

They all stopped – Guild out in front, Valkyrie beside Skulduggery, Fletcher and Shudder to her right, Ghastly to her left. Scarab didn't look at all alarmed.

"Aren't you a motley crew?" he said. "Detectives and desperadoes. Outlaws and agents. And so many of you. However can I hope to prevail against your combined might?"

"Give us the bomb," said Guild.

"You *have* the bomb."

"The *other* bomb."

"Ah," Scarab smiled. "You figured it out, eh? Of course, you realise this isn't going to end without a battle. You have your motley crew. I have my Revengers' Club."

"They seem to have deserted you," said Ghastly.

Scarab shook his head. "We've lost a couple along the way, but the big players are around. This is all part of our lovely little plan, you see. Everything we've done, it's all about revenge. And when it comes to revenge, timing is everything."

Skulduggery stepped past Guild. "Scarab, you're under arrest. Hand over the Desolation Engine, give yourself up and I swear you will get a fair trial."

"You slap those cuffs on me and I'll be dead before I get to a cell and you know it. The Grand Mage will have me killed. He might very well have *you* killed too. And your friends. We know too much, don't we, Grand Mage?"

"The Detective is offering you a peaceful way out," Guild

said. "I suggest you take him up on it."

"You prepared to give me a fair trial too, Guild?"

"Of course."

Scarab laughed. "For a born liar you're not very good at lying. You'd organised a little welcoming party for my release, hadn't you?"

Guild narrowed his eyes. "This is getting us nowhere."

"A nice band of specially chosen Cleavers, waiting for me when I got out of prison. Lucky for me the warden is no fan of yours, so he let me out a few days early."

"Take him down," Guild said to Skulduggery.

"Want to know a secret?" Scarab said with a grin. "I think the American Council is kind of hoping my little revenge plot succeeds. And the Russian Council didn't tell you that Billy-Ray had freed Dusk, did they? Seems to me a lot of folk are hoping I succeed. Everybody who's anybody wants you dead."

Guild stalked forward, clicking his fingers and summoning flame. "If you want something done," he muttered.

"Oh, good," Scarab said. "The fight." He turned and ran, and Guild ran after him.

The elevator door opened behind them and Valkyrie whirled round to see Dusk and Springheeled Jack stepping out. They brought up their silenced sub-machine guns and opened fire.

She dived, glimpsed Ghastly pulling Fletcher to the ground, and an instant later they had disappeared. Shudder dodged behind a pillar. Valkyrie looked at Skulduggery, but he was just standing there, hands out, and she saw the bullets appearing in front of him, coming into view as they slowed.

The gunfire cut off and she peeked out. Fletcher and Ghastly had materialised behind the enemy, and Ghastly had his arm wrapped around Jack's throat. Fletcher grabbed Dusk and they both vanished. Jack squirmed free and kicked out, catching Ghastly across the jaw. Ghastly pushed at the air and the gun flew from Jack's hands. Ghastly smashed a fist into him and kept on pummelling. Three punches sang in a short, sweet rhythm, the fourth knocking Jack's hat off his head. Jack stumbled away, straight into Shudder, whose elbow cracked against Jack's chin. Jack wobbled and went down.

"Stop hittin' me!" he cried. "This is hardly fair, now is it? Two of you against me?"

"You're the one who came at us with a gun," Ghastly said, standing over him.

"But that was for a giggle," Jack tried. "I wasn't *aimin'* at you, I swear."

Valkyrie looked back and saw Skulduggery running to catch up with Guild and Scarab.

"Besides," Jack continued, "we accomplished what we needed to." He looked up at Ghastly. "Are you usin' a new face cream or somethin'? You look different."

Shudder frowned. "What did you accomplish?"

"You got one unpredictable element in your little team," Jack told them with an exaggerated sigh. "The kind of power that could mess up everythin'. It was our job to take that power out of the equation."

Valkyrie paled.

"Where's Fletcher?" asked Ghastly.

Jack grinned. "He should be right—"

A fist of cold granite hit Valkyrie and she went tumbling. Shudder went to leap over her at Dusk, but Dusk threw Fletcher's limp body into him. They went down in a heap and Jack sprang, his knee smashing into Ghastly's face, then he leaped off him and landed behind Valkyrie.

He grabbed her, his hot breath in her ear. "I got someone who'd like to talk to you."

He shoved her at Dusk, who swatted her hand away as she brought it up. He didn't waste time with talk, or threats, or anything as mundane as enjoying the moment. He just sank his jagged teeth into her neck.

45

SEARCHING FOR SCARAB

For a time there was just the pain and the feel of her heartbeat thumping loudly and quickly. And when the pain stopped and her eyes refocused, Valkyrie saw Dusk holding her at arm's length. His lips were red with her blood, but his eyes were narrowed in confusion.

The window behind him exploded and Caelan came through, slamming into Dusk and lifting him off his feet. Valkyrie stumbled backwards, tripping over Fletcher's unconscious form and falling. Dusk seized Caelan and threw him into the wall, but Caelan came back with a snarl.

Valkyrie's hand pressed against the wound on her neck. Her blood was warm. She felt it trickling between her fingers. She glimpsed Caelan and Dusk fighting, and even from that one glimpse she could see that Caelan was completely outmatched. No matter how fast he moved, he couldn't hope to match the speed of a vampire like Dusk.

She lay flat. She was thirsty. Her thoughts were muddled. She turned her head in time to see Caelan drop to the floor. He didn't get up. Dusk slipped back to the side of Springheeled Jack.

Ghastly and Shudder closed in, forcing Jack and Dusk to retreat towards the elevator. Jack grinned. Dusk stepped back behind him.

"Careful," Jack said, "we don't want to hurt each other, now do we? I mean, who knows? After today, we'll probably be fightin' on the same side."

"I'd ask you what it is you're talking about," Ghastly said, "but I really don't care."

"Oh, come now, ain't it obvious? What do you think will happen when over 80,000 people are murdered live on air by a bomb that could only be described as *magic*? People are goin' to know, ain't they? They're goin' to believe in magic and they're goin' to believe in *us*. No more hidin' for yours truly. I'll be free to walk about on street level, do what I want, kill who I want... It'll be a little slice of heaven."

"That's why you're doing this?" Shudder frowned. "To reveal magic to the world?"

"That's why *I'm* doin' it, yeah. The others have their own reasons. They want the Sanctuary destroyed; they want the confusion of every sorcerer around the world scramblin' for a piece of what's left... I don't know, I didn't really ask them. We're not what you might call a friendly bunch. Ain't that right, Dusk?"

"That's right," Dusk said from behind him. "But I don't care about the Sanctuary or the war you're hoping will start."

Jack nodded. "Dusk's motives are pure. He's only interested in revenge. So, mate, did you do it? Did you bite her?"

"I did," said Dusk.

"Then has your thirst for revenge been sated?"

"Not quite," Dusk said. "Valkyrie Cain was only one of the people I sought revenge upon."

"Really? You didn't tell me that. Ah well, I suppose this is what you get when you don't talk, am I right? You get surprises. So come on, Dusk, who else is on your list?"

"You are."

Jack frowned and turned as the elevator doors closed and

Dusk was lost to sight. Suddenly alone, Jack turned back to Shudder and Ghastly just as they attacked.

Valkyrie forced herself up, one hand at the wound on her neck, and she ran. The wound was burning, but there wasn't much blood loss. She followed the corridor and took a left, jumping over the unconscious body of another security guard. Skulduggery came running back towards her.

"Where is he?" she called.

"Guild went after him. I lost them both." He started to say something else then grabbed her. "You've been bitten."

"Kenspeckle can cure me, right? So long as I get to him in the next few hours, I'll be fine. Dusk bit me and basically spat me back out. It's not even bleeding any more."

"Yes, it is."

"Well, it's not bleeding *much*."

"Valkyrie, you have to listen to me. Go back to Fletcher and get him to teleport you both out."

She pulled away from him. "What?"

"The Desolation Engine could go off at any moment. If it does, it won't care how strong you are or how tough. It won't be something you can fight."

"I'm staying with you."

"Damn it, Valkyrie, if it goes off, I won't be able to save you."

"I'm not going to need you to save me."

"I didn't involve you in all this just so you could die by my side, do you hear me?"

"You *didn't* involve me in this – I involved *myself*. I tagged along after Gordon was killed, *I* got you to teach me magic, *I* did it, OK? You didn't have a choice in the matter."

"For once, please will you do what I ask?"

"Not a chance. And the more we argue about it, the less time we have to stop Scarab."

Skulduggery looked at her then wrapped his scarf around his jaw. "He'll be among the crowd now," he said. "It's the safest place for him now that he knows we're after him. We'll have to keep each other in sight at all times."

"I'll be able to move faster than you. I don't have to worry about a disguise slipping off."

"You've got blood all over you."

She snapped up the collar of her coat. "Better? Now come on, we don't have much time."

46

ENDGAME

Guild watched Scarab move in off the steps and take a seat in the crowd. There was a time when an assassin of Scarab's calibre would never have allowed himself to be followed like this, but that time had drifted by while Scarab had been sitting in his cell. Now he was just an old man who thought he had escaped. There was an empty seat beside Scarab and Guild sat in it.

"Hello, Dreylan," he said. "Don't try to run. I wouldn't want you to embarrass yourself."

Scarab's jaw tightened, but he didn't move from his seat.

"Look what I found in the Repository," Guild continued, opening his hand. The copper disc he held was almost as wide as his palm and it had eight thin legs curled up against its underside like a dead spider. "Do you recognise it? I'm sure you do. You built it, didn't you? How many did you kill with this particular little weapon?"

"I didn't keep count," Scarab said.

"It just attaches to its target, isn't that right? And releases all this awful energy? So, for example, if I were to press it against you, the power it would release would be enough to give you a heart attack a hundred times over, yes?"

The eight legs flexed, as if the device had sensed a new victim.

Scarab swallowed. "Yes."

The crowd roared and people jumped to their feet around them. Guild and Scarab remained seated.

"Where's the Desolation Engine, Scarab?"

"In my pocket."

"Your near pocket?"

"Yes."

Guild smiled, carefully dipping his free hand into Scarab's coat. His fingers closed around the bomb and he pulled it out slowly. The liquid within the glass was still a calm green colour.

It hadn't even been armed yet. He held it under his jacket, away from prying eyes.

"You have caused us so much worry," he murmured. "It's a good thing I found you before you did something to actually trouble us."

"You're going to kill me," Scarab said, "is that it? Right here?"

"I think it would be for the best."

Scarab turned his head and looked at him. "Do you have what it takes? To look into a man's eyes and kill him? You've ordered deaths. You've orchestrated them, facilitated them, covered them up... But have you actually been this close when you murdered someone? Close enough to look into their eyes as they die?"

"I haven't," Guild admitted. "But I'm curious to find out what it's like."

"Can I be honest? I wish Meritorious were still alive. I would have much preferred *him* to do this."

"Well, we can't always choose who gets to kill us."

"That's true I guess. I mean, *I* chose you, but none of *these* people did."

"I'm not sure I follow your ramblings, Scarab. I'm not going to be killing these people."

"Actually, Grand Mage Guild, you kind of are. I didn't have this Engine built to set it off *myself*, you know. I did it so *you* could set it off."

Guild laughed. "And why on earth would I do that?"

"Because I'm about to tell you to."

"Two hundred years of loneliness has cracked your mind, old man. I'm not going to kill these people. I'm not going to kill myself. I'm only going to kill you."

"You'll kill me, you'll kill these people, but you won't kill yourself. I had the Professor make sure of that. The bomb's designed to spare your life and your life alone. I wouldn't let go of it just yet, by the way. That's when it'll detonate."

"What are you talking about? It's not even armed."

"Once it's been in *your* hand for more than ten seconds, Grand Mage, it arms itself."

Guild frowned and glanced down at the bomb in his hand. The liquid was red, churning and bubbling against the glass. Guild's heart sank into the chasm that his chest had become.

"Eighty thousand people," Scarab continued, "live on air. Rebroadcast around the world as the moment that changed everything. And the Grand Mage of the Irish Council of Elders is going to be the one held responsible. It's just... perfect, don't you think?"

"You're insane," Guild said. "I'll have it deactivated. I'll—"

"You'll walk out on to that football field," Scarab said, "and you'll drop the Desolation Engine. And all around you 80,000 people will be disintegrated."

"Why?"

The crowd roared again.

"I never liked Nefarian Serpine," Scarab said as if he hadn't heard Guild's question. "Vengeous was a good man. I never got to meet Lord Vile, but I couldn't stand Serpine. Couldn't see why Mevolent put so much faith in him. But credit where it's due – he knew how to get to people. That's how he killed Skulduggery Pleasant. Went after the family, you know? Made him so mad, so full of rage, he didn't stand a chance. Rage clouds the mind. Vengeance can make you blind. Which is why you have to wait, and choose your moment carefully. Timing, as they say, is everything."

"And this is your moment?" Guild snarled. "All I have to do is press this spider against you and this will be the *last* moment you ever have."

"My last moment's coming, don't you worry. But no, you miss my point. Serpine knew how to get to people. The family is an effective way of doing this. I'm going to reach into my coat now. If I were you, I wouldn't kill me just yet."

Moving slowly, Scarab took a phone from his coat.

"You might have to shield the screen from the light," he said as he pressed some buttons – "it's kind of hard to see the picture."

He held it out. Guild swallowed, hurriedly put the spider back in his pocket and took the phone from Scarab. He angled it out of the glare of the dull sun and saw what he knew he would see – his wife and daughter, bound and gagged.

"They're OK," Scarab said, looking back at the football game. "Unharmed. And they're going to stay that way too, if you do what I tell you."

"Let them go," Guild said, all breath gone from his body.

"Billy-Ray's with them right now and they're all watching TV. As soon as you drop the Engine, he'll release them. We got no reason to kill them, Grand Mage. Your family never did anything bad to us."

"I'm not going to kill these people."

"Yes, you are."

"You're insane."

"You've said that. Guild, you don't like these people, these mortals. From what I've heard, you never did. It's time to break the rules, Grand Mage."

"I won't do it."

"You are not only going to do it, but you're going to do it in the next three minutes or Billy-Ray will kill your wife and daughter."

"This isn't revenge. These people never did anything to you. You don't have to do this. You don't even *want* to do this. You want to make me pay, fine, make *me* pay. Not them. Not my family."

"It's all part of the same plan. With 80,000 deaths, every Sanctuary around the world will be shown just how vulnerable they are. The Sanctuaries should've been disbanded after the war with Mevolent ended. We didn't need you Elders setting up your fancy Councils, electing yourselves to positions of authority over the rest of us. I don't like people telling me what to do. I got a problem with it, point of fact. A system like that, well, it's open to all kinds of abuse. Miscarriages of justice as it were. Your system failed me and I got put in prison for killing someone I never killed, and because of that, you're going to go to prison for the murder of 80,000 helpless mortals. Let's see how *you* like spending the rest of your life alone in a cell. Grand Mage, you have about two minutes to walk to the middle of the field there. I think it's about time you started walking."

Guild had no breath to form words and Scarab was already looking back at the game. Guild stood, the Desolation Engine heavy in his hand. He thought he could feel it pulsing with a low and terrible life, but he dismissed the idea. The bomb wasn't alive. It had no consciousness, no sentience. It was not an object of evil – it was simply an object. The man who set it off, however, now he *would* be evil.

There was a gap between where he stood and the tunnel where the officials entered and exited. He could slip through and walk on to the pitch before anyone could even try to stop him. He looked back at Scarab. The old man wasn't even smiling any more. He was calm in the face of impending death. Of course he was. This was what he'd been waiting 200 years for.

Guild stepped down from the seats, his eyes fixed on the ground ahead. He didn't want to look up and see the tens of thousands of faces around him. He wished he could block out the noise – the cheering, the chanting, the thunder of living people – and yet if he'd had the option, he didn't know if he would. He was a man who was about to commit one of the single most monstrous acts the world had ever seen. Shouldn't he suffer for it? Shouldn't he invite that pain in at the earliest opportunity?

He realised his feet were still moving, that he was getting closer to the officials' tunnel, closer to the cameras and the football field, and still no ideas were coming to him. If he didn't think of something now, immediately, in a few seconds he would find himself either committing mass murder or sentencing his own family to death.

"Grand Mage," said a smooth voice in his ear, "could I have a word with you?"

Skulduggery Pleasant took his arm, the bones of his fingers digging into Guild's elbow like a vice, and suddenly Guild was in the officials' tunnel, walking through to where it intersected with the main utility tunnel that ran beneath the terraces. He pulled his arm free and turned, sudden panic setting in. Pleasant stood there, his scarf concealing his jaw, his hat pulled low and his gun levelled straight at Guild's gut.

"Sanguine has my family," Guild said. "You have to let me do this."

"Give me the Engine."

"It'll detonate when I let go. Where's Fletcher Renn? He can save you and the others. If you act fast, you can save a dozen people, maybe more."

Pleasant wasn't moving. "The lives of your wife and child in exchange for the lives of 80,000 strangers? That seems a tad unfair, doesn't it?"

"You, of all people, must know that I would do *anything* to protect my family. At least my walk to the middle of the field buys you some time."

"Time to save a handful of people and leave the rest to die?"

"If you try to stop me, I'll detonate it right here."

Pleasant nodded and put his gun away, but Guild knew what was coming. When Pleasant swept his hand wide, Guild was already pressing at the air. The space between them rippled and a breeze stirred. Within moments Guild's jacket was flapping in a hurricane force wind, localised to the tunnel and the tunnel alone. This wasn't going to work. He didn't stand a chance against someone like the skeleton.

As if to prove the point, Pleasant suddenly shifted position and instead of pushing against the air, he pulled. Guild stumbled forward and Pleasant got behind him, wrapped an arm around his neck and tried for a choke. Guild struggled against it and Pleasant broke off the choke and shot a side kick into the back of Guild's thigh. Guild stumbled, but Pleasant was right behind him, making sure the Engine didn't drop from his grip. Guild let him come closer then pressed the copper spider against the side of Pleasant's head. The spider's legs unfurled instantly and sank into the bone, and there was a crack, like lightning hitting a tree, and Pleasant jerked sideways and collapsed.

Guild didn't know how the skeleton detective registered pain – his very *existence* was a mystery still unsolved – but he doubted that even the great Skulduggery Pleasant could take a hit like *that* and get up again in time to stop him.

He turned to run for the football field and saw Valkyrie Cain coming towards him. He went to sweep her aside but she was faster, and a trail of shadows whipped into his face and he stumbled. His time had run out and he couldn't risk the girl getting in another lucky shot.

"I'm sorry," he said and tried to let go of the Desolation Engine, but his fingers wouldn't loosen.

He snarled, feeling the air closing in around his hand, painfully tight. Pleasant was doing it, propped up with his gloved hand outstretched. Guild ran to him, aiming a kick at his head, but Cain hit him from behind and took him to his knees. She wrapped an arm around his throat and wouldn't let go.

With his free hand, Guild tried loosening the choke. With the other, he smashed the bomb hard against her elbow, her shoulder, but her clothes were made by Bespoke. She probably didn't even feel it. Out of the corner of his eye, Guild saw Pleasant getting to his feet, his hand still outstretched.

Guild tilted, shunting Cain forward, then swung the bomb and felt it crack against her head. She cried out and the choke was gone. Guild pushed at the air and caught Pleasant full in the chest. Pleasant went flying back, the pressure around Guild's hand disappearing.

Guild stood, panting with exertion, his heart beating wildly. He opened his hand.

47

CRAZY

Guild vanished.

Valkyrie looked around. She'd glimpsed Fletcher running towards the Grand Mage, but now he was gone too and she knew instantly what he'd done. He'd seen Guild about to drop the Desolation Engine and he'd crossed the distance between them in the blink of an eye. Then he'd teleported them both away, somewhere safe, somewhere the bomb couldn't hurt any innocent people. But was he fast enough to do that and teleport away again before it went off? Guild's hand was open when he'd disappeared, the bomb already beginning its fall.

She helped Skulduggery up. He took something from the side of his head that looked like a metal spider and dropped it.

"Do you think Fletcher made it?" she asked softly. Skulduggery didn't answer.

Valkyrie took out her phone and dialled Fletcher's number. It went straight to voicemail. She nodded then, closing off her mind, struggling to get back to the business at hand, even though there was a part of her, deep down, that was screaming. She hadn't known how much Fletcher had meant to her. She hadn't *wanted* to know. "Scarab's still sitting there," she said.

"And Sanguine is holding Guild's family hostage," Skulduggery told her. Then he staggered and she reached out to steady him. "I can't go out there," he said. "I need a few minutes to recover."

"I'll take care of it." She ran out of the tunnel. An official scowled at her and she ignored him, got to the stairs and went straight for Scarab. He watched her coming. No smiles now.

"Guild is gone," she said, sitting beside him. "Fletcher teleported him away. Your little plan is over, OK? It's finished."

"Teleporters," Scarab murmured, shaking his head. "Never did like them."

"We've beaten you," she said with real, undiluted hatred.

"All these horrible things you've done and all my friends you've hurt, or killed, and it's all for nothing. We've beaten you and you've failed. Where is Guild's family?"

Scarab rubbed his eyes. His hand, she saw, was trembling. He looked so old now. Old and sad and pathetic.

She put her hand on his shoulder, and dug her fingers into a nerve cluster. He twisted in sudden pain, but she didn't let go. "Where's his family?"

"Billy-Ray has them," he spat.

"Are they alive?"

"Who knows?"

She dug in harder. "Where are they?"

"Don't know the street name. Call him. Ask him for directions if you're so damn eager."

She snatched the phone he took from his coat and as she did so, she snapped a handcuff around his wrist. She stood, stuffing the phone in her pocket and pulling him to his feet. She got him out on to the steps and cuffed his other wrist. She pushed him in front of her, heading back to the officials' tunnel. The same official who had scowled at her came up to block their way. Valkyrie raised her hand to his chest and snapped her palm. The air rippled slightly and the official shot backwards. The people around her, unaware of the magic she'd just used, thought this was hilarious.

She brought Scarab to the cover of the tunnel and shoved him towards Skulduggery.

"Guild's family?" Skulduggery asked.

"I'm going for them now," she said and hurried away, ignoring his protestations.

She ran up the steps and looked at Scarab's phone. There was only one number listed. She left the roar of the football crowd behind her and dialled it.

"I ain't seein' no thousands of dead people on TV," came Sanguine's voice.

"That's not happening today," she told him. "Your daddy's in shackles and the Desolation Engine is far away from here. All your little buddies have been beaten. There's just you left."

"An' you're comin' for me, that it, Valkyrie?"

"That's it. Just you and me, Billy-Ray."

"Is it my imagination or are you soundin' particularly angry today?"

"If Fletcher is dead, I *will* kill you."

"An' you're in a vendetta kind of mood, huh? Well, heck, a girl's gotta do what a girl's gotta do, am I right? Get a car to Howth. Number forty-one, Nashville Drive."

"I'll be there."

"I'll be waitin'."

She hung up.

The taxi made good time out of the city, and within minutes they were on the thin stretch of road to the peninsula of Howth. She could do this. She could take him. If he still had his magic, then no, she wouldn't be so stupid to come here alone. But he didn't have magic and Valkyrie did, and she was planning on using it. On the journey over she kept focused, kept her mind on what she was going to do, on what was about to happen. Not Fletcher. She didn't think about Fletcher. She couldn't.

Valkyrie paid the driver and hurried up to number forty-one. It was a nice house, like all the other nice houses on Nashville Drive. She didn't know how Sanguine had ended up here, but it didn't matter. The only thing that mattered was paying him back. He'd hurt her so now she was going to hurt him. If Guild's family was still alive, that was a bonus.

She wasn't going to be subtle. She didn't have the time or the temperament. She snapped both hands against the air, the space before her rippled and the front door flew off its hinges.

Valkyrie walked in, shadows writhing around her right hand, flames curling in her left. The living room was empty and so was the kitchen. She went in deeper, to the bedrooms. A woman and a girl were shackled together on the floor in the corner of the master bedroom, gags over their mouths.

She turned, expecting Sanguine to be rushing up behind her, but the hall was empty. With two pairs of frightened eyes on her, she stepped into the bedroom and nudged the door open fully. It swung slowly back and tapped the wall. She crossed to the ensuite, using the mirror inside to make sure it was clear, then she darted in, but there was nowhere for Sanguine to jump out at her.

She moved back into the bedroom. Her right hand flicked a trail of shadows under the bed. They didn't hit anything. Her eyes found the wardrobe, both slatted doors closed over. If he was in there, he was watching her right now and he could see how tense she was. How scared.

Valkyrie let the flames go out and abandoned the shadows. She pushed at the air and the wardrobe doors smashed to kindling. Clothes dropped from railings and hangers clashed, but when the debris had finished falling, there was nobody in there.

She went to the woman and the girl and pulled the gags from their mouths.

"Where is he?" she asked.

"I don't know," the woman answered. She was younger than

Valkyrie had expected. The girl looked to be about twelve. "He put us in here ten minutes ago. We haven't seen him since. Is Thurid all right?"

"I'm sure he's fine," Valkyrie lied. There was nothing she could do about the shackles, but she burned through the ropes tying their feet and helped them up. "Get your daughter out of here."

"What are you going to do? You can't face him *alone*."

"Sure I can."

Valkyrie used the shadows to break the window and she helped the mother and daughter out through it. Then she took out Scarab's phone and pressed redial. From somewhere else in the house, she heard Patsy Cline's 'Crazy'.

She stepped into the hall and held out her hand. The air's natural currents drifted by and she felt them and searched deeper. She barely noticed the shift in the air, but that was all it took and then she was walking forward. The phone was in the living room, on the table, and it stopped ringing when she neared. She waited until he was right behind her before turning.

The shadows stabbed at him, but Sanguine rolled, his straight razor flashing across Valkyrie's leg, but failing to cut through. Then he was up and she pushed at the air. It caught him in the shoulder and he spun right around, and came at her again.

He slammed into her and she sprawled over the coffee table, spilling the glossy magazines across the carpet. She tried to get up, but slipped on one of them. His knee came towards her. The world flashed and her head jerked back. He lifted her and threw her against the wall then he was up against her, his straight razor pressing into her throat.

"Hush," he whispered.

She couldn't stop him from cutting her throat if she tried. She stopped struggling.

"Good," he said and smiled. "You actually came here alone, by God. You must be really mad to leave the skeleton behind. Did you think you could take me?"

"Yeah," she said through clenched teeth.

"Now that, I think we can both agree, was a mistake. Do you think I'm going to kill you? I should. I definitely should. Do you think I should?"

Valkyrie didn't respond.

"You'd probably say no, even if you thought I should, so I don't know why I'm askin' you."

"Why didn't you kill *them*?"

"The broad and the kid? Saw no reason to. Only had 'em to

force Guild to detonate the Engine. Despite what you may think, I don't generally kill without good reason. It's usually money, but sometimes it's whim and I had neither. But killin' *you*, princess, now that is somethin' I have a very good reason for. You took my magic. You fouled up our plan. Where's my dear ol' daddy?"

"Skulduggery has him."

"So he could be in shackles or he could be dead – you never know with that guy, huh? Here's the thing I find amusin'– y'all call *me* a psycho an' yet you keep missin' the point. Your friend Skulduggery is an ice-cold killer. I mean, that guy is seriously unhinged. Takes one to know one, right?"

"He's adjusting."

Sanguine laughed. "Now that's a good one! That's one I should try! *'I didn't mean to kill all those nuns and orphans, Detective – I'm adjustin'!'* Oh, that is funny. But I think you're misunderstandin' me. It wasn't his recent trip abroad that sent him nuts – he's been nuts the whole time. Y'all just haven't seen it."

"If you kill me," she said, "he'll kill you."

"I have no doubt. Which is why it is a very good thing that I have decided not to kill you. Dusk called a few minutes before you rang – he was hightailin' it out of there before the bomb went off. He told me he bit you and I can see by the lovely wound on your neck that he wasn't lyin'. He told me he bit you and he told me that I should probably reconsider my whole *'I want to kill Valkyrie Cain'* thing, like he's doin'. Do you know why he told me that?"

"I don't."

"You don't? Do you want me to tell you why he told me that? Do you?"

"Sure."

He smiled. "He tasted your blood. You've got very special blood. Do you know that?"

She glared at him. "Yes."

"No," he said. "I don't think you do. See, you figure you're descended from the Last of the Ancients and that's it, that's the scope of your uniqueness in its entirety. I'm here to tell you, little lady, that that ain't so. You got a whole host of other things goin' for you. Not to give you too big a head or nothin', but everythin' about you screams important. And I'm talkin' *grand scale* important. Everythin' I hear about you just reinforces that whole idea that you, my dear, are a very special girl.

"When I broke into the Necromancer Temple, I heard some of 'em talkin' about you. They called you the Death Bringer. By the look on your face, I can see that you know what that is. You're their Great Dark Hope apparently, now that Lord Vile's gone. Imagine that. You and Lord Vile – one of a kind, huh? Ain't that somethin'?"

He began tapping the blade against her skin.

"It's a big responsibility now. The Death Bringer's the one to save the world, ain't that right? Are you ready to save the world, Valkyrie? And I don't mean save it from evil men or from twisted gods. I mean save the world from *itself*. Do you think you're worthy?"

"I don't know."

"Well, you're honest. I'll give you that."

He tapped the blade and she waited until it was no longer touching her skin, then she slammed the darkness into him. He flew backwards, head over heels, his sunglasses dropping to the ground.

"Damn it," he growled, "I said I *ain't goin' to kill you*, didn't I? Didn't I say that?"

"But you didn't tell me *why*."

He got up slowly, brushing down his clothes. He looked at her without needing eyes. "I get the feelin' bad things are goin' to happen, and I get the feelin' that *you* are goin' to be smack dab in the middle of it all. I ain't killin' you because, honestly and truly, li'l darlin', it's a lot more fun to keep you alive. That, I think, will be my real revenge." His smile returned and he nodded to the sunglasses at her feet. "You mind?"

She picked them up, thought about crushing them, but then tossed them to him.

He put them on. "Much obliged."

"The next time I hear that you're back in the country," Valkyrie said, "I'm going to assume you're here to kill me and I *will* go after you. And I *won't* let you walk away."

"I'm sure you'll do your best," he nodded. "Say goodbye to all of 'em for me, will you? Especially the sword lady. I've taken quite a shine to her, I ain't too embarrassed to say it."

"I'm sure she'll be thrilled."

Sanguine laughed. "Good luck to you, Valkyrie Cain. You got a lifetime of dark days ahead of you, if I'm not mistaken. I'd enjoy the quiet moments while you can."

He tapped a finger to his temple in a salute then turned and walked away.

48

A QUIET MOMENT

alkyrie took a taxi back to Croke Park just as the crowds were leaving the stadium. Half of them were singing; half of them weren't. She didn't know who'd won the game. She didn't care.

She called Skulduggery and he told her where he was. She went round to the back of the stadium, slipping by a Staff Only sign. She saw Cleavers loading Springheeled Jack into the back of a van. He was kicking and struggling. They closed the door and his pleas were instantly cut off.

Skulduggery stood with Ghastly and Shudder by the No

Entry door. Caelan stood apart from them. They all turned and watched her as she approached. She didn't say anything.

Davina Marr led Scarab to a second van. She got in behind him, a Cleaver joined them and the van followed the other one away. Sorcerers filed into the stadium, their job being to cover up whatever needed to be covered up.

"Dusk and Remus Crux are unaccounted for," Ghastly said. "Vaurien Scapegrace too, though I don't really know if he counts."

"I don't know about Crux or Scapegrace," Valkyrie said. "but Sanguine and Dusk are over their revenge thing."

Skulduggery nodded and didn't ask any questions. The questions would come later, she knew.

"Where'd you lot disappear to?" Fletcher Renn asked as he stepped out into the rain behind them.

Valkyrie turned, saw him there and the next moment she had her arms wrapped around him and her head on his shoulder. He laughed and hugged her back. He was soaking wet, but she didn't mind.

Thurid Guild hurried out after him and made straight for Skulduggery. "My family," he said. "Sanguine has—"

"They're OK," Valkyrie said, stepping away from Fletcher and composing herself. "They're in Howth, around Nashville Drive."

He looked at her, surprised. He was drenched too. "He let them go?"

"*I* let them go," she said. "But I don't think he was going to hurt them anyway. You're the one they wanted to hurt."

"What happened?" Shudder asked Guild. "Where's the bomb?"

"Mr Renn teleported us over the ocean somewhere," Guild said.

"I took this cruise once," Fletcher said. "Thought I'd like it. It was boring so I left halfway through. But I needed somewhere safe, somewhere without any people, and that popped into my head. I teleported there, dropped off the Grand Mage and teleported away again." He turned to Valkyrie. "Your window's fixed by the way."

She frowned. "You teleported into my *room?*"

"I didn't mean to. I didn't have time to think, you know? I just needed to get somewhere safe and I ended up there. No one saw me. Your room is still a mess though."

She scowled and he laughed.

"The Desolation Engine detonated," Guild said, picking up the story. "The blast left me unharmed, but I expect it vaporised every fish around me."

"Better fish than people," Ghastly said.

"Not if you're a fish," Shudder pointed out.

"I was in the water," Guild continued, "and I tried to imagine what it would have been like to have detonated that bomb with all those people around. You saved over 80,000 lives today, boy."

Fletcher's smile kind of froze. "I... I hadn't thought about it like that."

"I owe you everything."

"Uh... wow."

"I owe *all* of you everything."

"But mostly me," Fletcher said.

"Scarab is still alive," said Skulduggery. "Marr has taken him into custody."

Guild's face slackened for a moment. "Then she will learn the truth."

"She might keep quiet about it," Ghastly offered.

"No. No, she won't. And she shouldn't. After today, after what I was prepared to do, I think I deserve to be held accountable for my actions. If I am brought up on charges, so be it."

"Thurid," Skulduggery said, "we're talking about possible jail time."

"I am aware of the implications, Detective. But as for right now, I must go to my family. Thank you again, all of you." He walked away.

"But mostly me," Fletcher called after him and Valkyrie punched his arm. The moment her fist made contact they teleported.

She looked around. They were in Kenspeckle's Medical Bay.

"I thought you might want that bite looked at," Fletcher grinned as he rubbed his arm. His hair was flattened and spiky in all the wrong places.

"Your hair looks wonderful," she said.

He laughed and was about to retort when she grabbed his collar and pulled him into her. She clamped her lips around his mouth and mashed her face into his. He took a step back in surprise and she went with him, stepping in a patch of wet floor. Her legs went from under her and she flailed as she fell, whacking him in the throat on the way down. She looked up at him as he gagged and coughed, and from across the corridor she could hear Tanith laughing hysterically.

"I think I need practice," Valkyrie muttered.

49

ESCORTING THE PRISONER

"How many times have I saved your life?" Kenspeckle Grouse asked her. "More than a few, I'd wager. I've cleaned cuts and sewn wounds and fixed bones, and every time you leave here I tell you to be careful. Are you *ever* careful? It seems to me you never are. Do you think I'm joking when I tell you to take care? To stay out of trouble? To try and not get yourself killed? It appears to me, to poor, neglected, misunderstood, unappreciated little old me, that you *do* think I'm joking. This worries me. Apart from anything else, it credits me with a sense of humour I neither possess nor desire."

"I don't think you're joking," Valkyrie offered.

"A vampire bite," Kenspeckle continued. "You're a victim of a vampire bite. Do you really think this is an appropriate injury for a young woman to have?"

"Probably not, though now I'm curious as to what *is* an appropriate injury."

"You got yourself *bitten*, Valkyrie. Your magic clothes didn't stop that from happening, did they? Your sharp tongue didn't fend off those sharp *teeth*, did it? You could have died, you silly girl, or at the very least be turned into one of those *things*."

She looked at him and said nothing.

His craggy face softened. "The cure for a vampire bite is radically different depending on how long the victim waits before seeking treatment. You're lucky you came to me immediately afterwards."

"I'm cured?"

"You're cured."

"Does that mean you'll stop referring to me as a victim?"

He sighed. "Sometimes my bedside manner leaves something to be desired. I don't mean to lecture you all the time."

"I don't mind it."

"But I just *wish* you'd be more careful."

"So do I."

"And how is the headache?"

"Almost gone. I don't know what's causing them. Maybe my brain is leaking."

"For a brain to leak, you would first need a brain." Kenspeckle smiled, and his smile wavered. "I think Tanith Low is scared of me."

"Tanith's not scared of anyone."

"Fear and hatred are easily confused."

"Just give her time. She knows it wasn't you who hurt her. How are you doing though?"

"I'm fine. A nightmare or two, but that's to be expected. It's a blessing actually, the fact that I can't remember a thing that happened. I think that would be too much for me to handle. I never wanted to hurt anyone else ever again."

"You didn't hurt Tanith," Valkyrie said as firmly as she could. "The Remnant did. You're *you* now, the Kenspeckle who lectures me while he heals me. He's the only one that's real."

"You are wise beyond your years."

"I've always thought so."

*

Kenspeckle kept her confined to bed for two days. Tanith was transferred to the bed next to her. Skulduggery called by a lot and Ghastly visited on the second day. Fletcher was always around and China, true to her word, didn't put in an appearance.

By the time she was leaving, Valkyrie's wounds were healed and the scars were fading. Marr called to tell them that Thurid Guild had requested that Skulduggery and Valkyrie be the ones to transport him from the Sanctuary's holding cell to the prison. Skulduggery had agreed, more out of curiosity than anything else, and he picked Valkyrie up on the street outside Kenspeckle's building.

"We're early," she said as she buckled her seatbelt.

"I doubt Guild will care too much," Skulduggery responded, his sunglasses in place over his scarf and his hat pulled low. "He's looking at close to 300 years for his part in the Vanguard assassination and the cover-up. I don't think ten minutes is going to make that much of a difference to him, to be honest."

"Why do you think he asked for us anyway? Surely there are friendlier faces to see him off?"

"You would think so, wouldn't you? Maybe he wants to thank you again for saving his family. Or maybe he has something to tell us."

"A secret?"

"Confidential information perhaps. He is Grand Mage, after all."

"Was."

"Oh," Skulduggery said. "Yes."

"I wonder who'll take over. I wonder who'll *want* to. In the past three years one Grand Mage has been murdered and the other sent to jail. Who's going to want *that* job?"

"There will always be people who want power, Valkyrie. Never underestimate greed."

They stopped at a set of traffic lights and a group of lads stared at the Bentley until it moved off again.

"Sometimes I wish you could drive a less noticeable car," she sighed.

"I *can*," Skulduggery said. "I just choose not to."

"You know, I was thinking…"

"Never a good start to any conversation."

"Shut up. But I was thinking, maybe you should ask China to whip you up a façade tattoo, the same way she did for Ghastly. Then you wouldn't have to worry about your scarf and sunglasses."

He shrugged. "I'm considering it."

She arched an eyebrow. "Really?"

"If she can do it, why not get it done?"

"What kind of face would you have? Would it be yours? Your own one, I mean. The one you used to have?"

Skulduggery was quiet for a moment. "That face is dead," he said eventually. "Bringing it back would be..."

"Painful?"

He looked at her. "I suppose."

She nodded, then smiled. "Seeing you with a face would be weird. Do you think you'd have hair?"

"Oh yes. Hair is a must."

"Would you have a moustache?"

"Why would I have a moustache?"

"I'm not sure. What about your ears?"

"I'd have ears too, yes."

"I can't imagine you with ears."

A few minutes later they pulled into the parking lot behind the Waxworks Museum and got out of the car. They walked to the museum door.

"I'm with Fletcher," Valkyrie said quickly. Skulduggery turned his head to her and didn't say anything.

"We're together, kind of a boyfriend/girlfriend thing," she continued, all too aware of how stupid she was sounding. They walked through the museum corridors.

"Well?" she prompted. "What do you think? Do you have an opinion on it? Are you going to say something?"

"Yes," he said at last.

He nodded to the wax figure of Phil Lynott, who told them they were expected, and Skulduggery led the way down the steps. Detective Pennant greeted them at the bottom and told them to wait in the Meeting Room while he brought Guild to them. They started walking again and Skulduggery spoke.

"Valkyrie, ever since you brought me back I've been distracted. My concentration hasn't been one hundred per cent and my focus is... lacking. I knew there was something between you two, but I didn't see it. I needed you to tell me. Who knows how all this might have gone if I hadn't been so distracted?"

"The Faceless Ones hunted you and tortured you," she said. "That would distract just about anyone."

"But I can't afford to be distracted any more. Darquesse is coming and we need to be at our sharpest. Somehow, for some reason, you are intrinsically linked to what is going to happen."

"Ghastly's mother was a Sensitive," she said. "He told me about this just before you went through the portal. She looked into the future and saw you and me fighting a creature of darkness. Ghastly said it was unimaginable evil – the world on the edge of destruction."

"Sounds a lot like what Finbar and Cassandra are seeing."

They arrived at the Meeting Room and walked in. It was empty. Valkyrie took a deep breath and forced herself to continue speaking.

"Every vision we've been told about so far," she said, "they all end the same way. I die. I just want to be strong enough to save everyone else. I want to save my family."

Skulduggery looked at her.

"So this," she said, "what's happening and what's going to happen, this isn't your fault. You can't control everything and not everything is your responsibility. At Croke Park you said something about how you don't want to drag me around after you just so I can die beside you. I wanted to tell you then, but I didn't have the words and I didn't have the time. I'm here because I *choose* to be. You save my life. I save yours. That's how we work."

"Until the end."

"Until the end."

He stepped closer to her. "Thank you for saving me," he said softly, and wrapped the bones of his arms around her. Valkyrie smiled and hugged him back.

They parted as the door opened and Pennant led Thurid Guild in. Guild's hands were shackled before him.

"He's all yours," Pennant said and left them.

"You're early," Guild said. "Does the idea of my impending incarceration make you *so* eager you couldn't wait for the appointed time?"

"It's good to see you too, Thurid," Skulduggery said. "Are you ready to go?"

It looked like Guild was going to come back with another sarcastic remark, but then his face tightened and he nodded. Suddenly Valkyrie was feeling sorry for him. He was a man who had only been trying to do the right thing, and because of it, he was going to be taken away from his family and he'd probably never see them again.

They walked out, Guild between them, passing sorcerers who averted their eyes from the former Grand Mage. Valkyrie didn't feel right. This was too much like being an executioner, walking the condemned man to the chamber.

"How long before the Sanctuary is up and running again?" Skulduggery asked.

"A few more days," Guild answered, sounding relieved to be given the opportunity to talk about something other than his future. "Most of the artefacts have been returned to the Repository and some departments have already resumed work. The inmates will be taken back to the Gaol tonight, under heavy security of course. Not that they mind. I expect they're quite appreciative of any opportunity to be out of those cages. At least I won't be in a cage when *I'm* in prison."

"Good man," Skulduggery said. "Keep looking on the bright side."

Guild glared at him. "Why are *you* transporting me anyway? A feeble attempt to get in some last-minute taunts? It really is quite pathetic."

Skulduggery's head tilted. "We're transporting you because you requested it."

Guild laughed bitterly. "What is this nonsense? No, I didn't."

"I spoke to Detective Marr. She said you asked for us."

"Why would I ask for you two? I don't *like* you. I certainly have no wish to spend my last few moments outside of a prison cell *with* you."

They turned the corner and a man passed them wearing a raincoat with the hood pulled up. Valkyrie glimpsed his face.

"Myron?" she said, but he didn't turn.

"Myron Stray?" Skulduggery asked her.

"I'm pretty sure," Valkyrie said.

"It can't be," Guild said as they watched the man walk on. "The only people allowed past the Cleavers are people on the list – and Stray would *never* be on the list."

"I'm fairly certain that was him," Valkyrie insisted.

"Myron," Skulduggery called loudly.

Detective Pennant rounded the far corner, heard Skulduggery's call and intercepted the man in the raincoat, yanking down the hood. Myron Stray had trails of dried blood around his ears and his mouth was tightly shut, even as his eyes bulged wildly.

"He's punctured his eardrums," Skulduggery said.

Valkyrie frowned. "Why?"

"Because someone told him to."

Stray jerked away from Pennant's grip and his hand came out of his pocket. Pennant saw the Desolation Engine with its churning red liquid and he immediately backed off.

"He's being controlled," Skulduggery said. "Run!" he roared. "Evacuate the building!"

Valkyrie could see the tears in Stray's eyes and the bomb went off. It exploded with a soft *whump*. The liquid turned to a ball of red energy and the energy expanded. It seared the flesh from Stray's bones and boiled his blood to steam. It travelled across his body, his bones turning to ash. The ground he had been standing on was now a carpet of dust. Pennant tried to run, but he was far too slow. He didn't even have time to scream.

Skulduggery wrapped an arm around Valkyrie's waist – with

his other he gripped Guild – and they rose off the ground and flew. They flew through the corridor, whipping by startled sorcerers who saw what was coming, but were powerless to escape. Valkyrie watched the walls crumble and the people die, and still the ball of energy grew and chased them, faster than they could possibly move.

When the walls crumbled, the ceiling caved in and Skulduggery took them upwards. They veered to avoid falling masonry and the ball of energy found Guild and he screamed as his trailing leg disintegrated. They rose through darkness with his screams, then they burst into brightness and rain, and still they rose, and the ball of energy reached its peak and retracted.

They landed on a rooftop. Guild had passed out, the stump of his leg cauterised by the very energy that had wounded him. Skulduggery laid him down and joined Valkyrie at the edge. The Waxworks Museum cracked and tumbled into the chasm of dust. They watched the Bentley topple and crunch down below street level, the ground opening up to swallow it. The building they were standing on shook, but stayed solid. And then the rumbling was over, and there were only the clouds of dust and car alarms.

50

BACK TO HAGGARD

A little over thirty-two hours later, Valkyrie climbed through her bedroom window. The reflection stepped into the mirror and she absorbed its memories. She got dressed in the clothes it had been wearing and went downstairs. She made her mother a cup of tea and sat at the kitchen table and watched her father demonstrate the new baby seat he'd bought for the car. She did her best to smile at his antics.

The Sanctuary was gone. Destroyed. Twenty-nine sorcerers and twenty-one Cleavers had been killed. Davina Marr was missing and every surviving agent was hunting for her.

They'd questioned Scarab in his prison cell and he denied all knowledge. He claimed he had never been in contact with Marr. She was not part of his plan. He enjoyed the fact that such destruction was brought down by one of the Sanctuary's own agents.

Skulduggery didn't know *why* Marr had done what she did, but he knew *how*. The Desolation Engine that had been recovered at the castle had never been handed over to be deactivated. Marr had kept it and then given it to Myron Stray. She had made sure his name was on the list so that he could enter the Sanctuary without incident, and she had done her best to make sure that Skulduggery and Valkyrie were there also. Using Stray's true name, she had commanded him to burst his own eardrums so that he couldn't hear orders that would conflict with hers. Skulduggery theorised that she would have instructed him to keep his mouth shut and warn nobody of what he was about to do. She ordered him to do everything but be unafraid, and so Myron Stray had walked into the Sanctuary fully aware of what he was about to do, but completely unable to prevent it.

As far as the rest of the country knew, the old Waxworks Museum had collapsed all by itself, and it was a miracle that nobody was hurt. The truth had no place in the newspapers. The dead were mourned privately and quietly, the rubble was cleared and the giant hole was filled in In a few more days, Skulduggery had told her, there would be no sign that the Sanctuary had ever existed there.

Valkyrie went upstairs, pulled on shorts and a vest and went to bed early with the rain gently tapping the window. Within five minutes she was asleep.

51

WHISPERS

The nightmare woke her.

She sat up and slowly swung her legs out of bed. It was cold and her room was dark. The house was quiet. It was the middle of the night. Her nightmare clung to her with its smoky tendrils, clouding her mind, and she became aware of a low whispering in the room.

The dream whisperer Cassandra had given her lay on the shelf where she'd left it, and it was talking to Valkyrie in hushed tones that seemed to reach right inside her mind, bringing the nightmare back to her as a headache began to pound against her temples.

And now, finally, she could see it. At last, she could remember what had been plaguing her ever since she heard the name two days ago.

The whisperer kept whispering and Valkyrie saw her nightmare again in her mind. She saw Serpine and his glittering emerald eyes. She saw the fight in the Repository three years earlier, when he'd gone up against Skulduggery. The Book of Names had fallen and she'd glanced at it. She'd seen her own given name of Stephanie Edgley and her taken name of Valkyrie Cain. And, in the last column, the final thing she'd glimpsed that she was only now remembering...

She shouldn't have been surprised, of course. She had felt it within her, even before she knew of magic, that part of her that was descended from the god-killer. The Last of the Ancients had been powerful and mighty, and he had hurled the Sceptre deep into the earth – but there was no forgetting the fact that he was also a murderer. After he had killed his gods, he had murdered his brethren.

For now Valkyrie remembered where she had seen that name before. In the Book of Names, in that final column. Next to Stephanie Edgley, next to Valkyrie Cain. Her true name. The only name that ever really mattered.

Darquesse.

Oh hello, fancy meeting you here. You're looking well, I have to say. Really? Oh, you're making me blush. Well, I have been working out, it's true. Ah, you're too kind.

What am I doing back here? I'm here to announce something, but I'm not quite sure how to go about it. It is good news, yes. At least, I think so.

You see, the Skulduggery Pleasant series has always had an April publication date, but now we're moving the next hardback to September. Now hold on, don't start throwing things just—

OW!

Who threw that? Who was it? Was it you?

I'm keeping an eye on you...

As I was saying, before I was so rudely interrupted, this doesn't mean you're going to have to wait until September 2011 for Book Five. What it does mean is that, for one time only, you're going to get two Skulduggery books in the same year...

Skulduggery Pleasant: Book Five.
Coming September, 2010.

Derek
Somewhere in Ireland